tough enough  *to* tango

a SULLIVAN'S CREEK *novel*

BARBARA BARRETT

Previously published by the Wild Rose Press

First Champagne Rose Edition, 2015

Republished January 2024 by Barbara Barrett

Paperback ISBN: 978-1-948532-72-3

Sullivan's Creek Series, Book Two

Published in the United States of America

DEDICATION

Tough Enough to Tango features a father, Tim Harriman, who is so afraid of losing another child to an on-the-job accident he holds back the daughter who wants nothing more than to work alongside him in their general contracting business.

Like Tim, my own father, Richard Youngman, was in construction. Where Tim is bellicose and ambitious, my dad was more soft-spoken, and though he may have had aspirations of leading his own company someday, he spent his work life reporting to others.

But my dad believed in me, encouraged me to excel in my schoolwork and follow my ambitions. He wasn't the inspiration for Tim, but as a carpenter and later as a painter, he first introduced me to the world of residential construction. For that, I dedicate this book to him.

When I first met my husband, Veryl, he planned to become an architect. Though that didn't happen, he did design our last two homes, and I used what I learned from him as background for the first book in the Sullivan's Creek Series, *Saved by the Salsa*. But it has been this second book, which focuses on the building of Sullivan's Creek, where his knowledge and assistance has been invaluable.

CHAPTER 1

Shae Harriman swallowed, lifted her chin a fraction of an inch and pasted on her best sales smile as she approached the meeting of a lifetime. The meeting for which she'd been pleading. The meeting that had her so scared she couldn't finish a full breath because the desired result was so critical.

"Good morning," was on her lips as she and her colleague marched through the door to the conference room, but the words jammed in her mouth when she took in the room's occupants. Though three people rose, a woman and two men, the only person she saw was the tall entertainment god who'd dominated the news lately.

What was he doing here? Their client was supposed to be in a hospital somewhere following a collapse during a recent performance. He didn't look sick. In fact, in that tan jacket, crisp white shirt and form-fitting black jeans, he looked mighty healthy. Mighty.

Her brain momentarily shut down. Whatever she'd been about to say fled her thoughts. Her feet seemed cemented to the floor.

The trio moved toward her. The petite blonde extended her hand. "Lacey Rogers, Ms. Harriman. I'm one of the architects who drew up the design concept for the Sullivan's Creek housing development project. Thank you for agreeing to meet today and your willingness to come to the art gallery. It's a rather unconventional location, but we wanted to keep our discussion private."

Probably to avoid the media, who'd been in full pursuit since their client's breakdown.

Shae returned the handshake, remembering to keep a firm grip.

A guy whose dirty blond hair appeared to have been combed with a hand mixer stuck out his hand next. "I'm Mike Woodley, and this is Ned Collier, your client. Ned's had some minor problems with his throat recently and is under doctors' orders not to use his voice, so I'll be doing his talking today. I'm Ned's manager."

She greeted Woodley then grasped the entertainer's proffered hand, which exuded a delicious warmth, like climbing under the covers on a cold winter night. Better sense reminded her to let go about two nanoseconds beyond what would have been considered appropriate. "Good morning, Mr. Collier, or should I call you Jake, since your fans know you as Jake Bonneville? I'm sorry to hear about your throat but hope your presence here means you're doing better." *Lame, Shae. Very lame.* Could she sound more rattled?

His gray eyes studied her, apparently gauging her. His smile remained polite but uncommitted. For reasons that eluded her, she wanted to see his mouth curve up more.

"I see you've met Janice, Ned's mother." Lacey nodded toward the gallery owner, who'd led them to this conference room of sorts and now lingered in a corner. "She was kind enough to let us use her place, as long as we could do it today, because she's holding classes in here the rest of the week."

That explained the hurried nature of this meeting as well as the unique location. Shae gave herself a few seconds to study the room while she recovered from the shock of seeing the megastar. Pungent smells of paint and turpentine filled her nostrils. Half-filled book-shelves lined one wall and several folded-up easels were stacked along the facing wall.

She could do this, if Ned Collier would just stop gazing her way. She introduced Dave Hale, her construction superintendent, after which everyone but the mother took their seats. Janice Collier hugged one of the walls and remained in the background. Each of five places had been set up with a notepad, ballpoint pen and glass of water. A brown carafe graced the middle of the table.

Concentrate on your notebook. Don't stare at him. But she couldn't help herself. How was she supposed to focus on their proposal with this incredible male specimen so close? She gripped her hands to keep from touching her neck to assure the heat streaming through her insides hadn't seeped through her pores. Was his celebrity making her react like this? Surely it wasn't his overpowering presence? She admired attractive men as much as any other woman, but her insides rarely came to life as they were now.

Mike began the meeting. "We understand your father has been dealing with some serious medical problems lately."

Her cue. *Take your eyes off the superstar. Smile. Look like you know what you're doing.* She folded her hands. "My dad recently experienced a fairly severe attack of angina and was diagnosed with coronary heart disease. They were able to stabilize him without surgery, but his doctor has recommended a treatment plan, which, besides medication, dietary changes and exercise, also calls for absolute, stress-free rest."

Not enough to satisfy Woodley. "Ned's been working with your father for months and says he's quite the guy. Energetic, dedicated and very knowledgeable about construction."

She nodded. "He's all that. Plus, he's a workaholic. Probably what caused his current condition."

Mike cleared his throat. "His *condition*, yes. That's what we'd like to discuss. We're all rooting for his quick recovery. But if we read between the lines of your comments, Shae, that doesn't sound too likely."

She knew exactly where he was headed, but she wouldn't make it easy for him. "At this point, we really don't know how long it will take him to get back on his feet."

Mike exchanged a look with Ned and Lacey. "That concerns us. We're already into spring and ready to go into the construction phase of Sullivan's Creek, but it sounds like we may be without our key player."

"My dad's built up a solid business over the years, Mike." She remembered it was Ned who was actually in charge, so she redirected her gaze toward him, though she had to step up her concentration. "He's a great leader, but he's also put together an organization that can function without him for the short term."

Dave leaned forward, like he was about to testify before the grand jury. "We're in constant contact with him."

"He'll still call the shots?" Mike asked.

Shae sipped some water before she replied. "My father's doctors have told him to keep the tension in his life to a minimum. But he'll be a telephone call away for consultation as needed." This seemed to be the moment to reveal her own role during her father's recovery period. "My dad has named me temporary head of Two Rivers Construction."

Ned, Mike and Lacey jerked in unison.

"You?" Mike set his pen on the table. "No offense, Shae, but you seem to have come out of nowhere. Neither Ned nor Lacey has ever worked with you during the early phases of this project. What are your qualifications?"

Shae unclasped her hands and brought them to her lap as inconspicuously as she could. "I have a degree in civil engineering and construction management and, as Two Rivers' office manager the past five years, I'm thoroughly familiar with all the company's projects." Pause. The last part wasn't quite accurate since her dad kept her on the sidelines but for today, close enough.

Ned jotted something on his notepad and passed it to his buddy. Mike glanced at it briefly. "What about supervisory experience?" he asked.

Dave started to reply for her, but Shae chose to answer for herself. "I'm no stranger to the crews." If one counted the times crew members visited the office. "Plus," she patted Dave's forearm, "we're fortunate to have Dave. As superintendent, he probably knows the crew and subs better than my father."

"I have every confidence in Shae," Dave added, "but I'm there whenever she needs me."

Mike didn't respond to either statement. Instead, he fingered the document he'd pulled from his folder. "Given your dad's likely absence for some time and the size of this project, we felt it necessary to reexamine the provisions of our contract with your company."

She and Dave had discussed this contingency, and she was prepared to respond. Before she could say anything, Woodley continued. "Ned is making a huge financial commitment at a time when other developers are waiting to see which way the wind blows in the current economy. With your dad being out of the picture indefinitely, to protect his investment, Ned wants more direct involvement throughout the process."

Shae looked at her notes to avoid giving away her surprise. They hadn't anticipated their client would go this far. Her mind raced as she framed a counterproposal, something to defuse the ridiculous concession Ned Collier and his pal sought. "We'll send you status reports as frequently as needed."

"Not good enough. Ned wants the project manager to report to him."

Dave came out of his chair before she had a chance to quash the demand. "That's not possible. The project manager is on the general contractor's staff."

Easy, Dave. You're the one who's supposed to keep me under control. She struggled to maintain an even tone. "Dave's right. We understand your concern about your investment, but what you've proposed is highly irregular."

Mike tapped a finger on his notepad. "When the current contract was signed, your father assured Ned he'd be there for him twenty-four/seven. That's no longer the case. At least for a while. A period no one apparently can define. You're an unknown quantity, Shae. The alternative is for us to exercise our option to rescind the contract and find ourselves a new general contractor."

They were back in familiar territory. Not that she liked being here, but as office manager, she was the keeper of the contracts. Not the negotiator or the legal expert, but she was the one who built the milestone dates, cost projections and payment schedule into her computer program. Unlike the demand for the project manager to report to Collier, this was a contingency for which she and Dave had prepared.

"Changing contractors at this point wouldn't be wise. Two Rivers Construction has already entered into contracts with subcontractors, which would have to be terminated. At a cost. We've also expended sizeable resources providing preliminary construction services. Payment would be due immediately upon termination of your contract with us, along with a penalty payment to compensate us for having put other potential clients aside in order to work with you. Most likely, there would be a delay in the construction start date while you found yourself a new general contractor."

Mike held up a hand. "Okay, okay, we get the picture. It's obvious you've studied your options and come prepared to defend your position."

He glanced at Ned, apparently to seek further guidance, but his pal was otherwise engaged.

NED STUDIED the pair from Two Rivers, Shae Harriman in particular. He liked the way her long auburn ponytail swung back and forth every time she spoke, although it screamed amateur. Might have been a better idea to pin it up for this meeting to appear more professional. And what was with that outfit? Blue jeans, although clean, blue chambray shirt and work boots. Was it a costume to convince them she was one of the guys? Still, everything fit in all the right places.

Those deep aquamarine eyes reminded him of the Pacific on a calm day. Certainly weren't the eyes of a forceful leader who would bring in his project on time under budget. But they were hypnotic. Had to look away before he got caught up in them.

So, the daughter was standing in for Tim Harriman. Though her lack of experience was definitely a detriment, it might just play into his plans.

She appeared to sneak a peek at her superintendent, who had now returned to his seat after his outburst. "As for the project manager, I can't let the position report to Ned. Perhaps we can work out some other equally satisfying arrangement?"

Buying time. Not a bad tactic, although in the end, he needed for her to agree, because it was the only way he could manage his costs in light of his plunging revenues.

Mike paused a moment, as if to consider her response, although Ned had told him not to push this point today. Just soften her up with the threat to rescind the contract. "Fair enough. But we didn't throw it out there for mere discussion. We're serious." He closed his notebook. "That's all the questions we have."

Ned caught her—Shae, he liked her name—as she tried to read him. Probably wondered why he'd called this meeting before he could speak for himself. Or what in hell had possessed him to tackle this crazy project.

"Good," she replied in response to Mike's statement. But rather than appear ready to leave, she turned directly to him. "Now, tell us the status of your health, Ned."

All the table's occupants fell silent. Dave Hale looked away. Mike and Lacey would probably consider her question insensitive. But her cheek impressed Ned.

The Harriman woman continued, seemingly unaffected by their reactions. "We've discussed the impact of my father's health on this project, but we haven't addressed your situation, Ned. It, too, could become a liability to the project, if it persists. There's risk all around. Not just to you, but to us as well."

The lady was not only insightful, she also wasn't afraid to go for the jugular. Maybe not very tactful, but she was a fighter. He liked that, as long as she didn't fight him. But this wasn't the time to find out. He jotted "wrap it up" on his notepad and passed it to Mike.

"As you can see, Ned's doing fine," Mike said. "He's just not performing while his throat heals. With his newfound time, he plans to take a more active role in this project."

"Really?" Shae replied. "What does that mean?" she asked, still focused on him.

"That I'm sticking around and plan to be involved in this project every step of the way. Those are my terms, if you want to remain my general contractor."

The lady fell back in her seat, her face a study in shock.

What had possessed him to speak?

SHAE HOPPED into Dave's pickup and shook her head. "Can you believe that guy? He played us, letting us think he was under doctor's orders not to talk." She was a what-you-see-is-what-you-get kind of woman. She wasn't into game playing.

Dave held off turning on the car but instead switched his gaze to her, his expression incredulous. "He *spoke* because you badgered him with your questions. Your attitude caused the man to go against his doctor's orders and probably lost us the biggest project we'll ever have." He started the engine and backed out of their parking spot with a series of jerks.

"*My* attitude? For having less than a day to study the project plans, I'd say I was the picture of confidence."

"Maybe a little too confident. You don't attack a client with personal questions."

"Why not? We have as much right to know if he's healthy enough to participate in this project as they have to ask about Dad's projected return date."

Dave blew out a breath and returned his attention to the road as they pulled into traffic.

Why couldn't Dave see her point? Jake Bonneville, or Ned Collier, which apparently was his given name, had been swallowed up by Hollywood and all its phoniness. Right down to pretending he couldn't speak. "His hands-on interest is scary. Has he been like that all along?"

"From what your dad's told me, the guy tends to swoop into town from time to time, add new demands, change his mind a couple times and then head off for a concert or recording session just when we need him to make a decision."

Would have been nice to know this before their meeting. "Only now there won't be any concerts or recording sessions to get him out of our hair. He plans to be here. All the time."

Dave stared straight ahead. "So we tolerate him. This project is too important."

"I realize this is the biggest housing project we've ever handled. But if Ned Collier continues to be such a pain in the … we can survive without him."

Focused on driving, Dave pursed his lips, as if clamping down on words he didn't want to escape.

"What? What aren't you telling me?"

"Nothin'. We just can't afford to lose this guy."

"C'mon, Dave. I've known for some time that's something's off with the company, but Dad wouldn't share any of it with me. If I'm going to be in charge for a bit, I need to know everything there is to know about the company."

Dave checked the rearview mirror, adjusted it slightly and ran a hand down one side of the steering wheel. Though he valiantly attempted to divert her questions, she was pretty sure she'd worn him down.

"The last few years, the company's been struggling to stay in the black. While our competitors have cut back or even gone out of business, your dad has kept the lights on, but he was forced to dip into his reserves. That's why the office complex hasn't been remodeled, why your dad still drives a dated pickup and why we continue to use that rattletrap trailer for our mobile office."

If Dave had leveled a sledgehammer blow at her chest, he couldn't have sent more pain through her. The company was in financial trouble? Why hadn't her dad told her? Why hadn't she suspected? Probably because, until his heart problems forced him to put her in charge, she'd been so busy fighting him for more responsibility, it hadn't occurred to her that he withheld information to spare her the worry. "I didn't know."

"Didn't think so. Only told you now because you seem so all-fired set on fighting Collier at every turn."

"How bad is it?"

"Don't know for sure. Your dad only tells me so much. From what I can tell, we're still in the game, but we really need this Sullivan's Creek project to stay alive."

She tried to read his expression to gauge how much he'd tempered his words, but he stared straight ahead at the road. "Are you worried?"

He shifted his attention back to her. "Lots of things worry me these days."

"Like me being in charge of the company?" Did that sound too much like self-pity? Even if her insides were still jelly, especially after these new demands from Collier, she had to present the appearance of confidence to the staff, starting with Dave.

"Okay, yeah, if you want to put it out there like that. I wasn't sure how things would go when we first got there today, but you were great. You fielded their questions about your experience like an expert politician. Then you went and stuck your foot in it."

She slumped back. "I suppose you'll tell Dad?"

"That's your job."

"I don't want to worry him any more than necessary." Would Dave really leave it to her? This was his first test of loyalty. She didn't want her dad to know she'd possibly blown it before she could defuse the situation. "Okay, fine. I'll call him. But I won't tell him that last part. I'll tell him we did our best to represent his interests."

"Play it down the middle. Don't come on too gloomy or too hopeful. Tell him about the art gallery. That'll tickle him. Especially that name. Serenity. Real ironic these days."

Who'd have thought Dave was such a strategist? He could say so much and yet so little when called upon to skirt the issue. She'd remember for future reference.

CHAPTER 2

While his mother ushered the Harriman woman, her superintendent and Lacey Rogers to the front door, Ned remained behind in the improvised conference room with Mike to debrief.

Mike slammed into the same chair he'd occupied minutes before. "What the hell was that about? You deliberately let her know you could talk."

Ned settled a hip against the table, grinned. "Sure threw her off guard, didn't I?"

"Should have *thrown her out* after that insolent reference to your health. It's obvious she's in over her head. She could barely answer our questions."

Ned recalled how the woman had entered the room prepared to wow them and then froze in her tracks when she spotted him. There was something fresh and innocent about her. Probably why he'd found it so difficult to focus during the meeting. The hard-driven business-woman persona coupled with her otherwise ingenuous personality was a captivating combination.

"How soon should I call and tell them we've cancelled the contract?" Mike asked.

"Huh?"

"The thanks-but-no-thanks kiss-off."

Ned winced. Mike had gotten a little too carried away with his role of facilitator. Time to set him straight. "No need. I'll call her." He paused, debated whether to go on. Hell, why not? "I'm staying with Two Rivers." One part of him couldn't wait to witness Mike detonate, and the other part got ready to duck.

Mike spluttered, rose. "You've got to be kidding. It's because she's a looker, isn't it? Although I thought you'd sworn off women after Gillian and Julie."

His two former fiancées had screwed him royally, each in her own self-absorbed, scheming way. He wasn't about to set himself up for a third disappointment. Didn't mean he had to be a monk, though. All the same, his interest in Shae Harriman was totally different. "True, she's not hard on the eyes, but I have other reasons to stick with Two Rivers."

"She has no experience running that company. You can't let her use your project for on-the-job training. You're smarter than that."

Since he'd told Mike this much, he might as well fill in the blanks. "Gonna take advantage of that inexperience so I can play a more active role in the project."

Mike's sandy brow rose even higher. "*More active role?* Explain."

"I was serious about getting more involved. It's my money and my vision, so why not plant myself in the thick of things as their project manager?"

Mike scraped his hands through his perfectly styled disheveled hair. "You're kidding! I thought you were pulling her chain when you had me insist the project manager report to you. Have you ever even hammered a nail?"

"Uh, no."

"You don't know what decisions to make, how to make them or when to make them."

"Thanks for the vote of confidence."

"That's not all." Mike held up a hand and ticked off more reasons why Ned should reconsider. "You have absolutely no knowledge of the building trades, you hardly know this town any more, you're setting yourself up with an amateur and you've kept me out of all the financing that's gone into this bright idea of yours."

Ned released a huge sigh. He didn't want Mike to know, or even suspect, his diminishing financial resources, or the guy would insist on helping out. His millionaire friend could easily afford to get him back in the black, but Ned had sworn off visiting that well again. "I've told you, I don't want to lean on you. The last time, you nearly got thrown out of your family's business."

"My folks came around. Eventually. After your singing career took off."

"Which took a couple years, and in the meantime, your job was at risk, and you barely spoke to your parents or siblings because of me. You're just rebuilding your relationship with them. I'm not letting you jeopardize that again."

Mike returned to his chair and studied the ceiling for a few beats. Then he leaned forward and turned back to Ned. "What's going on with you? You've been so secretive about this project, I had to overhear you talking with Lacey and her partner before I had any inkling what you were up to."

"You mean when you eavesdropped?"

Mike had the grace to look away. "Wasn't that way. For weeks, you'd hang up suddenly whenever I came in the room. I simply chose to remove my shoes that day. Needed to air the tootsies."

Ned gathered his things. "Appreciate your helping out today. But your other clients on the Coast also need your attention. I'll be back in L.A. in a week or two. We can get together then and swap tales."

Mike grabbed Ned's arm as he swung by. "Not so fast. What's this about my heading west? You dismissing me?"

"No, not at all. Just don't want to take up any more of your time." Geez, what had he set in motion by asking Mike to be his mouthpiece?

Mike released his hold. "Actually, your housing development intrigues me. As long as you insist on doing this, I might as well stick around and see how it all unfolds."

Ned gulped. "Don't worry about me. I, uh, need to handle the rest myself."

Mike brushed away Ned's concerns with a swipe of his hands. "How about I at least sit in on a few more meetings? If you stay with Two Rivers, you'll need an ally whenever you deal with that woman."

Ned tugged at his collar. How to discourage Mike? "This will be a lot of boring contract details and preliminary layout."

"Right up my alley. Besides, someone has to make sure you don't overdo."

A cloud of suspicion caught Ned up short. "Did Mom ask you to do this?"

Mike shifted his gaze to the other side of the room. "No. I feel partly responsible for your throat problems, since I let you steamroll me into letting you perform at that benefit where you passed out. If I'd stood my ground like my gut told me, you might be singing today."

"Not the case. These nodules have been coming on for a long time. Even with medication and throat rest, the doc says it'll take a while for them to shrink. At least I avoided surgery."

"Just the same, I want to hang around and protect my interests."

"Be my nursemaid? I don't think so. I don't need round-the-clock care."

"Gimme a break here. Let me salve my conscience. You know me. I bore easily and will be off to parts west before you know it."

Ned had run out of excuses. The best he could hope for was to restrict Mike—Mr. Type A Personality—from taking over and just hope, as Mike had predicted, he'd soon grow bored. "If you insist on doing this, remember, we're not partners. Give me space to do things my way. Keep your opinions to yourself until it's just you and me. Even then, go easy."

Ned collected his things and headed for the door.

"Wait!" Mike slipped around him and blocked his way. "Got an idea. Come stay with me at the old Woodley homestead. The folks are still in Florida, and the rest of the family has cleared out for greener pastures."

Talk about being caught between a rock and a hard place, besides having his exit blocked. He could stay at his mother's and continue to fight off her smothering attention, or move in with Mike and give him a front row seat at his potential journey down the toilet, if his money situation didn't improve. "Thanks, but I can't do that to Mom. She's been so happy to have me at her place."

"Tell her you need privacy to entertain the ladies. She'll love that."

"She knows I'd only *entertain* a woman at your place if I was serious about her, and I've constantly reminded Mom serious relationships for me are off the table."

"Then tell her I'm loaning you free office space. You'll need a place for files and plans and whatever. Plus, you can hold meetings in the library. I should've thought of that before today, so we wouldn't have had to inconvenience your mom."

"She loved it. Notice how she stuck around in the background?"

"Since this whole project started out with her house, I don't blame her." Mike raised a brow. "Do we have a deal, then?"

"Deal."

They shook on it. "Great. Let's go tell your mom she'll be our guest at dinner."

"Dinner? It's barely eleven thirty."

"Later, you dork. She'll need time to get used to the idea of you moving out tonight."

Seven hours between now and dinner? A couple weeks wouldn't be enough time.

THE MORNING after the meeting at the art gallery, Shae slumped in her office chair. Even the fancy coffee she'd bought on the way in wouldn't help pump her up today. She'd twisted and turned all night, second-guessed her actions the day before. Even though she reassured her dad the meeting had gone well, niggling doubts crowded her brain.

Forty-eight hours before, when she accepted this challenge, Shae thought she could actually make it work and finally show her father she was capable of taking over for him. At least work alongside him.

Twenty-four hours ago, she'd been stoked about meeting with their client. And today? Though she still believed she could run the company, she wondered if she'd succeeded at her first task, to keep Ned Collier's business. Though she'd never admit it to Dave, questioning Collier's health probably hadn't been the smartest move.

If she had to wait much longer for a call from their client, she'd deteriorate into a puddle of stomach acid. How did her dad do this, court potential clients and then wait to hear from them? It didn't help, as Mike Woodley had pointed out the day before, that she had no management or supervisory experience. Now she was forced to punt, act on her own best instincts.

Around nine, Dave stuck his head in the door. "Want to go with me to see the crews? Before lunch, a good time to catch them."

"Might as well." Could she sound any more enthusiastic? She rose. "Sitting here waiting for the phone to ring won't make it happen."

"Wait. You can't go while you're in that mood."

"What do you want, Dave, smiles and giggles? I'm a nervous wreck."

"So am I. But life goes on. We've got other work to do. You need to get out there and talk to your crews. Though I've got everything under control, these guys are used to your dad stopping by every so often. You need to show them little has changed, even with him sidelined."

She remained planted behind her desk. "How do you do it?"

"Me?" He chuckled while he studied the floor. "Keep myself busy otherwise." He brightened, checked his watch. "We've got a few minutes to spare. I've got an idea."

Ten minutes later, in a park near their first inspection site in Clive, she threw a baseball back and forth with Dave.

"You've got a pretty mean pitch there, Shae. I don't remember you playing when you were in school."

"Didn't." She tried not to pant. Boy, was she out of shape. "Tagged after my brother so much, he finally relented and gave me lessons." Sean was in her thoughts a lot these days. If he'd lived, he'd be the one taking over for Dad. Or maybe her dad's health wouldn't have deteriorated at all, if he'd had Sean's help these past years.

When they took a break, Dave hauled out two bottles of water from his pickup. "Feeling better?"

She sagged against the fender, took a swig. "Feeling worn out." She laughed. "But yeah, you managed to take my mind off the job for a little while."

"Good! I keep that equipment in my truck bed for just such times."

"Ever play with Dad?"

"Uh, no. Sometimes I play *because* of him."

She winked. "I'll keep that in mind in case I drive by someday and find you out here again."

"Break's over." He retrieved a trash sack for their empty bottles.

As she climbed onto the seat, her cell rang. She shot Dave a hopeful look. "Cross your fingers."

"Ms. Harriman—Shae? This is Ned Collier."

Shae gulped air. This was it, one way or the other. And it was Collier, not his pal, Mike Woodley, on the other end. Good sign? *Take a breath, Shae.* "Uh, hello."

"Sorry our meeting ended the way it did yesterday. I startled you when I spoke."

He'd offered an apology? What did that mean? She didn't know how to respond.

"You may think we tested you."

"Uh—"

"Truth be told, that was sort of the case. If you're going to spearhead my project, I wanted to make sure you could handle it. Thought I could accomplish that best if I sat back and observed."

She cut straight to the point. "And? Did I pass?"

"I'd like to hear more before I make up my mind whether to continue the contract."

He was going to prolong her agony? "I thought we covered all the bases." They'd cut their profit margin to the bone. What more, other than concede to letting the project manager report to him, could she do to keep his business? "We offered you a solid deal. What else is there to discuss?"

"I'm not ready to decide until I gather some additional information. How about we discuss my ideas over dinner tomorrow night?"

Defend the contract over dinner? She didn't do dinners. Not social and definitely not business.

He mentioned a time and place. The information barely registered.

"You get first chance. Hopefully we'll be able to find common ground, so I don't have to go elsewhere."

She hung up, unable to move.

"That was Collier, right? Do we keep the job or not?" Dave's voice sounded like it was two blocks away.

She repeated the developer's statements as well as his dinner invitation.

Dave massaged his jaw. "Not the best news, but not bad either."

"Don't you get it? He wants to go over the sticking points tomorrow night over dinner. Just the two of us."

"Yeah? So? I heard you yesterday. You did fine until you got into the stuff about his health. Since you apparently didn't tick him off, sounds like full speed ahead."

She drew herself up. How could she tell Dave the thought of doing business in a social setting with anyone, but especially Ned Collier, aka superstar Jake Bonneville, curdled her insides? "I-I'm not prepared for this."

"So we spend the rest of today and tomorrow getting you prepared."

She shook her head. "No, that's not what I meant. I've never participated in a business dinner. I have no idea how to act. Or dress. Oh, my god! What do I wear?" Her voice rose, but she couldn't help it.

Dave patted her hand. "Calm down. Damned if I know what you should wear, but that's not important. As long as you stick to our plan."

Her wardrobe not important? She would be out in public with a man who knew his way around a place setting, who dined frequently with Hollywood starlets and dealmakers. How could she hold her own when she couldn't even remember if she owned a decent dress?

CHAPTER 3

Shae plopped her notebook on her desk and massaged her temples. Was the room buzzing or was that her head about to explode? Dave had quizzed her the last two hours. "Enough, Dave, enough. Thanks for skipping your site visits this afternoon to help me get ready for tomorrow night. But cost projections, staff levels and work schedules are going to haunt my dreams."

Dave set his folder down with less irritation than she'd displayed. "That was the whole point of this exercise. You can quote any part of the contract and work plan, even if you're in the midst of cutting a piece of steak—"

"Tilapia with mango salsa. Port of Call specializes in fish and seafood. I searched online for their menu so I won't appear overwhelmed as I decide what to order." Her research helped calm her nerves about dining while discussing business. Thanks to Dave, she was now more than ready to handle the data part as well. "I can't believe how little I actually knew at our first meeting with Ned Collier, given all I've learned since."

"Even so, you winged it pretty well. Now you can relax and enjoy dinner. You might even have enough energy left to defend whatever objections he raises."

"How has Dad dealt with these social things? He's no more into fine dining than I am." They'd lost her mother when she was just a toddler. She and Sean had been looked after by housekeepers while their dad built the business. There'd been no feminine influence in the house to expose them to a diet beyond basic meat-and-potatoes cuisine that either came out of can or a box.

It wasn't just that she had to adjust to a public appearance with a well-known personality. She had to do that while she ate gourmet food and simultaneously debated the merits of their current contract. And emerge victorious. How would she navigate those waters? Shae scrubbed her hands down her face and blew out a frustrated breath.

"Why not take the rest of the afternoon off?" Dave suggested. "The wife treats herself to a mani—her word—whenever she needs a boost."

Shae sneaked a look at her fingernails—chipped, uneven, ugly. Dave was proving to be more than a good superintendent. He was a pretty good counselor, too, his quotient of tact and subtlety rising as well. "Good idea."

Once the nail tech had stopped tsk-tsking and gotten down to work on the repair of Shae's nails, the manicure helped calm her nerves, despite her initial reservations.

Her newfound tranquility lasted all of an hour, until she returned to her dad's house, where she was staying, and checked her wardrobe. Blue jeans, slacks, a few pantsuits, but pretty light on dresses. She rarely wore them. But for some reason, a dress seemed appropriate for this business dinner, perhaps because she hadn't had time to dress more professionally for their first meeting and she wanted to show him she how professional she could be.

By late mid-afternoon on Saturday, within hours of the dinner, she had become desperate enough in the wardrobe department to make a trip to the mall. It only took fifteen minutes to wend her way around a maze of counters, shelves and racks of women's clothing before she wanted to collapse in the nearest chair. Other than exhaustion and confusion, the only other result of her efforts was a new blue blouse to wake up her trusty pantsuit.

"Got time for a makeup consultation?" a young woman's voice

asked, as if on cue. A blonde twentysomething with black hair extensions stood three feet away, makeup brush in hand, hopeful expression at the ready. Though the clerk's fuchsia and green eyelids shouted retreat, the makeup chair next to her beckoned.

"I don't use much makeup. It's a pain in my line of work, but I have a business dinner tonight night—"

"Say no more." The clerk adjusted twin mirrors that framed her station and pulled out one of the drawers in the cabinet below. "I know just what you need."

Sounded like a good reason to get back on her feet and flee, but it felt so good to close her eyes and shut out the blinding confusion of wardrobe overload. She relented. "I don't *need* much."

The young woman drew a fingertip across Shae's cheek. "You have a wonderful complexion."

"Thanks."

"I have something here that will highlight that asset."

"Highlight?"

"Make your complexion look even better. By the way, my name's Cecily, and I'm a certified makeup consultant."

"Is there a charge for this service, Cecily?" She'd willingly pay to sit here a few more minutes, but she'd better find out how much it would cost before getting too comfortable.

Cecily threw a small black drape over Shae's shoulders. "No charge, unless you fall in love with any of the products we use. Which I'm sure you will. Just sit back, relax and let me do the creating."

"Creating?" Yet another warning light flashed, which should have sent her sprinting.

Cecily moved in front of Shae, made an L with both hands, like a movie director envisioning her next shot. "Your face is a blank canvas and I'm the artist. A well-trained one, if I say so myself." She reached for a cotton ball, dabbed some kind of liquid on it. "First thing, we rid your face of all the residue that's built up since you last cleansed it."

The cotton ball was cold to the touch and tingled. The faint smell of alcohol reached her nose.

Cecily applied what appeared to be liquid foundation, let that set a bit, then followed up with something in a jar into which she dipped one of her brushes. She stepped back and appraised her work. "Not bad."

Shae merely smiled, fearful of the extent of her "makeover" if she gave Cecily the slightest encouragement.

"Ever worn fake eyelashes? I'd love to see how they look on you."

"I wouldn't. Skip those."

The makeup guru clucked. "Too bad. I don't see many women with such striking blue-green eyes. Do you have trouble getting people to take you seriously when you gaze at them directly?"

This was getting too personal. "Uh, sometimes." Always.

"What are you wearing to this business meeting?"

Shae shrugged through the shoulder cape. "I'm not sure. I looked for something here, but came up short. Now I'm out of time. Looks like it will be either the black or the brown dress in my closet."

"Black. Definitely black. Much more dramatic."

"I don't want drama. I just want to make my point."

"Of course. But black says you mean business and you're serious. Brown suggests you're vulnerable. I'm going to play up your gorgeous eyes to go with black."

Shae sat forward when she noticed the palette Cecily had selected. "Forget the eyes. I can't wear that paint. It'll smear and make me look ridiculous."

Cecily held up a hand. "Don't worry. I'll go light. But you need something. Just a dab here, a smidgen there." She set to work applying one color after another. "This will all blend together. It'll hardly be noticeable."

Did she really want to trust the word of this, what did she call herself? Consultant?

After another minute and several swift strokes of the brush, Cecily stepped back to survey her work. "If I do say so myself, another brilliant job on my part. You are one sexy woman."

Sexy wasn't quite what Shae had in mind.

Cecily reached for a hand mirror. "See for yourself."

"Sorry. Can't. Gotta run. I'll check it in the car." *When I'm alone and can grab a tissue to rub it off.* She reached in her purse for her credit card and handed it to the clerk. "I'll take a bottle of that foundation."

She finished the transaction and ran for the parking lot. Only then, in the presumed privacy of her vehicle, did she check her reflection in the overhead mirror. *Oh. My. God.* She looked like a streetwalker. Not that she'd ever seen one in person. She dug frantically in her bag for a tissue but couldn't find one. She flung open the glove compartment. Several drinking straws spilled onto the floor, but no tissues. Not even a paper napkin.

How could she have been so foolish? Cecily was a total stranger. Probably bored and needed something with which to amuse herself. *Okay. Fine.* She'd be home soon enough. Even though she was running short of time, she'd make time to rid herself of all this color. What had she been thinking?

"WINE?" Ned lifted the bottle in anticipation. "I asked the sommelier to recommend one of their best reds."

Shae put a hand over her glass. "No, thanks. But you go ahead." She needed to keep a clear head for the discussion to come.

Ned poured himself a glass and set the bottle back in its holder. "Maybe later?" He swished the contents of the glass, gave it a slight sniff and took a sip. "Umm. The sommelier knows his stuff. Sure you won't change your mind?"

"Not now. But if we can find common ground, I'll be happy to toast continuing as your general contractor." She hoped her words would remind him they were here to do business. Not drink. Not for chitchat.

He glanced around the room. "I asked for a semi-private spot. I had no idea they'd give us a room all to ourselves."

"Why are we meeting at a restaurant anyhow? I thought you wanted to keep a low profile."

He leaned in and cupped a hand around his mouth, conspirator fashion. "Truthfully? I'm staying at Mike Woodley's family home, and the walls were closing in. A guy's got to get out sometime."

Get out? Good one. His actions this evening meant she had to hide out in a private dining room, arrive in a chauffeur-driven car, and slip in the side door. "Do you ever tire of the star treatment?"

He shrugged. "It was fun at first. But these days, I prefer to stay away from the crowds when I'm not on stage. I use my celebrity sparingly, when I need a little privacy."

"It certainly got a workout tonight."

"How's your fish?"

She had no idea. She couldn't taste a thing. Her meal was easy to cut and consume, the only positive aspects of her selection. The mango salsa slid right down her throat, once she figured out which fork and which knife of the ten assembled utensils to use. "Uh, fine."

"By the way, you look very nice tonight."

She touched a cheek. "Uh, thanks. I, uh … thanks." He couldn't be serious. Even though she'd removed most of her *makeover*, she still felt she must look like a clown in judge's garb. What had she been thinking to trust that woman with her makeup?

She'd wanted to look good this evening. So much for that. His expression when she arrived had almost sent her back to the door. His smile had morphed from startled to amused to sympathetic, as if he was fighting off pity for her abysmal sense of style.

She tugged at the dress's high satin collar, which constricted her breathing, and glanced up to find him watching intently. "Feel all right?"

"I'm fine. It's just—" *Oh, hell, tell him.* "My collar's a bit tight."

"Loosen it. Undo one or two of those top buttons. I won't report you to the house mother." He leaned toward her. "Do you need help?"

She backed up in her chair, and her hand nearly toppled her water glass. The thought of him touching her, even for so innocent a reason, sent waves of heat through her private parts. "No, no. I can manage." He propped his chin into his palm and eyed her. "I've wondered about that collar ever since you arrived. Who would design something so uncomfortable?"

Did he have any idea what efforts she'd put herself through to look like this tonight? Then the absurdity of the situation hit her, forced her to laugh too. "Wardrobe isn't one of my strong suits. I bought this dress for a job interview a few months back."

"How'd that work out?"

She tried to recall. "Now that I think about it, I got the Dallas job with my other dress, the brown one."

Ned raised a brow. "Your *other* dress? You only own two dresses?"

What had possessed her to be so candid? Might as well go down with a little humor. "What can I say? I'm a fashionista."

"I'm impressed. Most women's closets are packed so tight they can barely remove a hanger."

"And you're an authority on other women's closets, how?" Oh God, oh God, oh God! Could she have picked a worse response? She didn't want to appear to flirt. As if she could pull off the femme fatale thing anyhow.

"Hypothetically speaking, of course." God, he was smooth.

"If you got a job in Dallas, why are you still here?"

It was such a mistake to have dinner alone with this man. She couldn't trust herself around him. Something about him disconnected the filter in her brain from the circuitry that controlled her mouth. "Like I said, my dad asked me to step in for him while he recuperates."

"I know. But why were you leaving Two Rivers in the first place?"

How could she answer his question without impugning her father? "Dad's a real hands-on sort of guy who fought hard to build the company to where it is today. He's had to control everything under his nose, which hasn't left much room for me to participate as fully as I would have liked."

"It must be killing him to let you run the company now." The words were no sooner out than he must have realized their inappropriateness. "Sorry. That was—"

"Don't worry about it. Actually, it probably would have killed him if he *hadn't* let me or someone else run the company right now. Probably why he decided to keep it in the family."

"Let's talk about your continued role with this project. Your dad's heart problems have placed you and your company in a tough position. But I'm sure you can understand why I have to protect my interests, if I decide to remain with Two Rivers."

He was actually getting to the point. Hopefully, her stomach would be satisfied with the few bites of fish she'd taken, because further consumption of her meal wasn't going to happen. She forced a positive smile. "How do you propose to *protect your interests*?"

"First item, suppliers. From now on, I want to review all contracts with suppliers before they're signed."

"You want to review their contracts?" *Stay cool, girl.* This was just his first demand, and it was a doozie.

"I studied the list of suppliers you plan to tap as construction gets underway. Others outside this area can underbid them."

"Even with shipping charges?" This was solid ground for her, given her previous responsibilities. "I don't think so."

"I've located some high-volume dealers who want the business enough they're willing to absorb some or all the shipping costs. Rayburn Hardware in Milwaukee. Cram's Plumbing Supplies outside Chicago. There's more, if you want to hear about them."

"That won't be necessary." She forced herself to take a breath. "Unacceptable, Ned. We need our local suppliers. We can't let you undercut them."

"This isn't a request, Shae. I can get us some better deals." His continued to smile, but his chin jutted out a little more than it had a minute ago.

"With all due respect, you don't know enough about construction to make final calls on the purchase of supplies and materials." Had she really said that? She'd come here tonight prepared to hold the line with her knowledge and charm so Ned would have no other choice but to stay with Two Rivers. Instead, he'd asked for additional involvement, and all she'd done so far was say no. Some negotiator she was.

"You're an authority on the purchase of supplies and materials?"

She kept her gaze steady. "Actually, yes. Purchasing has been one of my responsibilities."

"I, uh, didn't know that." He paused, as if to regroup. "I also want to approve the work schedule."

She rolled her eyes. This was getting ridiculous. "We'll certainly involve you at every step of the process."

"Not good enough."

"I'll have some wine now." She hadn't realized that would come out.

INTERESTING. After her earlier refusal, he would have bet she'd make it through the entire meal without any alcohol. Did this mean he'd backed her into a corner? Or was it a brilliant negotiating strategy on her part?

She sipped her wine, unconsciously running her tongue over her lips after she put her glass down. God, did she have any idea what she was doing to him? How could this woman wearing such puritanical garb be so seductive? *Focus, Ned.* Time to make his announcement. "I want those review and approval provisions because I've decided to be my own project manager."

She clamped a hand over her mouth. "What? Why?"

"Mike told you I wanted the project manager to report to me. Although you weren't particularly crazy about the idea at the time—"

"I said 'no way'."

"I believe you said you needed time to think about it. I'm serious about being project manager. With this throat thing, I'll be available. I definitely have the interest. And with your lack of experience—"

"If you became the project manager, you'd compound that situation even more. I at least have grown up in this business and have the appropriate schooling. You don't have the least idea what a project manager does."

She was right and clever enough to use that particular liability to weaken his point. "I'm a fast learner. Plus, I've got more to lose than you, since I'm the one paying the bills."

"Have you ever pursued a project like this?"

"No."

"Been a part of one? Worked with subcontractors?"

"Had my home in Brentwood remodeled a few years ago. Subcontractors were involved."

"Did you have direct contact with them?"

Man, did she have to get so picky? "I, uh, left that up to the contractor I hired."

She didn't reply, although she did hold up her glass as if to say, "Touché!"

"You've made your point, Shae. I admit I have very little—okay, no experience with construction. But *my* point is, that doesn't matter. I'm the client."

Had to get this settled fast. With each passing minute, it had become more difficult to remain on point. Whenever he looked her in the eyes, he saw the verdant waters of Fiji, which enticed him to throw caution to the wind and come swim in their depths. His groin reacted involuntarily, made him squirm in his seat.

He refilled her glass. "Good stuff, isn't it?" Hoped she hadn't noticed him going light on the stuff after his first sip, designed to encourage her to join him. Wine, any alcohol, was on his doctor's no-no list.

She stared at her glass as if she'd never seen it before. "Yes, it is. But I really shouldn't." Nonetheless, she continued to sip.

"We seem to be at an impasse. What do we do about it?"

A crooked smile slanted across her face. "Arm wrestle?"

He felt the underside of her arm. "What kind of muscles are you hiding from me?" As soon he'd touched her, he knew it had been a bad idea.

She eyed his hand on her arm, but she didn't pull away. "What do you think? Could I beat you?"

She stared him down, as if issuing a challenge. And challenge it was, to keep his wits about him. He'd gone too far. He'd underestimated how little wine it would take for her to relax. She was in no condition to continue talking business, even though it would probably net him the deal he wanted. Maybe her, if he were cad enough to take advantage of her semi-inebriated state.

Before he could settle their bill and pour her into a cab, though, the easy listening music in the background switched to a vocal. One of his, the management obviously catering to his good will. As the music began, the vocal split into two totally unique tracks, one rasping and the other clear and penetrating. They wove themselves together to produce yet a third melodious sound.

"That one of yours?"

He shrugged. "Guilty."

She sat up straighter, eyed her wineglass. Her eyes narrowed as if some new thought had struck her. "You set that up, didn't you? Plied me with alcohol so I'd let down my guard. Softened me up with that romantic song. Acted like you actually cared what I thought."

"No, Shae. I never meant to, well, okay I did try to help you relax with the wine—you seemed so stiff and unsure of yourself—but I had nothing to do with the—"

She flung her linen napkin on the table. "I can't think straight. Too much wine.

She rose abruptly, knocked the chair backward. In her attempt to steady it, she bumped against the table and toppled his wine glass. Since he'd hardly drunk any, the contents streamed across the tabletop and dripped down on him.

"Sorry. I'm no good at this," she paused long enough to murmur.

Then, with studied effort, she headed for the door. Surprised, Ned remained seated while he stared helplessly at the red stain growing on his slacks.

So much for settling this tonight.

CHAPTER 4

Ned slipped out of his wine-drenched slacks and the navy jacket which had miraculously escaped the spill and hung them on the small valet chair in his room at the Woodley mansion. Under a hot shower, he slaked soap over his body to wipe away the smell of wine while he replayed the events of the evening. What happened? He'd been making progress renegotiating the contract the way he wanted it. He was sure of it. Then his song came through the sound system and she'd fallen apart.

In all fairness, she hadn't dumped the wine on him. At least, not intentionally. His glass just had the misfortune to be full when she knocked against the table as she fled the room.

So where did tonight's debacle leave him? If he broke the contract with Two Rivers, the other general contractors in the area probably wouldn't buy into his serving as his own project manager. He needed that degree of participation to keep costs down. He picked up the phone and punched the number.

"Dave?" Shae replied in a somewhat muffled voice.

"Uh, it's Ned Collier."

No immediate response. "Oh. I, uh, hi. If this is about your ruined pants, I plan to make full restitution," she said finally.

"Appreciate the offer but not why I called."

"No? Then why did you?"

Did this woman really want his business? Her directness threw him. "I plan to drive out to the property tomorrow. Would you like to ride along? You've probably been there several times as the infrastructure went in, but it would give us another chance to discuss the contract free from distractions."

At first, she hesitated. "Discuss business in the car?"

"I just thought … never mind. I'll meet you at your offices Monday morning."

Brief silence. "No. I'll go. I've, uh, only been there once. When Dad first signed the contract."

Really? Her old man hadn't seen fit to keep his daughter in the loop about his biggest project ever? Just how much had the guy told her about Sullivan's Creek before he handed the reins over to her?

One more reason he should drop Two Rivers as his general contractor. But if he started over with another outfit, the time required for them to come up to speed would slow completion of the first plat. He needed to complete and sell those unsubscribed houses as soon as possible to see a return on his investment. "No better time than tomorrow morning for you to meet the site of what could prove to be the most important work you'll ever do. Providing we can come to terms."

They made plans for him to pick her up the next morning at eleven. Her reluctance to be alone with him was puzzling. It wasn't like he was going to ply her with liquor when they got there. Couldn't be his celebrity, if her pluck at their first meeting was any indication. Whatever. She must really want to keep the contract to get past her hesitation and agree to accompany him.

SHAE TIED her hair back in its usual ponytail the next morning and donned an old pair of blue jeans, a red T-shirt, a tan windbreaker and work boots. No need to obsess over wardrobe today like she had the day before. Look where that had gotten her. She experimented a little with the foundation she'd felt obligated to buy from Cecily. The woman hadn't been completely mad. This stuff really did improve her complexion.

Despite the comfy apparel, though, once ensconced in Ned's tiny sports car, the body wearing it was anything but relaxed. She tried to focus on the proposition she was about to make. The one she'd practiced in her head all morning. But Ned hadn't been sitting twelve inches away then, and his aftershave, or whatever scent he was wearing, hadn't clobbered her olfactory senses like it was now.

Once they were underway, she willed her voice to sound natural. "I did some thinking after I got home last night." He didn't need to know she'd been sleeping off her drunk when he'd called or that she downed three cups of black coffee this morning. The hangover more or less under control, she'd called Dave and made him late to church brainstorming additional ways to cut costs.

She removed a piece of paper from the pocket of her windbreaker. "I've diagrammed the gist of our negotiations thus far. A column for your requirements and another for Two Rivers' responses. It's not comprehensive. But it's a start at consensus."

He lifted a brow, and the effect nearly made her forget what she was about to propose. How could someone so challenging be so intriguing?

"Come up with anything we can use?" His tone was nonchalant, but she was sure he was interested by the way his eyes flickered.

"Maybe." She paused, then plunged in. "Every point you've brought up seems to either revolve around reduced costs or more direct participation by you." She held her breath, waited for him to reply, but he remained silent. "Why not turn over the supplier data you've compiled to us and let us go after similar deals with our local vendors?"

"You think they'd agree to lower their prices?"

"They won't be happy." An understatement. It would place years of hard-won affiliations on the line. Moreover, she hadn't run this past her dad, although Dave had reluctantly conceded it was the best, and maybe only, way to keep the deal. "But when we point out to them that they risk losing business they may never regain to outside competitors, I think they'll go along."

He returned his attention to the road. They drove in silence for several minutes, until Shae's impatience got the better of her. "So? What do you think?"

"Interesting thought. But so far, just a concept."

She was ready. "Here's the thing. I can't guarantee we can get these concessions, but if we do, they'll be on an ongoing basis. The suppliers you've talked to were probably ready to give you a short-term deal to get your business, but I doubt they were willing to agree to the quoted prices for more than the first six months."

He liked her proposal. The way the fingers of his right hand tapped on the steering wheel and the fact he speeded up told her so. This time, she made herself remain patient, not push for a response.

"Why didn't you bring this up last night?"

Unexpected question. Her case rested on his trust in her and her ability to pull off what she'd proposed, so she had to be totally up front with him. "Dinner meetings aren't my cup of tea. I wasn't at my best last night. Anything I was about to propose was put on hold when I realized how tipsy I'd become."

"Didn't mean to make you ill at ease. I do a lot of business over meals. Apparently that's not your thing."

"I, uh, no, it's not."

"I'm glad you agreed to try again today."

"I'd like to get this settled as much as you." That didn't sound very friendly. She tried again. "I really did want to see the property."

She had one more item to broach, but they were slowing. Must be nearing the property. Shortly, a small sign saying "Future home of Sullivan's Creek" appeared. The scene caused her to catch her breath. She had expected a flat farm field. Although the area before her had surely been that not long ago, now it was a vast network of winding roads, several hills, trees, and even a few small footbridges. Of course, there was no green grass yet, which would not appear until each housing unit was finished.

"Ned, I didn't expect anything like this. It's so …"

"Extensive? It's going to be quite the place to live when it's done."

It hit her like a wrecking ball. She wanted to be part of this. A major part. Not just to keep the company afloat and not just to show her father she was capable of making this happen. She wanted this for herself, to make this man's dream happen in this incredible place. Her next proposal had to clinch the deal with Collier.

Ned unlatched the gate that protected the property from outsiders, then drove the car a little farther on to what appeared to be a temporary parking/staging area. She threw open the door and jumped out to get a breath of air and a better look. Ned followed behind.

She pulled her jacket tight to ward off the day's unexpected chill and smelled late spring in the rich, loamy scent of the soil and the emerging vegetation across the road, where the fields were under cultivation.

When she'd learned Sullivan's Creek was several miles out of town, she'd pictured cornfields, barns, silos, cattle. All great for the Iowa economy but not exactly her idea of a residential community. The landscape was rolling prairie, primed for summer vegetation.

Her ace in the hole could wait a few minutes more. First, she wanted to explore, take in her surroundings.

"Beautiful, isn't it?" Ned had come up next to her while she'd been engrossed studying the land.

"Yes. It is. I understand your passion for this project." Time to launch her idea. "One more thing. We're willing to accept you as project manager."

"Yes?"

"Provided we can agree on certain conditions."

Ned had moved a few paces ahead. At her words, he stopped and turned. "And those would be?"

"Dave or I sign off on all your decisions."

"What good does that do me?"

"It gets you a title and a reason to hang around the site without intimidating the crews with your developer status. That's what you really want, isn't it?"

He booted a clump of dirt out of his way. "How can I make decisions with those limitations?"

"You can. You just won't be able to execute them until Dave or I buy in. That safeguard is in your best interest. Otherwise, you'll set yourself up for certain failure with your lack of experience."

"What if neither of you signs off?"

She'd anticipated this reaction. "Then you call a meeting of the three of us and state your case." She tried not to sound too anxious, but either he agreed to her proposition, or Two Rivers couldn't go ahead with the deal, as much as they needed his business and as much as she wanted to prove herself capable of leading a project of this scale.

He stuck his hands in his pants pockets and wandered off.

She gave him his space. Away from town, away from everyone else, with just this deal to consider, she hoped he'd realize the gem she'd offered him. He probably wouldn't obtain any arrangement quite so permissive with their competitors.

She tried not to watch him pace. Didn't want him to see her own tension. But despite the do-or-die nature of the moment, she was tempted to catch a glimpse of his back end every so often. He looked good today. Damned good. His black jeans seemed molded to his body. How had he been able to sit in his tiny car? At least the warmth generated by admiring his body helped cut the chill in the air.

He returned after a few minutes. "You're a tough negotiator. Your dad would be proud."

"Do we have a deal?"

"We're close. I want to see it on paper first."

She clapped her hands. "That's fantastic."

"Didn't say yes … yet. But I like your ingenuity. I want to build in some kind of fallback position for me, should you and your superintendent nix something I really think we should do. I think that's possible. Don't you?"

No. But she wasn't losing the contract over it now. "I think so. Shall we shake on it?"

"Let's shake on getting this far." He held out his hand.

As they made contact, as if on cue, the sun came out and caught him in its shimmering rays. For a second, she forgot about the deal. She simply stared at this gorgeous creature and enjoyed how the light blue pullover hugged his chest, revealing high, tight pecs.

He noted her gaze and edged toward her, the glint in his eyes going smoky. A bolt of panic seized her. *Omigod. He's going to kiss me. If he does, he'll find out what a fraud I am when it comes to sex.* She could fantasize about his buttocks all she wanted, but following through on that daydream wasn't in the cards. Especially with a guy like Ned Collier. Or should she say Jake Bonneville? She and Jake lived in different worlds.

She had to do something fast to avoid embarrassing them both. "Tell me more about this place. Why the name Sullivan's Creek?" she asked in the instant before his lips would have touched hers.

"Huh?" Ned attempted to adjust gears. He'd almost kissed her. In the middle of a business deal. What had gotten into him? Fortunately, Shae had the presence of mind to avert disaster. But why? She'd been the one with the come-hither look. He'd merely—okay, he'd willingly, been ready to follow through. "Jake Sullivan was my grandfather. I took my performing name from him and his favorite car. The creek you've probably seen on the various plats in the project file."

"You inherited this land?"

"It should've gone to my mother. But she prevailed upon Gramps to deed the land over to me on his death. My parents' art gallery was doing pretty well by then, and she wanted me to have something to fall back on if my music career tanked." How ironic. His mom might have been psychic, except now it was this very land that might tank him.

Shae shielded her eyes with a hand to screen out the sun. "It's so peaceful." Her voice had gone soft. Almost reverential.

"Yeah, well, that was his idea. When I was kid staying here one summer, Gramps taught me how to drive a tractor over these rolling hills. At the top of a rise, he turned off the motor and pointed back toward town and asked if I heard the same sound he did. I thought he meant the sound of corn growing, thinking myself so smart for regurgitating what Gramps had told me about crop growth at that time of summer.

"He chuckled at my response but shook his head. Told me it was the sound of *civilization* creeping toward us. I'd learned in school that the great civilizations of the world had given us religion, and printing, and, unable to come up with anything else, threw in tractors." Though he didn't disagree, he pointed out how modern society had added things like fast food, car washes and shopping malls to the list, which in turn had meant that one field after another had disappeared to become ticky-tacky buildings. I'd been so confident then that he could successfully fight off anything. It would be a few years before that bubble burst when Gramps succumbed to cancer.

"He admitted he couldn't fight encroaching gentrification, but if it had to happen, he wanted it to be his terms. He didn't want the land ruined, the land that would someday be mine. Since he'd no longer be here to guard it against unscrupulous developers, he was going to trust me to carry out his dream. Make sure it was developed the right way, retaining as much of its pristine prairie grandeur as possible."

Damn! Hadn't meant to tell her so much.

Shae did a three-sixty taking in their surroundings. "Pristine prairie grandeur. That's almost poetic."

"Gramps wasn't much of a poet. More a pragmatic environmentalist."

"A pragmatic environmentalist." She nodded, as if she knew exactly what he was talking about. "Why now? You probably could've held off doing anything with it yet for years."

"My mom came home from the gallery late one night and surprised a burglar. Scared him off, but just the thought of her vulnerability in that part of town frightened the crap out of me. Her response was to install a security system, mine was to strong-arm her into moving."

"But why out in the country? Seems like someone living out here would be pretty vulnerable, too."

He nodded. "Exactly. That's why I pulled out Gramps' plan.

Thought I could convince her if I put an emotional spin on the idea and gave her neighbors."

"That's terrible. And brilliant."

The sun disappeared behind several dark, ominous clouds. In the distance, the slight rumble of thunder signaled a surprise late spring storm. Though she'd worn a windbreaker, Shae rubbed her arms to ward off the chill.

"Cold?"

She studied the clouds. "I'm not a big fan of storms."

"Then let's go back to town and flesh out your proposal so we can re-sign the contract tomorrow."

Although they had barely explored any of the property, Shae didn't disagree.

He gazed out over what used to be his grandfather's fields one more time. Shae was right about the peaceful thing. Every time he visited, he felt like his dad and grandparents walked the fields with him. He could really use their counsel right now.

What he could also really use, after their near-kiss, was to get out of here. Didn't dare admit to himself his feelings for her were changing, evolving into something else. Something he dared not consider because of where it might lead. Shae was one of those women who'd demand serious if she ever got involved with a guy. He didn't plan to get serious with any woman for some time to come. If ever.

But he also wanted to seal this deal while she was open to compromise. "When we get back, we'll go to your office, if that's okay." He opened the door for her and moved around to his side of the car. "We should be able to knock out the revisions within a couple of hours."

She nodded but didn't say anything. Nor did her face reveal whatever thoughts were running through her head. She kept looking out the window, up at the sky. He wasn't sure if she was angry, frustrated or frightened of him and his out-of-control libido.

He tried to start the car. Instead of the steady purr he was expecting, though, it choked. What the … He tried again. Same response. Then a third time with no success. He sank back in his seat. He'd wait it out.

"Problem?" Shae asked.

"Won't start."

She frowned but didn't comment further. Instead, she clasped her hands in her lap and stared out the window again.

Her self-control ground against his impatience. His hand itched to start the car again, but he wanted to give it a full two minutes before trying. When he finally did, yet again, nothing happened.

Didn't that just cut it? He wanted to throw something but settled for pounding his fists against the leather-clad steering wheel instead.

"How's the gas gauge?"

"Filled it before I picked you up."

"Battery?"

Couldn't she leave the checklist to him? Her questions grated. "Battery should be fine."

She bit her lip and resumed her vigil of the heavens.

Cars weren't his thing, but he needed to do something. "Stay here. I'm going to check up front." He fiddled around with the knob he thought released the hood. Nothing happened. He kept searching and finally found the pull under the dash. He gave a nervous laugh, like he'd known where it was all along and had just been killing time.

She returned a strained smile.

Under the hood, he pulled at This and twisted That and prayed the car would start, because he didn't know what more he could do, other than call the rental agency to come get them. He tapped on Shae's window, indicated she should lean over and try the ignition again. He returned to the front to see what happened. Nothing.

He emerged from under the hood and motioned for her to hold off doing anything while he messed around some more. This time he twisted That in the opposite direction and pushed in This. When she once more turned the key, the engine still didn't turn over.

His mind and body had now officially gotten past almost-kissing his general contractor. But the remedy was a little too extreme for his liking. His back was cramped from bending, and he felt like chewing nails. But he wasn't ready to concede defeat. So he examined one part of the engine at a time. Perhaps he'd spot something out of place. Turning green. Or smoking.

"What's up?"

He jerked, smacked his head against the hood. For a split second, he nearly blacked out. A sharp pain shot through the area of impact. *Ow, ow, ow, ow!*

"Sorry. Didn't mean to sneak up on you. I thought I could help."

He eased out from under the hood, straightened to get the kinks from his back and rubbed his head. "Help? You're batting a thousand against me so far."

She winced. "Why don't you go back to the car and let me tinker with this?"

"You? You know about sports cars?"

"Not exactly. But I do know pickups and my own SUV. Let's see how closely the engines resemble each other."

"Don't bother. You'll get your hands dirty. I'll call the place where I rented this ton of junk."

"Getting a little dirt on my hands is in my job description. Let me play around here a few minutes, and if I can't figure it out by then, you can make your call."

She was just being helpful. What could he say? His macho pride could take it. Yeah, right. But what was she going to do that he hadn't already tried?

Two minutes later, she signaled him to try the ignition again. Why not humor her? She actually thought she'd been helping. He gave it a try, and to his surprised mortification, the engine kicked in and purred like the softest kitten.

When she appeared at his window, she beamed, two thumbs up, almost beside herself with glee.

Reluctantly, he turned one thumb up in congratulations. Beginner's luck. Or else he'd primed it for her. That was it.

She must have sensed his lack of enthusiasm, because her smile died and she rounded the front of the car and got in her side again. "The end clamp on the battery terminal wasn't secure enough to start the car, so I took the rubber ends off a few hairpins and stuck them between the clamp and the battery post. That's all the car needed to start. I just wanted to get out of here before the storm breaks."

The trip back to town was spent in silence. He wanted that contract. They'd been so close to making it happen. But now he wouldn't be negotiating from a position of strength, thanks to his talent at car repair.

It wouldn't be so bad if, when she wasn't studying the sky, she'd cover her mouth with her hand as if trying not to smirk.

Okay. He'd use this to his advantage. Should he ever again be tempted to pull her into his arms and plant another one on her, he'd remember that smirk. No self-respecting Lothario, horny or not, kissed a smirk.

CHAPTER 5

"Ned! What a nice surprise." His mother unbent from her position over a shipping box and brushed away foam peanuts that clung to her apron. "I'm in the midst of unpacking."

"Mike told me you stopped by to see me yesterday. Sorry I missed you."

"I wanted to see how your voice is doing."

He hadn't seen his mother since he moved to Mike's house the week before. Preliminary dig plans occupied his time instead. "I'm taking my meds and drinking gallons of water daily."

"No singing?" she asked. Her tone was a little too intent.

"No, although sometimes I forget and hum a snatch of a tune only to remember I can't go there yet."

"Please, please don't push your voice. It will come back in its own good time." She picked up a canvas leaning against the crate. "My latest find. Darren Williams. Traditional subject matter this field of daisies, but a bold color palette. You'd expect lots of white and yellow. Instead, purple and green dominate."

"Reminds me of Sullivan's Creek."

She held it in front of her. "It does, doesn't it? I'll have to ask her where this is located. She doesn't live too far from here, so it's probably somewhere in the state."

"How about going out to dinner tonight?"

She replaced the canvas in the box, then touched his cheek. "Not necessary, dear. Besides, I'm going to be tied up here for a while cataloguing this shipment." Her face brightened. "But here's an idea. I'm doing a special showing of Darren's works next month. For once you'll be here to take it in. Will you come?"

She immediately turned away from him, as if she didn't want him to know how important his attending was to her.

"Ah, Mom!" He didn't feel the least bit guilty groaning. He hated these staged events, as much as he knew how important promotion was for his career.

"One night. A couple of hours. I'd really like for you to be here, but suit yourself." Her tone hadn't quite reached the begging stage, but it was certainly entreating.

He counted to ten mentally, hoped she'd mistake his silence for resolve. Firm resolve she couldn't erode. Right. He was putty in her hands and they both knew it. "Okay. But just this once."

She twisted back to him, beaming. "You won't regret it. You might even enjoy yourself."

"Don't gloat."

"Let's talk about you, then." She drew him across the room to a small sitting area.

"Me?"

"Mike told me you've decided to keep Two Rivers as your general contractor. That's the outfit being run by the young woman I met at your meeting, right?"

Ah, Mike. Not only had Mike taken an immediate dislike to Shae, he thought he detected sexual attraction on his part to their female contractor, which just didn't exist. No telling what Mike had told his mom.

"I liked her," she said.

That was news. His mother had refrained from talking about any of his women since she'd advised him his second fiancée, Julie, was marrying him for his money. He should have listened to his mother then, but he didn't. He couldn't believe his unassuming fiancée could be so grasping, so he'd accused his mother of interfering in his life. Then Julie's sister drank a little too much champagne at a bridal shower and revealed how Julie planned to use her new husband's money to start her own company. That had been that, as far as their marriage, or any marriage for him, was concerned.

"Wow. You rarely comment on my lady friends."

"She impressed me when she didn't let you get away with the silly scheme you worked out with Mike. For him to lead the meeting while you sat back and watched her in action? Like one of those judges on those television competition shows."

"Ms. Harriman does have a way of making me say things I hadn't intended."

His mother tilted her head and gave him one of those you're-kidding-me looks he'd received almost every day when he was a teenager. "Also doing things you don't intend? Like taking her to dinner or giving her a private tour of your grandfather's property?"

Apparently she'd stayed long enough at Mike's to get an earful. "All business. Plus, I got the deal I wanted. Pretty much." Time to change the subject, before she pumped him for more details about Shae. Instead, he'd let her in on a few of his plans for the development. "I'm going to stick around town while the construction phase of the project gets underway."

She nodded. "Yes, dear. I know. That's why I thought you would be available for my showing next month."

"I'm going to be the project manager."

Her mouth puckered into something close to a frown. "Mike told me about that as well." That was all she said, although it was obvious there was more on her mind.

"Go ahead. Say it, whatever you're so valiantly holding back."

"There are so many other activities you could involve yourself in during this period. Why take on something you know nothing about?"

"Granted, I don't know a two-by-four from a ... whatever. But I know what I want in this development, what Gramps would have wanted. I also know how to read a financial report and negotiate for myself in a business meeting."

"Why not let Mike continue to do that for you, like you did at the meeting you held here?"

"Don't you think I can do this, Mom?"

She returned a vigorous shake of her head. "You can accomplish anything to which you set your mind. But why invest so much of your time and energy in something someone else is better prepared to do while you could concentrate on your real work—your music?"

"Haven't forgotten my music. I'm currently working on a couple of movie scores. Which I need to get back to." *Before you begin to guess at my financial problems.*

"Ned?" she called on his way to the front door. "Invite Mike to the showing, too, will you? It's the twenty-seventh. I'll send you both engraved invitations."

Engraved invitations, from his no-nonsense mother? What was his world coming to?

"DO WE HAVE A DEAL, MR. BLALOCK?" Shae kept her voice even and firm as she attempted to sound as authoritative as her dad to convince the elderly supplier she meant business.

"Deal, young woman?" the voice on the other end grumbled, "Deals are made between equals. Not by wimps in bulls' clothing trying to force something down the throats of their business connections."

Wimps in bulls' clothing? New one. Had she really turned into the bitch he described in the two weeks since Ned Collier had decided to keep them as his general contractor? No. Not her. She was simply holding her own with the man with the reputation for bullying his clients. Her father had often complained about the man's churlishness. Imagine. Tim Harriman offended by someone else's truculent manner?

"We've been through the draft agreement twice, and I've checked off all the points with which you took issue. There's nothing left to debate."

"You're certainly not your father. May growl like a polecat, but he at least listens to my concerns."

Did Blalock not get it? Instead of finding someone who'd supply the weatherization barrier for less, she'd cut the man a break. Sure, he'd have to reduce his original bid, but he still had the job. "My father would have thrown the phone against the wall a half hour ago."

"Ah, hell! I don't wanna mess around with this any longer. I've already wasted more time talking with you than your business is worth."

"Good! We'll send the revised agreement over this afternoon."

"Hmmph." He hung up.

Shae set down her phone with a triumphant flourish and checked Blalock and Company off the list. Amazing. She'd convinced the old guy to shave three percent from his cost.

Not bad for a half hour's work. Ned would be delirious. Not that she cared what he thought, other than it would be one more way to prove she could handle this job.

She ran her eyes down the list, assessed her morning's accomplishments. Ten names. Seven contacted. All but one had been willing to lower their estimates when she told them she could do better with their competitors. Like Blalock, none of them had been particularly happy until she reminded them of the potential for future business, or lack thereof, from this project.

Shae stretched her back against the chair and attempted to relax the taut muscles.

She allowed herself a drawn-out sigh as she picked up the phone to tackle the next name, but her arm went limp, like a deflated tire. She'd hit the wall. But since her morning's efforts had produced results, she could afford a break.

She reflected on the events of the past several days. Should be relieved the contract between Two Rivers and Ned Collier had been signed and the construction phase of the project was underway. Instead, regret plagued her mood. She touched her lips, memories of the kiss she'd deflected when he took her to Sullivan's Creek continued to haunt her. What if she'd allowed it to happen? Would that have been so bad? Ned was such a well-known, powerful man. What would it have felt like to have his lips on hers, if only for a moment?

"Good. You're here." She jerked. Ned lounged against the open doorway, the door that had been closed just seconds ago. "We need to talk."

"Did we have an appointment?" She hadn't seen or talked to him in days. His appearance just as she'd been thinking about him was eerie. She fought the urge to feel her cheeks.

"Didn't realize I needed one."

"Well, no, but—"

He sank into a visitor chair and dropped a black leather valise on the floor. "I've been playing with the project plan." His opening comment emerged a little too fast.

Her stomach clenched. Good-bye, fantasies about the man. Hello, pain in the—As project manager, of course she should expect him to be working with the project plan. But the way he'd said *playing with it* made her nervous. "Oh?" she finally managed to say.

He watched as if to gauge her mood. Then, like he just then remembered the purpose of his visit, he leaned over and pulled out a folder, flopped it on the desk. "Take a look."

What had he found? "Looks okay to me," she said after she'd perused the document inside the folder.

"To you, maybe. But not to me. This is so confusing. I don't see how you folks get anything built."

Her spine stiffened. She'd prepared the plan. It was her baby. "Confusing? How so?" She really didn't want to know.

He drew his finger across the open page. "Here, for starters. All these columns."

"Columns? This is standard action plan format— who, task, completion date, status, actual completion date."

"It's just so confusing."

"So you said."

"Too much information crammed together."

"You read sheet music and scores all the time. How is this any different?"

"Music follows a very rigid formula. A B-flat note always appears in the same place. Four-four time always has the same number of beats to a measure."

She waved her hands. "Notes, measures, whatever. Those things make sense to you. Why would you expect to understand construction terms when you've never built anything?"

He straightened. "It's not the terms I don't understand," he said in an exaggerated huff.

"Then what's the problem?"

Deep intake of breath. "Like I said before. The columns." He rose, moved swiftly around the desk and leaned over her. "They're so close together, so tight, they're difficult to follow." His finger touched her hand as he showed her. Was he talking about the project plan or her?

She sensed his taut pecs and abdomen less than an inch away. Her frustration with Ned's nitpicking fought with her body's awareness of the man. Her lower parts woke up and reminded her they were there and ready for business.

She breathed out the words. "You want more space?" She could use a little more space herself at the moment. Despite his ridiculous concern, she gave in to the force field that surrounded the man and turned her head to face him.

Ned's lips were mere inches from hers. For the first time, she noticed the broad bow of his mouth. So inviting, so … *Don't go there, Shae.*

His eyes met hers and held.

She had to do something. Either end it or give in to her impulses and let happen whatever was about to happen. Just minutes before she'd wondered, daydreamed about such a thing. Now the opportunity had reappeared. She knew what she wanted, but she didn't dare. Her father would cut short his recuperation and pull her off the job in an unrecovered heartbeat if he discovered something was going on between her and Ned.

~

NED WATCHED the battle rage within Shae's eyes. She glanced away, as if afraid of him. Then she turned back, unable to shut him out. She blinked fast several times, as if surprised by her own audacity. Finally, those gorgeous orbs went a blurry, inscrutable teal.

What on earth had made him approach her? It was impossible to concentrate on the document, because he was so focused on that lovely face and upturned nose. And her beckoning mouth. Ah, hell! This was the last place in the world, the last female for whom he should have this kind of feelings. But he'd checked better sense at the door. *Carpe diem. Go for it!*

In one swift movement, his arms went around her, pulled her from her seated position into his embrace. God, she smelled good. Unlike every other time he'd first kissed a woman, he paused, studied her expression, a combination of surprise and invitation. His eyes went to the mouth he was about to ravish and then sought her eyes, checked for acquiescence.

She stared back at him, her mouth forming a tiny *o*.

All the signal he needed. He wanted to crush his mouth against those luscious lips, but he took his time, started slow and sweet. Contact. Glorious days! He forgot his resolve and pressed her closer, deepened the kiss.

He was about to explore the inside of her mouth when she shoved out of his arms and backed away, a stricken expression slashed across her face. She brought a hand to her mouth. "What was that?" Her voice, though croaky, rose in alarm.

Surely she'd known what would happen? "I kissed you. Thought you wanted me to." Okay, he'd wanted it, too. Initiated it. But a guy didn't need cold water thrown in his face to know when he'd read a lady wrong.

She continued to finger her lips. "How'd … why?" Her eyes, though still wide, reflected alarm. Even a tinge of shame.

She hadn't been openly flirting, but he knew the look he'd seen in her eyes. She'd wanted him to kiss her. But he was a gentleman. He wouldn't push. "Sorry. I must have misread—"

She closed the folder and handed it back, all the while not looking at him. "I'll have the plan reformatted for you," she said in an unsteady voice. "Revise the spacing. So you can read it better."

He was at a loss what to say. Obviously, she didn't want to pursue the kiss let alone talk about it. He was here under false pretenses. He'd manufactured his concern about the project plan because he wanted to see her again. For some unknown reason, he'd been compelled to check out the vibes he'd felt the day they'd gone to visit the site.

He'd crossed the line. Embarrassed her. She'd been right to back off. With as much dignity as still remained, he headed for the door. He paused. "Thanks." She could determine for herself whether he referred to redoing the report or for forestalling the kiss. He made himself take several steps down the deserted corridor. "Stupid, stupid, stupid!"

SHAE STOOD to the side of her office window and watched Ned head to his car, his gait fast and determined. No looking back. Once inside the vehicle, he slammed the door and burned rubber in a speedy exit.

Mentally, she waved good-bye to what might have been while she swiped at the tears running down her cheeks. Damn! They wouldn't stop. She was no better than a mopey teenager. Her dad would consider it a sign of weakness. But she'd been strong, hadn't she? She'd ended it, regained her business persona.

She'd enjoyed the kiss, oh God, how she'd enjoyed it! All those things she'd heard about physical attraction were really true—escalating heartbeat, insides going to jelly, even her toes had curled. But she'd had to stop herself, curtail the direction things were leading before it was too late and she was hopelessly enmeshed in an affair she had no idea how to handle. No way would she jeopardize this deal.

He was a big star, probably accustomed to casual affairs. He might be curious about this hometown honey, but once the novelty of hooking up with her waned, Shae would be left to pick up the pieces.

Couldn't risk that or her dad's wrath over such unprofessional behavior. So she'd stopped it. Not as soon as she should have. To herself, she could admit she hadn't wanted to stop it at all. But she couldn't let it go on. *You have no idea the sacrifice I just made for this company, Dad.*

Would it be worth it?

CHAPTER 6

In the days following Ned's visit to her office, Shae threw herself into construction planning so she wouldn't speculate about what might have been if she'd allowed Ned's kiss to continue. But thoughts of him intruded nonetheless. At first, she worried her rebuff of his advances might cost them the contract. But when Dave told her Ned had called to ask the date and time of today's orientation meeting with the project crew, she knew they'd at least survived that incident.

Since Dave was more familiar with the crew members, he'd handle the meeting. All she had to do was be there and look boss-like. She'd been so busy with the Sullivan's Creek project, she hadn't been able to get out to the sites to visit the crews and get them used to her new role as much as she would have liked. Of course, she knew some of them from their infrequent trips into the office, but she'd been office manager then.

Her phone rang. It was Dave. "Dave, I'm glad you called. I'd like to go over the agenda one more time before the meeting. We only discussed it in passing the other day."

"Uh, that's why I'm calling. I'm at the emergency room at the hospital with the wife. They think it's her appendix."

"Oh, Dave. I'm so sorry. Don't worry about a thing. Your place is with her right now."

"Appreciate your saying that. But what about the meeting? I suppose we could postpone,

but most of them are probably already on their way."

"I'll handle it."

"You sure you're up to it?"

"Sure. Why not? I'm not you, but they'll realize it's an emergency and go along with it."

"I'm not much of an agenda man, but there's a list on my desk with my talking points."

"Okay. I'll go find it. Now, you get back to your wife. Give her my best. Call when you can." She put down the phone, considered the task ahead. Even though she wasn't much of a person for speeches, she could do this. Right? Dave's notes should be enough to get her through.

As if she didn't have enough on her mind, she ran into Ned on her way to Dave's office. The memory of his kiss flooded her mind, despite her best efforts to forget it. How was she supposed to act around him now? She waited for him to provide a cue.

"Understand there's a crew meeting. Thought I'd sit in."

"Right. Dave told me you planned to be here," she said, rather than tell him his presence wasn't necessary or even desired.

"Where is he, anyhow? Wasn't in his office."

"Dave has a family emergency."

He frowned. "That's too bad. You still going through with the meeting?"

"I'm going to lead it."

"You?"

"I'd postpone it until Dave can be here, but it's too late." She crossed her arms in front of her. "We wouldn't want to lose valuable time, would we?" Did she sound too sarcastic? "It's quite routine, really. We're just going over what we'll need from them and who'll be assigned what jobs. That kind of thing. Pretty boring." She ducked into Dave's office. To her relief, Ned didn't follow.

Dave kept an orderly desk, and his notes lay in the middle. Unfortunately, Dave was also a man of few words, at least on paper. She'd have to improvise. No problem. She was up to speed on all the project details since her disastrous dinner meeting with Ned.

She approached the all-purpose meeting/banquet/ break room from the rear to assess her audience before she took center stage. Ned stood behind the rows of seated crewmembers and shook hands with a couple stage-struck well-wishers. Apparently he'd forsaken his preference for a low profile today.

She breezed past them and made for the front. "Good morning, everyone. Dave Hale was called away unexpectedly with a family emergency. I'll be filling in for him." She went on to tell them they had signed on for what was to be the most ambitious building project the area had ever seen and they should feel honored to have been selected. She was about to thank them for signing on, when a hand went up in the front row.

"How's your dad doing, Ms. Harriman? Is he coming back soon?"

Rude, but his concern seemed genuine. *Be nice, Shae.* "My dad had a close call with his heart. He is recuperating at a local rehab center. His doctors haven't given him a return to work date yet. But thank you for asking. And I'd like to thank—"

"How soon can he have visitors?" another guy asked.

"Visitors?"

"Yeah. A bunch of us would like to check in on him. See for ourselves how he's doing."

Just what she needed, crew members who'd report her every move to her dad. It was difficult enough to keep Dave's visits and contact with her dad to a minimum and not deprive either of the other's company. *Smile. Don't shut them out entirely, or they'll push back.* "That's, uh, very kind of you. I'll tell him you asked. But for now, his visitors are confined to Dave Hale and me."

"Speaking of Dave, why isn't he here today?" The first guy again.

In a steely tone, she said, "Like I said already, Dave was called away for a family emergency. It was too late to cancel, so I'm here in his place." She attempted a reassuring smile.

Not good enough. "Do you know enough about construction to lead this meeting? Maybe we should postpone until Dave's here," first guy replied.

Her entire body tensed, her throat constricted. How dare he question her credentials? Tim Harriman wouldn't take such treatment from a crew member. Her father would put this guy in his place.

"What's your name?" she asked the disrespectful man.

"Pete Martin. If you were out on the sites half as much as your dad was, you'd know my name by now."

"I agree, Pete. I should have visited more. Instead, I've been busy planning for the largest project in this company's history, a project that's going to keep you employed and well-paid during what is an otherwise serious downturn in our industry." She took a breath, gave her words enough time to sink in before continuing. "Moving on, I wanted to say—"

"No disrespect, ma'am," the second crew member cut in, "but Pete just had the balls to ask what the rest of us have been thinking. Are you qualified to lead this monster of a project while your dad's out?"

The room went absolutely quiet. Everyone had diverted their eyes in embarrassment during the first question. Now, they all turned to her to hear her response.

She gripped the edge of the lectern to keep her balance. Didn't they get it? She was in charge, and they weren't supposed to question why or how. She didn't have to justify herself to these people. She was here as a favor to Dave. In fact, she had half a mind to walk out on such disrespect. She fought off the urge to check out Ned, because she knew he was taking in this apparent mutiny, waiting to see how she'd deal with it.

Shae fought to keep her cool. "Just when did the crew start questioning the credentials of their superiors?" she couldn't help but ask.

Almost to a person, the group moved back in their seats as an audible, collective gasp swept through the room.

What was so shocking? She'd merely told them the way it was.

She attempted to stare down the entire assemblage, but her tear ducts betrayed her. No, no, no, no! She couldn't cry now. Not when she had to hold her ground. Especially not in front of Ned Collier.

She had to get out of there.

"I was going to welcome you all to the project before I was interrupted," she said in the steadiest tone she could manage. "Despite your misgivings about my qualifications, that still holds. Welcome, all of you. A copy of the preliminary schedule is on the table in the back. Further details can wait until later."

She didn't say good-bye or thank them for coming. She seized hold of whatever dignity she still possessed and charged from the room. Back in her office, she leaned against the locked door to stop shaking. When the shudders didn't abate, she staggered to her desk and slumped into her chair. First objective: get her breathing under control.

Why hadn't they listened to her? Or given her their respect. Because she was a woman? Sure, she didn't know them as well as she might have hoped, but this Sullivan's Creek project had eaten up so much of the time when she could have been out visiting the crews. So she had no management experience? Her dad had picked her. He owned the company. His decisions shouldn't be questioned.

Brisk knocking cut into her thoughts. "Go away!"

No go. The knocking continued. "Shae? Open up." Ned.

"Not now, Ned."

The noise subsided, but she was sure he was still there. "This can't wait. C'mon, let me in."

"No! Go away. I need privacy."

"No time for that. We need to talk." The determined edge to his voice signaled he wasn't listening to her any more than the crew had.

She dragged herself to the door. "Oh, all right!"

He burst into the room as soon as the lock tripped, then immediately closed the door behind him.

She didn't know what to do, other than stuff the tissues with which she'd been swabbing her face into her pants pocket. She leaned against the front of her desk. Couldn't give him the impression he could simply barge in and demand a meeting every time he had a question. "Okay, I'm listening. What's so important to justify your intrusion?"

"Have you heard from Dave yet?"

"No. But I haven't checked my messages."

"How soon can he get back here?"

"His wife is probably having an emergency appendectomy by now. I doubt we'll hear from him until at least tomorrow."

"That may be too late."

He didn't shout, but it was clear he was more than a little concerned about the scene she'd just escaped. "Why? What's going on?"

He pursed his lips. "Several crew members are talking about signing on with other crews."

Just because she'd left the meeting abruptly? "Let them. Work is pretty scarce right now."

"They said there are still a couple medium-sized projects in progress. Nowhere near as massive as this one, but they think they can get along with those general contractors better. I tried to persuade them to hold on another day until Dave returns."

"Until—" Was it that serious? Just because some impertinent crew members couldn't stomach the way she'd treated their questions?

Ned went to gaze out her window. "You apparently stepped on some toes a little too hard back there. It seems construction workers are almost as superstitious as musicians. They felt bad vibes in that meeting. They don't want to stick around to see how those pan out."

HE WATCHED a small group of crew members gather in the parking lot. From their animated state, arms flailing, leaning in to each other, he doubted his reassurances had done much good. Within a minute, two more joined the three, then two more. Dissention was spreading fast. He needed to move faster to counteract Shae's tantrum. Finding new crew members would take time, time he couldn't spare. Those first phase homes had to be on the market soon, so he could get his money back. Since Dave Hale wasn't here to do clean up, he'd have to rely on her.

He turned back to find her seated at the desk, going through a notebook. "What are you doing?" he asked.

"Contact information for others we've worked with over the years. We don't have to cave to those guys' demands or attitudes."

Didn't she realize none of this would have happened if she'd kept her cool? He shot to her desk and placed a hand over one of the pages but didn't touch her. That had brought him nothing but trouble the other day.

"Those guys as good?"

"Of course. No. I don't know." She lifted her hands in surrender. "I haven't worked directly with the crews. Must have been obvious in the meeting. They, their questions, got to me."

She was nursing a case of damaged ego. He didn't have the time or the inclination to deal with such sensitivities. "File that information away. There's still time to keep the crew you have, or had. But you need to regain their allegiance right away."

She crossed her arms in front of her and tilted her head toward him. "Really? How do you suggest I do that?"

Sarcasm. She still didn't see how much damage she'd done herself.

"Have your support people call everyone who attended today's meeting. If you're sure Dave Hale can make it, invite them back for a follow-up confab tomorrow. Throw in food. A generous spread around the lunch hour."

"Since when have you become such an expert at staff relations?"

How could she be so blind? He took a breath so he wouldn't say something he'd regret. He had to keep her reasonably pliable until he could get with Hale. "I have a small group of musicians and producers who've worked with me for over five years. I'm tough on them, too. There are times when you have to be. But other times it makes more sense to go with the flow, give in to their wishes."

"Didn't you hear them challenge me?" Her voice rose.

Surely she recognized her inexperience was just the kind of opening salvo employees liked to throw at their new employers? Just to see what they'd do. And she'd done plenty. "How do you account for their actions?"

She thought about it. "That first guy, Pete, seemed miffed because I hadn't spent much time in the field with them."

"Legitimate point?"

"Legitimate or not, he was out of line to bring it up."

She wasn't listening, because she was still bristling at the guy's rudeness. "Put his comments aside for now. Do you think your lack of field visits bothered him so much he'd risk his job to mention it?"

She opened her mouth as if to say, "Yes," then shut it.

"If you were out there mucking it up with them every day, would they be pleased?"

"I admit I should have spent more time with them. But I've been so inundated with—"

"Yeah, yeah. With my project. I get it. But these guys aren't upset because they think you've ignored them. They'd much rather deal with Dave. He's a known quantity and one of them. Their complaints about your absence were just their way of testing you."

"They seemed to want a show of strength. That's what I gave them."

It was like the early morning California fog he knew so well had suddenly cleared. Shae thought the fact she was in charge meant everyone would blithely follow. She was clueless about what it meant to lead. Mike had been right to question her lack of supervisory experience. But, hey, wasn't this the very reason he'd stuck with Two Rivers? If he could help her manage her people better, he could manage her. God, that sounded insensitive, even to him. But if he was going to keep Sullivan's Creek solvent, he had to guard his expenses with an iron hand.

He turned away from the window, settled in one of the visitor chairs and repeated her statement. "Show of strength, huh? How did you do that?"

She blinked several times, as if she couldn't believe he would even ask such a question. "I told them I'm in charge. I make the decisions. I didn't let them rattle me."

Ned reclined, crossed one leg over the other. "Really? Let's recap. You ended the meeting abruptly. Didn't cover anything you'd planned to say. Walked out before anyone could ask any more offensive questions. Sounds like you were rattled to me." She didn't answer.

"While we're on the subject, when you walked out, it may have seemed like a power play to you, but to your audience, me, for instance, it said you didn't feel you could stay and fight it out. Like you weren't tough enough to tango."

"I did what I thought my dad would do. I've seen him storm out of many a meeting."

"Which you attended?"

"Well, no. I wasn't always included."

Interesting. Her training seemed to have come long distance from the School of Dad. "How do you know such tactics worked?"

"Because … because—"

"From my experience with him, your dad can sometimes blow off a little steam. But his crew seems to respect him anyway, and his clients have stuck with him because of the quality product he delivered."

Elbows on her desktop, she leaned into her tented hands and seemed to think through his words. "If I hadn't walked out, how would I gain their respect? If I ran after them and begged them to come back, it would seem like I caved."

He placed his hands on the front of her desk and leaned in. "If these guys are the best, why not let them think they've won this round? You've got the rest of the project to let them learn otherwise."

She bit her lip. "Do you have any idea what you've asked? It won't seem like I'm in charge at all if they think they've put one over on me."

"Yes, you will. If they see Dave defer to you. Same as I did when we first met at my mother's art gallery. I never would have considered your company if I hadn't seen the exchanges between the two of you that day and believed you able to take charge." Not totally true, since the very weakness he'd read in her then had been a deciding factor in sticking with this company, but she needed something to hang onto. For now, he'd give it to her.

"You did?" Her tone sounded incredulous.

His opinion seemed important to her. Surprise.

"Okay, I'll give it a try, but I'm not convinced."

He'd worn her down. "Good luck."

He was at the door when she called, "Ned? See you tomorrow."

He raised his brows in surprise. How had she known?

For the first time since their aborted kiss a few days back, she smiled at him. "You were planning to sit in, right? Even though I hadn't invited you. I might as well let you think you won this round, too."

CHAPTER 7

"Crew walked out on her, huh?" Dave swiped his fingers over his chin. It was an hour after the unsuccessful crew meeting, and Ned had sought him out in the surgical recovery room at the hospital.

Ned clarified. "Actually, Shae walked out on them first."

Dave's hand hit the armrest of his chair. "I shoulda been there. But there wasn't much choice. Couldn't leave my wife."

"Of course not. No one's blaming you. I'm a jerk to come here and dump this news on you, but too much is at stake to let it go. I overheard several crew members talking about signing on with other projects rather than deal with Shae. We need to act fast to pull things back together."

"No one's ever walked out on Two Rivers before."

"Shae Harriman has never been in charge of Two Rivers before."

Dave angled his head at Ned. "With all due respect, Mr. Collier, that's unfair."

Ned slumped in his chair. "Call me Ned. You're right. I knew she had little leadership experience when I continued my contract with you folks. But I didn't realize she had virtually no experience. Today was a real shocker. She seemed more concerned about their lack of respect than the possibility of a walkout. Even when I tried to tell her she could lose her crew, her response was to call in new people rather than attempt to get her current crew back."

Dave leaned forward, palms on thighs. "Shae takes people at face value. If they said they're leaving, then her response would have been to replace them. Probably never occurred to her to coax them to reconsider."

"Look, man, I like Shae. She got a terrible deal, being thrown into this job and expected to swim. As a topper, she found herself in charge of the largest project your company has ever tackled. But that project is my project, too, my money. I can't afford to see it go down the tubes or be delayed because the boss got her feelings hurt."

Dave narrowed his eyes. "She know you're here?"

"No."

Dave didn't reply but instead stared at his hands. His silence spoke volumes.

"Okay. I hear what you haven't said. I have no right to interfere. If I'm not happy with how things are going, I should find another general contractor."

Dave still didn't respond, as if he waited for more from Ned.

"I don't want to break the contract," Ned felt compelled to add. "I know it's unusual for the developer to be so, uh, underfoot. But this project has been a lifeline for me as I've struggled to get my voice back." *As well as given me a back door to keep my costs down.*

"I understand. But she won't be happy."

Ned hung his head. "I know. A bit presumptuous. She'll tell you about this sooner or later, once she calms down, but I didn't want to take a chance she'd put it off. To keep your crew, time is of the essence."

In a resigned tone, Dave asked, "What do you want me to do?"

"Come lead the meeting tomorrow, provided your wife's okay. Shae needs to be there, not just to watch you and see how it's done, but also to show those guys they didn't scare her. She really did try to answer their questions today. At first. But when they questioned her ability to head up the project, she got defensive. So tomorrow she has to show she's gracious enough to step aside and let you run the meeting."

"Did you discuss any of this with her?"

"Had to almost break down her locked door to get her to talk to me, but in the end, she agreed to a second meeting. Over the lunch hour. With food."

Dave chuckled. "Food, huh? She gotta cook too?"

Ned sat back. "Might've gone too far with the food, although it seemed like a good idea at the time. Deals in L.A. are usually made over lunch or cocktails." He added an afterthought. "After I left, I texted her the names of a couple caterers my mom uses. Thought Shae wouldn't talk to me on the phone."

"You seem to have it all figured out. Except the part where she sits there without opening her mouth. You really think she can do that?"

"I do, if we can convince her keeping her mouth shut is not a sign of weakness. I'll stick close to her tomorrow and nudge her if she forgets. I invited myself to the meeting, although she'd already antici-pated I'd be there."

"She must feel so alone. Confused. I let her down," Dave said, at length. The crew more or less told her she wasn't up to the job and threatened to desert her. Now she has to concede to a do-over."

"She's not too crazy about me at the moment, either," Ned added. "But if we can help get her crew back and retain a little pride in the process, it'll be worth her ire."

THOUGH SHE WAS TEMPTED to confide in her father about her problems with the crew and get his advice about how to deal with them, Shae didn't want to raise his stress level. Couldn't risk it. If she was really honest with herself, she also didn't want to lose his confidence and possibly her only opportunity to show him her stuff. Nonetheless, once she'd set the wheels in motion for the next day's meeting, later that afternoon she found herself a participant in a father-daughter checkers match at Blackhawk Hills, the rehab facility where her dad had reluctantly agreed to be taken.

Even though he won, Tim Harriman's fist pounded the game board and sent several checker pieces onto the floor. "How much longer do I have to be cooped up here? This place is the pits." Thankfully, his outburst didn't have anything to do with the crew's pending desertion. Now in his mid-fifties, with his salt and pepper hair, near six-foot height, and penetrating blue eyes, her dad was still quite handsome, when he wasn't complaining, which seemed to be quite frequent since coming to the care center.

It was almost a relief to listen to his tirade. This was behavior she knew and understood, the most familiar thing she'd dealt with of late. She retrieved the checker pieces and set them back on the board. "What does your doctor say?"

Her father grumbled to himself as he hunched over the board.

"What was that?"

"Nothing. How'd things go today?"

She felt for her dad. He was frustrated with the restraints and inactivity imposed by this regimen. However, he seemed to be on the upswing. His complexion had returned to its normal color, not the deathly pallor she'd witnessed in the hospital. "You're changing the subject again. What did the doctor say?"

"I'd rather hear about Collier's project."

"Okay, but first, was Ned Collier as hands-on with the project before your heart problems?"

He sat back, seemed to consider her question. "No more than other developers. They all think they know better than the experts they hire." He stopped, rubbed his chin. "Now that I think about it, though, he seemed to become more intense as the project progressed. Once the actuals on the sewer system and streets and the rest of the infrastructure started coming in, his attention switched to the financing. Couldn't believe the costs could be so high, stuff like that."

So it wasn't just her being in charge that had Ned concerned about costs. Although such reassurance didn't ease her mind completely, it helped to know she wasn't the cause.

"Why do you ask?"

She kicked herself mentally to have opened this door. But Ned's little lecture after today's meeting still grated. Yes, it was his project and he was footing the bill. But she was the one in charge of Two Rivers at the moment, and she had to find a way to get the point across to him soon, or both of them were in for their own breakdowns.

"No way am I going to slop baked beans on a plate for those guys." Just prior to the crew meeting the following day, Dave informed Shae the two of them would also serve the free lunch they provided. "I might as well put a bone in my ponytail and wear an animal skin. Both shout Neanderthal woman. Slave. Subservient."

"We'll be servers, Shae." Dave said. "Not just you and me. The rest of the office staff as well. Even Ned said he'd be happy to help. The idea is to show how much we value our crews."

"Maybe you do. I can't say the same after yesterday's meeting."

"Ah, yes. Yesterday's meeting." He steered her away from the food containers the caterer had just delivered. "I'm sorry you had to go through that without me."

"Not as sorry as me, to relive it again today. With you in the lead. Am I allowed in the room?"

Dave placed a comforting hand on her arm, then, as if he remembered his place, removed it just as fast. "These aren't bad guys. They just take a little getting used to. They need to get used to their new boss as well."

"Ned said they had tested me. And I failed."

"Don't let them get to you. They have no more idea how to relate to you than you do to them. Sounds like both sides went a little out of bounds yesterday."

She stuck out her chin. "You didn't answer my question. Am I welcome at my own meeting?"

"Of course, you are," Ned said from behind her as he joined them. "You're the boss. If it helps, think of yourself as the owner of a number one basketball team. Is it the owner who calls the plays? Well, maybe. But behind the scenes. On the game floor, the owner lets the coach deal with the team."

She actually understood his analogy. Basketball was one passion she shared with her father. She tried to recall where the owner sat during games. On the sidelines with the coach? In a skybox above the crowd? She wasn't a *skybox* type of person. That would be Ned, even though these days he seemed to relish the sideline post more.

Finally, she gestured toward the food. "Do I have to wear an apron?" she asked in a begrudging tone.

Dave bit back a smile. "Of course not. You don't even have to *slop* beans, since we're serving tacos. On the other hand, you might want to wear something to protect that pretty blue blouse."

Her pretty blue blouse. Last night, she'd studied her closet long and hard as she debated what to wear today. Until she'd assumed the reins of this project, she'd never paid the slightest attention to what she wore. Probably because she'd grown up in a male-dominated household. After yesterday, it was important she appear comfortable and in charge. Maybe, since the guys seemed to use her being female against her, it was time to take advantage of her gender. So out came her trusty, no-nonsense navy pantsuit with the light blue blouse. And Cecily's makeup.

In the end, despite Dave's words of warning, everyone except Shae wore a butcher apron as the hungry crew filed past them to be served.

"Hey, Dave, glad to see you're here today," one guy said, as the superintendent placed two taco shells on his plate.

"I'm glad you came back, Marty," Dave returned.

"Hamburger or chicken, Marty?" Ned asked.

"Hamburger, thanks."

Shae followed Dave and Ned's lead. "Shredded cheese, Marty?"

Marty started to reply, but a crew member behind him appeared to nudge him, so instead, Marty just pointed.

Shae forced herself to keep her smile intact. She gave Marty a generous serving of shredded cheese, then turned to the next person in line and asked him the same.

When Pete Martin appeared, she was the first to speak. "I gave my father your regards when I saw him yesterday. He asked me to tell you and all the guys how much he appreciated your cards."

After a long pause, Pete finally grunted. "Uh, thanks."

Reluctant acquiescence. "I asked his doctor how soon he can have visitors. He told me it would probably be another week. But as soon as visitors are allowed, we'll let you guys know."

Pete's eyes widened. "Good. Thanks."

Next to her, Ned moved closer and tapped her elbow slightly with his own. Finally, he approved of something she'd done. If she'd had more time to compose her thoughts before the meeting yesterday, she probably would have thought to check on this and brought it up herself. But that bridge had already been crossed. All she could do now was anticipate the road ahead.

Splat! A blob of taco sauce shot through the air from the plastic squeeze bottle a foot away and landed on her front. On her new blue blouse. She stared at the growing stain before she realized what had happened.

The crew member who'd thumped the bottom of the squeeze bottle, apparently to loosen the sauce, gave her a "my bad" grin. "Oops. Sorry. The stuff came out sooner than I thought it would."

"Those guys were just testing you," Ned had told her yesterday. Was this another *test* or was it just an unfortunate accident? What would her dad do? Hell, her dad didn't own a new blue blouse. Her reaction was up to her. She wanted to clobber the guy. Better yet, retaliate with her own shots of taco sauce aimed his direction. But she wouldn't let herself be suckered into a mindless reaction again. Not when the whole point of this second meeting was for her to show restraint.

She grabbed a couple napkins and dabbed up as much of the sauce from her blouse as she could. Wouldn't prevent the stain—had to suck up the fact the blouse was ruined—but she needed to get as much of the stuff off before it dripped on her pantsuit. But first she scooped up a bit of sauce with her gloved index finger and took a taste. "Not bad." She smiled at the crew members still in line, gawking at the show. "But better on your tacos, I'm sure."

She plucked the offending crew member's name from recent memory. "Good shot, Jimmy." She leaned across the table toward the man and fixed a mischievous glint in her eyes. "Just to be on the safe side, let me help you with that sauce."

Jimmy took a step back, held up one palm while he protected his plate with the other hand. "Uh, that's okay, Ms. Harriman. I got enough." He scuttled away.

While she still held the bottle, she turned to the next man in line. "How about you, Bob. Can I offer you some taco sauce?"

Bob shook his head and sped away as fast as Jimmy. She'd made her point, so she set down the squeeze bottle and went back to spooning out shredded cheese and lettuce as if nothing had happened.

"I'll take a heaping helping of that cheese, Ms. Harriman," the next man said. "That's what makes the taco." She ladled it out for him. "Not the sauce."

She looked up from the container of cheese just in time to catch his hint of a smile. *Well, what do you know?* Maybe she'd passed this test.

As soon as the line cleared, Ned leaned over. "Great save! I held my breath there for a moment, wondered if we were in for a food fight. But you came through like a pro."

"How's your blouse, Shae? Did it survive the taco sauce?" Dave whispered.

She turned away from the serving table to check. "It's a goner, but if it regained the tiniest ounce of respect for me, it'll be worth the loss."

Once the crew members had eaten and the remains of the meal were cleared away, Dave called them to order. "Welcome *back* to Part Two of our orientation meeting, everyone." Before anyone even thought to snicker or interrupt him, he went on. "Hope you enjoyed the meal."

Polite applause.

"We'll do this kind of thing more often as the project unfolds, to celebrate the conclusion of various milestones along the way."

More applause. More enthusiasm.

"You can thank our interim boss, Shae Harriman, for the idea. Just one of the small innovations she's introducing. With her dad's full approval, of course."

Everyone glanced over their shoulders at Shae seated in the back of the room. *Just look gracious, Shae. Don't correct Dave by telling them the food was Ned's idea.* What innovations? First she'd heard of them, but she'd come up with something. For now, the crew had to believe she had their best interests at heart as she introduced her own small touches. With her dad's blessing, of course. She hated that last part, but after yesterday, the crew wouldn't take kindly to anything with just her name on it. Plus, it was in *her* best interest to keep her dad informed.

Though difficult, she kept her mouth shut, remembered Ned's coach-owner analogy.

Before Dave moved on to the main agenda, he returned to the subject of Shae one more time. "I also want to thank Jimmy, who made me look good with our new boss." He paused, allowed everyone's attention to drift to their fellow crew member. "I tried to talk her into wearing an apron today without success." The room exploded in laughter.

Dave waited for the room to grow quiet again. "Just so you know, we've now removed all the taco sauce from the premises." More laughter, at Jimmy's expense this time, as those around him nudged him to make sure he'd heard.

Dave, you showman. She released her breath.

"Okay, let's return to the real reason for this meeting and talk schedule and workload." For the next twenty minutes, the group listened while Dave laid out the plans for the project. No one interrupted. No one walked out.

At first, Shae's defensiveness got the better of her as she sat there and absorbed Dave's words. *I said all that, too. How come no one's questioning Dave when he says it?*

But then she broadened her observations and noted not only Dave's body language, the nuances in his presentation style and the sequence in which he laid out the plans but also the group's reaction to him. He took his time at first, started with humor. At her expense, he'd found something that put them all on common ground, and that shared experience resulted in a positive outcome.

The day before, she'd been so anxious to get started and have the meeting over with, she'd not given herself time to relax and play to her audience. Truth be told, had she not experienced the grilling, it never would have occurred to her, even now, how important it was to relax.

"That's about the size of things. At least for the moment," Dave concluded. "Any questions?"

The room went silent for a few beats, and then, as if the group had elected its own designated spokesperson, Pete Martin raised a hand. "Uh, Dave. We all appreciate your coming in today to go over things again. We heard about your wife. We're glad all went well with her surgery."

Tiny steel bars threaded their way through her veins. For all the good will they'd attempted to generate with the free meal and Dave's presentation, the crew's mood had returned to this. She sensed the next question before Pete Martin opened his mouth again.

"Thanks, Pete. All of you. It was a fairly routine surgery, although it came on fast. My wife is doing quite well."

"Good to hear," Pete continued.

Shae held her breath.

"With old Tim out for the time being and you dealing with an emergency yesterday, it really drove home the point that we're all working under jerryrigged leadership. No disrespect to you, Ms. Harriman," he gazed back at Shae but added, "Shae, we realize you're just helping out your dad, but too much is at stake here for someone who's never led a project like this to be in charge."

"That's what I'm here to explain—" Dave said.

Shae stood and faced her people. "No one is more aware of my supervisory and management inexperience than I am, Pete. But I do have legitimate credentials for this job. Like a civil engineering degree from Iowa State. I'm familiar with this company and all it stands for, because I've worked in the administrative office the past five years."

"I, uh, didn't realize you were an engineer," Pete replied.

She stuck her chin out just a tad. "I really want us all to succeed." She inhaled, exhaled. "Yesterday was a great lesson for all of us. Painful, but informative. Now that it's out in the open, I hope we can accept the fact I'm here, at least for a while. Whenever I appear to go the wrong direction, I hope you'll work with me to correct it."

Speech concluded, she took her seat again. She'd really set herself up for a letdown now, even though she'd felt compelled to make the statement.

Pete bit his lip, wiggled in his seat. "I, uh … sure."

Dave quickly cut in. "Thanks, Shae. We all appreciate your commitment to this project."

She willed herself to appear professional and gracious.

A few chairs away, Ned nodded and gave her a discreet high sign.

When Dave glanced toward the back of the room, Shae turned that way as well. A few of the office staff held trays of champagne flutes ready to move in as soon as the meeting ended. Who authorized champagne? The crew may have been treated to lunch, but they were still on work time, when alcohol was off-limits.

"Come on in, folks," Dave called, as if not quite sure what else to say. The staff moved among the audience, distributing the drinks.

After everyone had been served, Dave took hold of a glass. "Uh, well, wasn't expecting this, but our, uh, developer, Ned Collins, apparently wanted to add his touch to today's meal. If the weather permits, we break ground next week." He raised the glass. "To clear skies, a little luck, God's good graces and the construction of Sullivan's Creek."

Everyone held their glass aloft, joined in.

Toast over, champagne consumed, the group began to file out. Shae rose to shake hands with people, wish them well in the weeks to come. But those who remained either went up to congratulate Dave or stopped by Ned to thank him for the champagne.

She should be relieved, happy. They had their crew back. At least the crew members had been civil. Even laughed a bit. Instead, she stood there like a pillar of stone, a frozen smile belied the rage growing within. This meeting had been aimed at the crew, Dave, her and their reconciliation. But Ned couldn't leave well enough alone. No, the superstar, who apparently craved an audience, had been hell-bent to remind her and everyone else he was the one who paid the bills.

Couldn't let her enjoy even this tiny victory.

CHAPTER 8

Within ten minutes, the room emptied except for Shae, Ned and Dave. Since the office staff had cleared away the remaining food, there wasn't much cleaning up to be done.

Dave drifted over to the chair where Shae now sat attempting to process what she had just observed. "Looks like things have settled down here. I'm going back to the hospital. Call if you need me."

She came out of her reverie. "Thanks, Dave. You really turned things around."

He lifted his shoulders. "You did your part, too. You kept your calm when you needed to. Even joked with the guys a little."

"Speaking of jokes, you weren't so bad yourself. I've never seen you lead a meeting let alone defuse a potentially explosive situation like that. Impressive." She shook his hand, held it a fraction to convey her appreciation.

"Uh, you're welcome," a somewhat surprised Dave returned. "See you tomorrow."

"That was very gracious of you," Ned said, after Dave left.

"Even I have my moments."

"Some meeting," he commented. "Twenty-four hours ago, I wasn't sure we'd ever get to this point."

"We?"

He returned a puzzled look. "Well, yeah. I was right there alongside you in the serving line. And then, there was the champagne at the end—"

She gritted her teeth, still seething. "Yes, the champagne. Fairly high-ticket item for someone who has nickel-and-dimed everything else. Did you find a liquor store with a two-for-one sale?"

"Actually, I raided the Woodley wine cellar at my friend's invitation. Alcohol on the job probably isn't the best idea, though."

"No, it isn't."

"It was just a small flute, Shae."

"Champagne may be the drink of choice in the entertainment world, but not in construction. Even I knew these guys are generally beer drinkers, unless they're at a wedding or anniversary party. All you did today, besides one-upping me, was demonstrate how little you know about this world. Not the best start for the guy who wants to be his own project manager."

He grimaced, stared at the floor momentarily. "Okay, point taken, although I was only trying to help you seal the deal."

"Why? You weren't the one they threatened to walk out on."

He leaned so close she could smell his woodsy after shave. "Oh, really? It was my project in jeopardy. If I hadn't—" He stopped and sucked in his lips.

"If you hadn't what?" A tiny bubble of suspicion poked her brain.

"Never mind."

"Never mind? What did you do, Ned?" she challenged, letting her misgivings underpin her tone.

He didn't answer at first. "I'm glad Dave was able to be here."

"Uh-huh?" She lifted a brow.

"I wasn't sure he'd understand the gravity of the situation. Especially since his mind was probably on his wife. As it should have been."

"What does that mean?" She couldn't keep her voice from rising.

Backing up a step, he placed his hands in his pants pockets. "I, uh, went to see him at the hospital."

"You did what?" She was almost shrieking now.

"His wife was still in recovery. He was just sitting there, waiting to hear about her condition. He welcomed the distraction."

"You went to the hospital? Intruded on his privacy?"

"It was a bit, uh, irregular, I agree. But I called first to make sure he was okay with seeing me."

"People don't do that to other people."

"I said I checked with him first. Made sure I wouldn't be interfering. It worked out well in the end."

"It was my job to contact him. Which I did."

He shifted his stance. "You had your hands full setting up today's meeting. I had the time to check in with him."

She didn't know which was worse, his interference or his belief he hadn't. "You went way beyond your bounds."

He narrowed his eyes. "Maybe so. But face it, Shae. You were in over your head yesterday. I had too much at stake to risk you not following through on this plan."

She drew in her lips. He had no confidence in her?

These past weeks, she'd been so focused on keeping his involvement to a minimum, she'd forgotten the concerns he had about her when she took over. "I did follow through with Dave. I also proved myself at this meeting, as you said yourself."

"Only because Dave was here to lead."

She couldn't dispute his point. Dave had saved the day. But it cut that their client still doubted her. Damn! She'd been working so hard to make a go of this assignment.

Unable to come up with an appropriate rejoinder, she reached for her bag and stomped off.

"There you go again," he called from behind her. "Ought to get yourself some running shoes for faster takeoffs."

Déjà vu. Only yesterday she'd felt the same way at her office, slamming, then locking the door. Shouldn't have walked out. Should have held her ground. But his lack of confidence in her had shaken her own confidence so much she couldn't talk.

She grabbed a coffee mug on her desk and threw it across the room. It caromed off the side of a file cabinet—her dad hadn't yet digitized all their records— and shattered. It took a couple of beats for her to realize what she'd done. Then the tears arrived. A deluge she couldn't stop. Who was she more upset with, Ned or herself? One thing was for sure: working with him, having him as project manager was proving to be more difficult than she ever imagined.

Better sense told her to get out from under this project now. Two Rivers couldn't afford Ned Collier's way of doing business. But it couldn't afford to lose his business either. With her dad on the side-lines, it was up to her to figure out how to make this work.

From now on, she had to be on guard and watch Ned much more closely. But how was she supposed to do that without risking her heart?

TWO DAYS LATER, Shae sat in her car and watched the stakes go into the ground to mark where they would dig Ned's mother's lot. The weather, which had turned cold and windy, reflected Shae's mood. Why was it taking so long? They should have finished an hour ago. Old Man Todd, the despot whose company was responsible for the excavation, had probably drawn out the process in return for having to discount his fees.

A knock on her side window startled her. "Miss Harriman?" One of the crew. From his puckered eyes, things weren't going well. None-theless, she chose the high road. "How's it going, Marty?"

"Slower than we'd like. But this outfit is known for doing a cracker-jack job. Mr. Todd wants to know if you want to check the first section."

How considerate of Todd. Was this for real or was it a set-up to make her look like a rank amateur? She'd never witnessed this part of a project before, except as in intern in college. But she was game. She could read site plans with the best of them.

"Good idea. I'll be right there."

Marty gave her startled look. "You will?"

"Sure. Give me a minute to put on my jacket and I'll join you."

"Look. If you want, I'll do it for you."

Was he attempting to help or save them the embarrassment of her ignorance? "Thanks, but I can handle it."

"You, uh, ever done this before?"

"It's been a few years, but I haven't forgotten." She sure hoped she hadn't. She closed the window and grabbed her windbreaker.

"Don't let Old Man Todd get to you," he added when she emerged from the car. "He's a bit crusty, but he's like that with everyone. Even his own crew." He nodded the direction they should go and set off ahead of her.

Ned had arrived shortly after she pulled up, but thus far, they hadn't spoken. Not surprising considering how they'd left things earlier in the week. He stood off to the side and spoke with crew members and signed autographs, but Shae was sure she felt his gaze on her when she wasn't looking.

"Here she is, Mr. Todd," Marty called as they approached a ruddy-faced older man who gazed at a roll of site plans.

"The GC usually checks the placement of the stakes around the lot lines and the footprint of the proposed construction," the older man stated, his tone gruff.

She forced a smile and debated if a handshake was in order. She decided against it when he continued to stare at the maps. "Let's get started then." She waited. He didn't move.

Finally, he did look at her. For all the crevices etched into his wind-blown face, he had the most blazing blue eyes she'd ever seen. Cold blue. She could have sworn she heard a snarl. He took his measure of her in an instant, then returned his attention to the site maps. Without a word, he pulled one off the top of the stack and held it out to her.

Though tempted to ask, "Now what?," she instead lifted the map to chest height. At first, all she could make out were strange scrawls like a foreign alphabet. But as her eyes focused, one familiar symbol after another emerged. She made her way to the GPS device to assure the stakes lined up with the coordinates.

She was nearly finished with the various markers when she ran into one stake that didn't check out. She rechecked it three more times.

"What's the matter?" Todd had come up behind her.

"Huh?" Should she tell him? The last thing she wanted was to make a big production over nothing. She'd save those times for when she really needed them. "I, uh, must have messed up the alignment. The point I've referenced doesn't compute."

He scowled, like he didn't believe her. "Let me see." He pushed past her to check the GPS himself. His eyes returned every so often to the map she still held. Finally, he grabbed it away from her and studied the instrument again. "Hmmph!"

So the marker had been placed incorrectly. Would he admit it? Or had he thrown in a ringer to see if she'd find it?

The answer came shortly. Todd backed away a few feet and waved over a couple of his assistants. With their lowered heads, they resembled a football team huddle. First one and then the other took a shot at the alignment. Each sneaked peeks her direction, then they'd resume their inspection.

Finally, Todd came over to her, a sheepish look having replaced the earlier haughty one. "Good call. It's corrected now." No thank you, no apology, but his tone sounded different. Acceptance?

She'd been right! *I knew it, I knew it, I knew it!* A wave of pleasure swept through her, and made her almost want to dance a jig. Better sense kept her feet in place. But damn! It felt so good for once to have bested these defenders of the construction world's male bastion.

Todd turned to go, his lieutenants flanking him and spoke to them. "See if the lady wants some coffee."

"I'll get it for her." Marty, her own man, materialized from out of nowhere.

What do you know? She'd consumed coffee from her own thermos all morning to keep warm, but she wouldn't waste this invitation. Nor Marty's nominal acceptance of her. She started for the small silver van that served as the crew's snack wagon and passed within fifteen feet of Ned. He didn't say anything, but she could tell from his knowing expression he'd witnessed the scene.

THEY BROKE ground for the first group of houses a few days later. Shae watched, unable to speak, as the earth was scooped up and pitched to the side. This was really happening. This huge building project was actually underway. With her at the helm.

She pivoted and caught the look of wonder on Ned's face. "Exciting, isn't it?" she asked, despite their recent differences.

He nodded. "Is it always like this?"

How would she know? This was her first groundbreaking as well. Her dad downplayed stuff like this. But for her, this was a major high. But Ned didn't need to know. It would be one more sign of her inexperience. She swung her ponytail, attempted to appear less intense. "Enjoy the high but save some awe for the other steps along the way."

The mound of earth grew higher. Conversation wasn't necessary. History unfolded before them. History in which they both were major participants.

NED'S MIND went back in time to the summer when he was ten, just shooting up, his shorts hitting his thighs higher each passing week. Both grandparents had been alive then, Grandma Cathy hadn't passed away until a few years later. She spoiled him with great comfort food and Grandpa Jake lavished him with attention, taught him the elements of farming.

The vision was almost too much to take in today. He needed to escape the dig before he got too sentimental. He slipped behind some of the equipment that wasn't in use and settled on a large boulder dug up earlier.

Tomorrow, he'd bring some camp chairs, maybe even a tent. Set up a portable office. Some place where he could watch over things yet keep his distance from Shae, although she'd been the one who'd avoided him since her outburst after the second crew meeting the week before.

He reached inside his windbreaker and brought out his phone to reread the email from his banker, Zoe Johansen. She wanted to meet and discuss the status of finances. Despite Ned's previously spotless record, her board of directors was asking questions. He'd already read the note several times this morning, but, like the prey frozen by the hypnotic stare of the cobra, he couldn't seem to leave it alone.

"That the only place to sit around here?" Mike stared down at him, a quizzical look on his face.

Ned shifted sideways while he slipped his phone back inside his jacket. "Make yourself at home. This is probably the most comfortable spot, aside from our vehicles."

No sooner was he situated alongside Ned than Mike shoved a hand in his slacks pocket, brought out his own cell phone and checked for messages. "Thought you'd be over at the dig," he said when he'd finished. "That female GC ban you? I've still got the contact information for the other general contractors you considered, whenever you've had your fill of her attitude. Has she pissed off any more crew members this past week?"

Ned kept his eyes focused on his hands. "Can't say. Haven't been around her much."

"Ah, so she's pissed you off, too."

Though Mike was spot-on with his assessment of the situation, Ned wasn't about to agree with him. Shae's reaction to the champagne at the second crew meeting still rankled, even though she'd handled herself pretty well in the meeting. So he'd left her alone. "She's more than pumped today, this being the first day of excavation. I hung around to watch the first few loads of soil come up, congratulated her and then came over here to take it all in."

Mike studied him a moment. "It's a bigger day for you. Does she know about this land?"

Ned recalled the day a few weeks before when he'd brought Shae out to see the site. "A little bit. Told her how Gramps had entrusted it to me, and now I wanted to put his plan into action to get my mom back here. I wasn't sure Mom would ever consent to live on the land where she grew up after she defied Gramps to marry my dad. Grandpa Jake really wanted her to marry a farmer and carry on here."

"I liked your grandfather, the few times I saw him before his death. He never struck me as the vindictive type."

Ned swiped dirt off his jeans. "He wasn't. He never said so, but I think he and Gram long suspected Mom wouldn't be content to live in the country. She was too much into the cultural scene that went with her art."

"So she set down roots in Des Moines?"

"Yeah, well, that was Dad's doing. His parents were older. He wanted to be in town near them. I considered bringing her out here today to witness the dig for herself but decided to wait a little longer, until it's framed and she can begin to visualize all the color and design she wants to put into it."

Mike gave him a small nudge. "You're turning out to be a pretty good son. Despite the way you put yourself down for not being here when your dad died."

He fought off the urge to hug his friend, who'd clobber him if he did. But Mike's reassurance really helped. "Your turn's coming. One of these days your parents will tire of the social scene in Palm Beach and come back home. Long before the urge will hit your siblings. They'll need you then."

"Yeah, right." As if to change the subject, Mike checked his phone again.

"Expecting a particular message?" Ned asked, only slightly curious.

Mike placed the gadget back in his pocket, then stuck his hands in his pockets as well. "So aside from Hardhat Harriman's temper tantrums, how's everything else going?"

"The crew showed up today, so it appears she got past that challenge. Remains to be seen how they'll treat her now that construction has started. A lot depends on her attitude. At least we're pretty much on track. As long as this weather holds up."

Mike nodded, seemingly satisfied with the response.

"What brings you out here? You're not into anything rustic. Did you manage to get me that movie scoring gig we discussed?" He tried not to sound too hopeful, but he could use about ten scoring gigs to keep his head above water.

Mike turned away. "Uh, not exactly."

"*Not exactly?*"

"Uh, well, I haven't heard. Yet. I expect to hear from them soon. That's why I've been checking my emails."

"Okay. I can wait. I've got my hands full here for the time being." True enough, although he really couldn't wait much longer on the scoring project.

"Yeah. Uh, well, it's the other deal we need to discuss. The one you finished a few weeks ago?"

"Oh. That. They want rewrites?"

Mike shifted his gaze to his pants. "They've dropped the project."

His words didn't register. "It's been postponed?"

Mike faced him at last, his expression an attempt at studied nonchalance. "No, man. It's off. Done for. It ain't gonna happen."

"But it had already gone into production."

"Leading lady went into drug rehab. Claims she'll be out in a few short weeks and threatened to sue if replaced. Rather than mess with her attorneys, they pulled the plug on the project, which they can do without fear of a lawsuit."

"But they've already invested so much. How can they afford to walk away?"

Mike shrugged. "You know how these things work. They may recover more in insurance than they would have made on the film. Or a year from now, a similar project with a different title will show up with a different actress as lead."

Ned rose, his gut ached. That score had been his reserve for over-runs on this project. He tried to recall the details of his contract. "They're paying me whether they use my music or not. Right?"

Mike made a face. Not a happy one. "You'll get to keep the initial fee, but the rest of the deal was based on production and release."

Ned's stomach fought him, as if he'd eaten spoiled meat. "So that's that?"

"About the size of it. If they do pursue a similar project down the road, they may contact you then." Mike pushed off the boulder. "This is a setback. But you, we've, got other irons in the fire. That other movie deal could break any day now. Just be patient and keep your spirits up."

"Patient? Keep my spirits up?" Even though he was supposed to take it easy on his vocal cords, Ned's voice rose. "I was depending on that deal now that my personal appearances are on hold."

"It's a disappointment. But you're fixed quite well with all the residuals coming in from your last tour. Plus sales of your CDs." He paused. "Hey, how far along are you with that song for Renee Dechamps? Want me to turn up the heat there?"

"Not yet. I need to work on the coda and the bridge." Plus a decent melody and a hundred other things. The creativity needed for scores was one thing. But to produce another chart-climber for Renee was not easy when so much of his mental energy was currently invested in this project.

Damn! The bulk of his residuals and royalties as well as a large part of his bank account were tied up in this building project. He thought he could swing the rest he needed with these two movie deals. Hopefully a few others. But now that the one had netted only a fraction of what he'd anticipated and the other was still just a possibility, his remaining options were fast disappearing. He still owned property and a somewhat healthy stock portfolio, but his liquid assets, those he'd used as his equity stake to finance this project weren't going to stretch far enough. He owed that banker, Zoe Johansen, a response. What was he going to tell her now?

Mike stared at him, his brow wrinkled in concern. "Hey. It's not the end of the world. We've got more than these two ventures on the horizon. I'll just have to ratchet up the charm with my next pitch."

Ned attempted a smile. "Sure. That's all we need. For Mike the Schmoozer to hit the trail."

Mike thumped him on the back. "Couldn't have said it better myself. I need to get back to town. Work some more angles."

"Yeah, you do that. Keep me posted." And then, partly because he wanted to pay Mike back for the *good* news and partly because misery loves company, he announced his latest commitment to his mother. "Mom's got this big reception for some new artist in a few weeks. I agreed to go."

"Uh-huh. So?"

"So, you can be my date."

"Ah, you know I dig your mom. Even that faux hippie look. But those artsy things drive me wild. My parents dragged me to too many New York galleries when I was a kid."

"C'mon, Mike, gimme a break. I'm not crazy about them, either."

Mike lifted a brow. "You're serious, aren't you? You must've finally run out of excuses. That lady's tried countless ways to get you there. Okay. Guess it's the least I can do after my less than positive news."

"The very least."

Mike headed off, his pace increased with each step, as if he couldn't get out of there fast enough. Before he'd gone more than twenty feet, his phone was once again out of his pocket.

The humming sound of excavation equipment in the background made Sullivan's Creek actually seem real. Hadn't been the case when he'd returned to town several months ago to check out the infrastructure. Utilities, sewers, newly laid streets had seemed oddly alien, unrelated to his building plans. But watching the beginnings of actual homes emerge from the soil took his breath away.

Ned rubbed his hand along the boulder's rough surface, examined the gray residue on his fingertips when he finished. Iowa dirt. He was the steward of one of the world's most valuable natural resources. "Do you see all this, Gramps? Catch the irony—on the day excavation begins for the homes you envisioned, I discover I may no longer be able to pay those in charge of the dig, if I can't get my finances straightened out."

He slapped his hands together to remove the dust. He felt like such a failure. Maybe this was God's way of reminding him that fame, and the wealth that came with it, could be temporary and indifferent. Had he taken it for granted and squandered his chance to realize his grandfather's dream? It wasn't just the pipedream of an old man who fought to retain a dying way of life. No, Grandpa Jake had foresight. The guy had been ready to surrender to the inevitable, *embrace* the inevitable and shape it to the needs he anticipated. Do it the right way.

Maybe Mike would strike gold in the days ahead and find him more work, but Ned couldn't count on that. He had to take care of this himself, although his alternatives were more limited now than an hour ago.

"What do I do, Gramps? I'm down to two choices. I either convince the bank to increase their backing, near impossible but worth the attempt, or find additional backers. The first option means I have to bite the bullet and contact this Johansen woman. Or I swallow the bullet and call Irv Farley." Hadn't been in contact with Farley since he'd collapsed at the guy's fundraiser in Malibu.

"Of course, there's always Option Three: let Mike invest in the project."

But he couldn't risk harming Mike's relationship with his family. At the beginning of Ned's musical career in Europe, he'd made the mistake of allowing his first fiancée, Gillian, to manage his band's affairs. She claimed she knew what she was doing and he'd trusted her. The result? She'd signed them to an ironclad contract that kept him in England during his dad's illness and then left him when a job for her came up in the States. Ned had barely been able to return home for the funeral until Mike loaned him money to buy his way out of the contract.

Mike had taken the money from his trust fund without his parents' knowledge at the same time he refused to join the family business. Even though his parents wouldn't have begrudged Ned the money, Mike's defiance of his parents' wishes infuriated them so much they threw him out of the house and had very little communication with him for months.

It had taken Ned years to get past his guilt from causing friction between his friend and his family. He'd been almost as relieved as Mike when the Woodleys began to come around a few years back. Though Mike was still a bit skittish about anything concerning family, these days the reconciliation was almost complete. That is, if Mike didn't loan him any more money.

Had Mike's showing up here today been a message from his grandfather? "Sorry, Gramps, if that's what you were up to. I'm not ready to listen."

CHAPTER 9

"What do you mean we aren't using pans to form the basement walls?" Shae struggled to keep from screaming at the foundation sub. It was the day after they'd finished digging. Overnight, the weather had grown cold again and the wind had picked up.

The sub squared his shoulders and pulled at his denim jacket. "We're going with preformed foundation walls instead."

"I can't recall the last time we used preformed walls. I'm sure your bid didn't include them."

"Didn't."

The man seemed reticent to shed more light on this change in plans, but Shae wasn't content with his terse replies. "It didn't? Then how did it get changed?"

The sub glanced behind him. "Mr. Collier threatened to go with another company unless we reduced the bid. Best we could do was offer a cheaper alternative, preformed walls."

"He did what?" Ned had stuck his nose into operations again? She couldn't believe it. Just the thought accelerated her pulse rate. "We'd already accepted your bid. Did you remind him of that?"

"Tried to, but the guy wouldn't listen. I didn't want to lose the business of our local celebrity, so I found an agreeable substitute."

She couldn't fault the sub. Jake Bonneville might be known for his smooth vocal tones, but Ned Collier was a bulldog, apparently one with quite a bite. "Okay, I get the picture. Mr. Collier can be rather persuasive. But I can't let you proceed with this method. Preformed walls may work, but they're not up to our building standards."

"Sorry, Ms. Harriman." The man's face turned as red as the kerchief around his neck. "Guess I should've confirmed this change with you, but he led me to believe you'd given him that authority as project manager."

She didn't want to discuss Ned's role as project manager with the sub. "How soon can you replace this stuff with the pans we originally specified?" she asked instead.

The sub checked his watch. "Depends how much I've got on hand. I'm pretty sure I can get enough back here after lunch for at least the first couple houses."

"Okay, let's make the switch then."

He rubbed his chin, as if hesitant to go on. "You realize this'll cost more than the original bid?"

She blew out a puff of air. She'd suspected as much, but there was no way around it. "Understood. Sorry about the mix-up," she said, though it pained her to apologize for Ned's poor judgment.

He started back to his truck, shaking his head.

If the increased cost wouldn't also affect her profit margin, she'd almost feel vindicated that Ned's cost-cutting measures had backfired. This time, acting on his own bore no relation to her inexperience or his lack of confidence in her. She'd extracted a pretty good deal from these folks. But apparently it wasn't good enough for Ned. Why hadn't he'd stuck by their agreement and brought his concerns to her and Dave?

She didn't want to jeopardize their contract, but Ned couldn't continue to make independent decisions on this project. They had to talk. Now.

She entered the army surplus tent Ned had installed as his "field" office that morning and found him going over some papers. A card table rammed up against the center pole served as his desk. He looked ridiculous. Any self-respecting developer who thought he needed to be around every minute of the day—and there were a few—would have invested in some kind of trailer or motor home, like the company used. Not Ned. His penny-pinching had reared its ugly head yet again.

"What brings you here?" He shuffled the stack of papers into a pile and set a folder on top.

So nonchalant. Barely interested. She gobbled air to hold back her mounting anger. She'd learned a lesson from her first crew meeting: she couldn't let anger get in the way of her leadership. She had to stay firm but keep her cool. "What have you got there? More changes to the bids we've accepted?"

"Huh? What do you mean?" So innocent.

"I just talked to the foundation sub. His crew is enjoying an extended break because they have to switch out the preformed walls they brought for the pans we originally ordered."

He jumped from his chair and went to look out the tent flap. "That's what they were supposed to use. You changed back to poured walls?"

"I didn't have a choice. We don't use preformed walls anymore."

"But they're a hell of a lot cheaper."

"Maybe so, but foundations are critical to safe and enduring construction. Two Rivers won't challenge that principle on my watch, and preformed walls don't cut it. They're supposed to be made of green wood. In recent years, some suppliers have taken liberties with how they defined *green*, which further reduces the quality of construction."

He sidestepped her and returned to his impromptu desk. His eyes avoided hers.

"Well?" She bit back her aggravation, strived for a patient tone.

He picked up one of his numerous documents and appeared to study it. "Okay. I didn't know. These guys always pad. We shouldn't have to pay for their greed, so when I called them on it, they proposed this alternative. If it's such a poor practice, they should've said so."

She suspected the sub had warned him about the probable impact and Ned had chosen not to listen. "Instead of saving money, we're going to pay for your tight fist."

He drew his brows together. "How so?"

She came closer. "For starters, there's a crew out there being paid to stand around. We'll also have to pay their supplier a fee to take back inventory that most likely was special-ordered. Finally, there's the cost of additional transport and unloading."

He stared as if her laundry list hadn't penetrated his brain.

"Don't you get it, Ned? You may have thought you were reducing costs, but your tampering will probably double what you thought you were saving."

He licked his lips and hunched further over the makeshift desk. He still didn't look at her. His response caught her up short. She'd expected more debate. While she waited for a reply, she held her arms tight against her chest to keep from trembling. When no response was forthcoming, she prodded. "Ned? Did you hear what I said?"

He dropped the piece of paper and folded his hands. "I may have a thick head, Shae, but I can still hear."

His quiet tone unnerved her. She dropped into a metal folding chair opposite the card table. "You, you're admitting you were wrong?"

He turned eyes the color of slate on her. "Is that what's been eating you? That I made a mistake? Put that energy into figuring out how we're going to absorb the added expense."

"Me?"

He gave a deep sigh and ran his hands through his hair. "I, uh, seem to need more technical assistance than I thought."

"Technical assistance?" Was he actually admitting he didn't know everything?

"To evaluate whether my ideas will fly."

His last words were nearly inaudible. Must have cost him. She leaned into the table, still suspicious, but her agitation had subsided. "What did you have in mind?"

He grabbed the stack of documents and shifted them to the middle of the tabletop. "Sit." She continued to stand.

"Please."

Her curiosity got the better of her. She did as asked. "Okay, now what?"

He pushed the papers across to her. "Take a look at these. I may have, uh, overplayed my hand slightly."

The first document was an order for lumber. Already, she was confused. Why would he have this in his possession? The subs took care of this sort of transaction. "How did you get this?"

"I, uh, told the framing sub we needed to see it."

"And he gave it to you?" She was incredulous. "What did you do, turn that celebrity magnetism on him?"

"I, uh, told him it was for you. You wanted to make sure we received the quoted prices."

She considered his words. They didn't compute. "You could snip away to your heart's content. That still wouldn't change the quotes." Then it dawned on her. "Unless you went back to the suppliers again?" Her voice rose on the last word and her heartbeat resumed its earlier erratic rhythm. Surely he wouldn't have done such a thing without informing her, let alone the subs?

The tent flap blew in abruptly, buffeted by a sudden gust of air.

"Wind's picking up," Ned said to no one in particular.

She glanced toward the tent opening but remained seated. "I hope that doesn't mean a storm's on the way. The crew needs a couple hours to set the pans once they arrive." What else could go wrong today?

She resumed her review of the papers. The more she read, the more the bile rose in her throat. His audacity and single-minded cutting of costs were too much. She'd come here to have it out with him, but at the moment, her first priority was to salvage their profit margin. "Here. Start splitting them out." Shae shoved the papers across the table to him.

"Why?"

"I'm going to review your handiwork, first. Once we've isolated the ones you've changed, I'll assess the impact."

"You mean halt my cuts?"

She edged forward on her chair. "Maybe. Maybe not, if they make sense."

"Gee, thanks."

While she waited for him to finish sorting through the documents, she studied him.

He glanced up and caught her. "Why are you staring at me?"

"I've never worked with anyone quite like you."

He laid a group of stapled sheets to one side. "As I recall, you've never worked with anyone. But I'll bite. What's so different about me?"

"I've never encountered anyone so thrifty, tight."

"I'll take that as a compliment." He placed another stack to the other side of the table.

"Wasn't meant to be. Besides undermining me and being a pain in the backside, your actions are bordering on the ..." She searched for the right word. "Manic."

"You think I'm a nut case?"

"You tell me." She pointed to the three piles.

"I'm saner than most people. How else would I have been able to find these potential savings?"

"But why?"

He started to reply, but she cut him off. "I know, I know. You're a businessman. Only the bottomline counts. So you say. But given the scope of this project, these changes will barely make a dent in the overall cost."

HE ROSE ABRUPTLY, strode to the tent opening and noted the angry black clouds in the distance.

She never let up, although he had to admit, she'd been somewhat reasonable about the changes he'd made, after he'd stalled enough to get her to calm down. But did she have to be so intense? And persistent?

Yeah, he'd used poor judgment. But he had to do whatever he could to make this project happen within his reduced financial limits. From now on, he'd try as much as possible to involve her and Dave in whatever additional cuts he made. At length, he pivoted and faced her. He owed her some kind of explanation. The trick was to tell her about his financial problems without revealing too much. "My, uh, circumstances have shifted somewhat since I undertook this project."

"I know about the problems with your voice."

He nodded. "Which prompted me to postpone all personal appearances for the next six months."

A tiny line stretched across her forehead as she digested his statement.

"Those were a major source of income for me."

"Uh-huh."

"Income, I was, uh, planning on to finance the project."

"Oh."

Did he hear disappointment or alarm in her tone? He moved over to within a few feet of her. Close enough to take in the clean, fresh fragrance of bath soap that had overpowered his senses since her arrival. "Just *oh*?"

She backed up in her chair and lowered her eyes. Then she turned their full aquamarine force on him. "I didn't realize you were having money problems." She kept her voice low. "I thought it was simply how you operated, your inability to leave well enough alone." She stared at her hands. "Does this mean the project is off?"

Hadn't expected so direct a question. But then, this was Shae. What else should he have anticipated?

He straightened the tent's ceiling cord, a needless task, because it simply curled back the way he'd found it as soon as released. The futility of the gesture reminded him of the hopeless state of his finances.

Yet again he considered telling Mike about his money troubles. Mike was a financial genius. He'd had plenty of practice playing with his family's wealth over the years. But how could he confess the mess he'd made of things to the guy who'd never known a setback?

"Ned? What about the project?"

Damn! Why did she keep pushing? Couldn't she see how this was eating away at him?

He swiveled back to her, nearly dislodged the center pole holding up the tent, ready to tell her to mind her own business. "Wait," she said, before the words were out. "No one likes to talk about their money problems. Especially to those they owe the money."

Her comment caused him to pause, cool his jets. He forced a smile across his lips. "I'm pretty sure I can still handle this, although I may need to pursue a few other financial avenues that weren't in my original plans. But it's difficult for me to work through this with someone as persistent as you on my case."

Her expression softened somewhat, her nose wrinkled. "Is that how you see me?" She appeared to consider his comment. A brow rose to accentuate her contemplation. "I guess I have been on your case. But can you blame me? You've used your position as project manager to take actions independent of either Dave or me, despite our agreement. Why would you take such chances when you know nothing about construction?"

"Now you know. No threat of a lawsuit? No *how-could-you-be-so-stupid?*"

She blinked, obviously thrown by his words. "No. I didn't realize you were under so much pressure. I-I'm concerned about you."

Her admission disarmed him. He fought the feeling. Didn't like having her worried about him. Although it was a relief to be able to talk to someone about his money problems, he couldn't allow himself to let down his guard. He wasn't used to sharing his private life. Not with his mom. Barely with Mike. Certainly not with Shae Harriman, a business associate.

He was her client, for God's sake!

"Now that I've told you, can we drop it?"

She blinked again, as if she'd been struck. She folded her hands in her lap and studied them. "Okay.

He couldn't help himself. "What?"

"I'm sure you've got a team of high-priced financial experts to advise you. Plus you've got your friend, Mike. But if you ever want to talk, kick around some ideas to generate more revenue, I'm here."

Her sincerity, her caring, was almost more difficult for him to take than the chewing out she'd given him minutes before. It would be so easy to say, "Great, let's discuss how to find me more money," but something held him back. Something he couldn't name.

She must have sensed his reticence, because she returned to the topic at hand, the changed bids and supply orders. "I understand these better now. At least, what prompted them. We might be able to salvage some of the cuts you proposed. Let's focus on those a while. It may be nickels and dimes, but it's a start."

She seemed so optimistic and helpful he gave in to her suggestion and, along with her, huddled over the stack of papers.

They kept at it for some time, debated, argued, each threatened to quit at one time or another, and then took up the gauntlet again.

"Here you are!" Dave held the tent flap to the side. "You didn't answer your texts, Shae."

"Sorry. I got so involved here that I must not have heard them come in. Guess you'd better call from now on." She didn't explain what they'd been doing.

"The pans have arrived."

"Great. Now we can finally finish," she replied.

Dave swiped a hand through his hair. "Uh, yeah, as soon as the weather permits." He raised his brows. "Haven't you paid attention to the sky? There's a bad storm on the way."

"Uh, yeah," Ned filled in before Shae let Dave know too much. "We're about ready to pack it up."

"Good. Wouldn't want to get caught out here in the middle of nowhere in a harsh summer storm." He turned to Shae. "The pans have been unloaded and covered with tarps. But with this storm on the way, I've released the crews for the day and I'm headed out myself. Don't want to worry the wife any more than necessary these days."

"Give her our regards. We're out of here ourselves soon," Shae said.

As soon as he left, they returned to their work. No mention of stopping. The sides of the tent flailed as the wind intensified. "I suppose we should pack up and get out of here," Ned said finally, as the canvas snapped and rain beat on the tent roof.

"Just a little longer. We're almost done. That lantern is battery-powered, right? In case the light goes out."

"Yeah. Straight from my dad's old camping gear. I put a new battery in the other day."

"Then let's stay. What's a little rain? My windbreaker's in my car if I need it."

The tent flap succumbed to the now howling wind, fluttered back and forth several times. Ned went to strap it down. He stuck his head outside just long enough to realize this was no genteel early summer rainstorm. The wind made him catch his breath, and he shut his eyes tight against it to shield them from bits of blowing debris.

He backed into the tent and struggled to latch the flap. "Whew! We may have overstayed our escape time. We'd better get going."

Shae charged to the tent opening to check the weather for herself. When she returned, her eyes had grown dark with alarm. "You're right. That's a major storm out there. What do we do now?"

He considered. "We could probably make it to one of our cars, but we'll be saturated. The way the rain is pummeling the tent, I suspect the dirt roads out of here will soon be mud." Then he noted the streams of water that gushed under the tent. Before long, the ground would be a swamp.

Another gust of wind took its vengeance on the tent, actually ripped up one corner.

"We've got to get out of here. My car's closer than yours." He gathered the papers and shoved them into his valise.

"Wait! How about the mobile office instead? The company trailer? It's closer than our cars. Who knows how far we'd get in them anyhow."

Her suggestion made sense. "Okay, we'll head there. At least it'll have a dry floor."

"And the dry clothes Dave keeps there for emergencies."

He clutched his case under his arm and reached for her hand with his other. "Ready?"

She sucked in a deep breath. "Let's go."

CHAPTER 10

Shae and Ned spilled into the front part of the dark vehicle, banged the door to shut out the menacing wind and driving rain. The gloom of semi-darkness and the moldy smell of rotten food and aged paper greeted them.

Shae fumbled around the wall near the door to find the light switch. She panted, exhausted from her flight through the growing muck outside. She bent to catch her breath, then straightened, slapped rivulets of water off her jacket. "I'll check the bathroom for towels. I'm drenched and freezing." She headed down a small hallway to the left.

"Dry clothes, too," Ned called. "Late spring, and it's like—" He didn't—couldn't—finish, as a fit of coughing overtook him.

She came right back. "You okay?"

He waved her off, though his hacking continued.

"Sure?"

"Go!"

Ugh! Wrong time to play tough guy, Ned.

In the miniscule bathroom, she grabbed towels, then seized what dry clothes she could find from a closet tucked into the hallway. "Only found two of these," she said as she returned to the front office. She threw one of the towels to him.

She held up a small bundle she clutched under her other arm. "Dave's knit pullover and jeans. Here, you take them. With that cough, you need them more than I." She undid her ponytail, which already hung by its life, and toweled off her matted hair.

Stifling another cough, Ned returned the clothes to her. "You take them."

"What'll you do?"

"Any blankets or sheets back there?"

"Two in the closet. Probably more on the bed in the back room."

"Then I'll wrap myself in those," cough, cough, "while my clothes dry."

"We'll split the difference. Give me the top, you keep the pants, and we'll both wrap up with blankets."

"Fair enough."

Ned's cough alarmed her. Had his throat problem returned? If it had, he certainly hadn't wanted to discuss it, so she'd back off. For now.

Heavy sheets of rain drummed the top of the trailer like giants working out. The rain had already become a deluge of major proportions before the fireworks even got to them. Would the trailer stay anchored if the ground got too muddy? She pictured them floating away in their modern-day ark.

Put it out of your mind. You've got to shed these wet clothes.

Five minutes later—after Shae used the bathroom and Ned used the front part of the trailer to get rid of their soggy duds, lay them out to dry and don their dry ensembles—they turned their attention to the next order of business - food.

Shae checked out the desk drawers. "Surely Dave has something edible stashed in here."

"Like a steak dinner?"

She pulled out a box. "Would you consider peanut butter and crackers instead?"

"That's good. For starters."

Next, she brought out a plastic sandwich bag, contents unknown.

"This is the only other possibility I see, but don't get excited. It's gray underneath." She gave the package a cautionary sniff and flipped it into the wastebasket. "Eeuw! Forget this."

"Is there at least running water in the bathroom sink? If there even is a bathroom sink?" he added as an afterthought.

"Yes. And"—she riffled through one of the drawers she'd just inspected and withdrew a package of paper cups—"we even have something to drink it with."

"No coffeemaker?"

"Dave usually brings either a thermos from home or buys the expensive stuff."

"So. We have a box of peanut butter and cracker sandwiches."

"Three apiece."

"And unlimited water."

"As long as the contents of the water tank hold up."

He grabbed two cups from the package and headed to the back. He returned a minute later and offered her one. "Cocktail?"

"Is it that time already?" She checked her watch. "Oh, my God! It's almost seven. No wonder I'm hungry."

He pointed to the box of snacks. "Time for our first course." With the blanket folded tight around her, she sat in the desk chair and opened the first cracker sandwich. Ned remained by the hallway.

She took a few swigs of water. "Umm. Hits the spot."

"Want more?" he asked over his shoulder as he returned to the bathroom.

"Not yet."

His attentiveness threw her. A few hours ago, when she confronted him about the bids, he'd been defensive, obstinate, secretive. But ever since they'd taken up residence in this trailer, he'd been nothing but considerate and helpful.

"Guess I'll give one of these crackers a try," he said, with his second cup of water in tow. He took a bite, chewed and then set the remains back on the desk.

"I'd forgotten how good these can be. Haven't had one since," she thought back, "the times I'd come to visit Dad at his office when I was a kid. He'd put his work aside and snack along with me."

"How about your brother?"

"Sean got more of what little time Dad gave us. They hunted, fished. Even bowled."

"That bother you?"

"I adored my brother. Thought he could do anything. But the amount of time Dad spent with him hurt. I tried to fit in by doing the same things. Became a bit of a tomboy."

"That why you went into civil engineering?"

"No. I'd grown out of that phase by the time I was a teenager. I changed my major from accounting to civil engineering after Sean's death."

Ned rose, picked up her cup along with his and wandered back to the bathroom for another refill. When he returned, he picked up her story where she'd left off. "You never planned to be a general contractor?"

She offered a sort of chortle. "Me? I was a girl. Girls weren't expected to head construction businesses. That had been drummed into my brain since I was little. They tolerated my tomboy antics, but it was clear Sean was Dad's golden boy, his heir apparent."

"What about after your brother's death?"

"He never said so, but it was like Dad resented me for still being alive. He spent even more time away from home."

"Think that may have been the start of his heart problems?"

She angled her head. "I hadn't made that connection. Anyway, I was a college sophomore at the time and thought I could help bring him out of his grief if he knew I had changed my major so I could take Sean's place someday."

"And?"

She held up her palms. "I'm here, right?"

"Yeah, but—"

"We both know I'm only here because Dad was desperate. Desperate enough to put me in charge while he recuperates to keep me from taking the job in Dallas and reassure you a Harriman was still in charge of the company."

HER CHEST TIGHTENED as she realized how much he now knew about her. She wasn't one to share so much about herself, but confined here in this trailer in the middle of a storm, information flowed from her tongue as readily as the torrents of rain fell to earth outside. Time to change the topic.

"For dessert, I'll split the candy bar in my purse with you as soon as I figure out where I put the thing." She waddled about the trailer in her blanket cocoon to search. "My purse isn't here," she had to admit after a few futile minutes. "I must have left it in your tent. Besides the candy bar, my phone was in it."

A chill iced through her as the impact of her discovery dawned. No purse, no phone, very little food. They could be stuck here all night, if the storm kept up. Even if the rain stopped, their cars might get stuck in the mud. Just the two of them. Confined in this tiny trailer alone…together.

"Hey, it's not the end of the world. There's not a living soul out there to steal it. I doubt any of the night critters will be out and about this evening, either."

Shae blew out a breath, attempted to calm the feeling of vulnerability that engulfed her. *No one but you and me, Ned.* "I need to let Dave know where we are."

"I'll call him. Should probably let Mike know where I am, too." He pulled his cell from his valise. "Damn! Battery's dead." He rooted through his briefcase for a few seconds. Shortly, he retrieved the charger. "Ta-da! Where's an outlet?"

"Good question." She scanned the small office until she discovered a plug-in along a wall strip hidden by the side of the desk. "How long do you think the storm will keep up?"

"Hard to tell."

"Even if it stops, we'll probably be here all night, won't we?" she asked needlessly.

Ned blinked, like this was news. "I thought we could make a run for it."

"We could try. But until the ground dries, I don't know whether our cars will make it through. Even if we could get to the highway, there's no telling if we'd run into downed trees and power lines."

"So we're here for a while?" he asked.

"Better than being out there. Besides, our clothes need to dry, unless you want to ramble around the countryside in that get-up."

He slumped back in his chair. "It's not that I don't like the company. You've been a real sport. I'm concerned about the delay in construction this storm could cause."

"Actually, the water in the excavated holes could work to our advantage. It will settle the dirt and put moisture under the concrete, once it's poured, so it will cure harder although slower."

"Go ahead and say it," he said.

"Say what?"

"Remind me we might have gotten in the foundation for my mother's house today, at least the footings, if we'd had the pans."

"I'm tempted, but since it appears we're sharing each other's company the next several hours, I'll let it drop."

He didn't respond. Instead, he opened his blanket and used it to fan his chest several times and reveal tight pecs and a six-pack, which she'd only suspected existed. Only then was the point driven home to her she was entirely alone with this exacerbating, exciting man for the next several hours. Alone and half naked.

"What's with this place?" he asked. "It's like an inferno."

She pulled at the neck of her shirt. Did that explain the sudden flash of heat that had zapped her? "Residual heat probably builds up in these tight quarters. We were too chilled to notice at first. It's almost summer, though you'd never know it today."

He rose. "Does this thing have AC?"

"Both AC and heat. I think I saw the controls in the hallway."

Ned set off toward the back of the trailer yet again, came back shortly with more water. He cocked his head, as if he listened for something. And shortly, that *something*, the AC system, kicked in.

He sipped his water and then let the blanket slide to the floor. "You mind? I feel like a furnace in this."

"Uh, no," she croaked. He was hot? Did he have any idea what his exposed chest did to her? In college, she'd let her roommate talk her into going to a male strip club once. Just once. She hadn't been able to take a full breath then any better than now.

Another burst of light outside. She counted the seconds before the roll of thunder. Less than the last time. The storm was almost upon them.

The lights flickered and then went off.

She waited for them to come back on, but they didn't. As each second passed, a living rigor mortis immobilized her. *No, no, no! Not now.* She'd successfully kept her problem under wraps since the storm began.

"Shae? You okay over there?"

Had he picked up on her fears? That her old nemesis had seized her. "I'm fine. How about you?"

"Didn't expect to lose the lights. Spilled water on my blanket. Geez, it's really dark in here in between streaks of lightning. Does this place have its own generator or did they just stretch a power line over here?"

The rumbling outside increased along with ever more constant flickers of light. A loud boom nearly punctured her eardrums.

Shae sat pinned to the chair gripping her arms. The darkness that surrounded them unnerved her, but the frequent shafts of light also made her crazy. All the old fears took over. *No! Go away. I'm stronger than I was as a child. You're not going to win this time.*

"Shae? The generator?"

She forced herself to answer. "Somewhere outside. Don't know where."

"It'll have to wait then. I'm not going out there in this downpour unless absolutely necessary. Guess we won't cool off after all."

She no longer noticed the heat. The minute the lights had gone out, ice permeated her veins.

She heard a faint rustling nearby, then a click and more rustling. Ned was in his briefcase again.

Suddenly, a tiny beam of light appeared, aimed directly at her. She screamed.

"Sorry. Didn't mean to scare you. I remembered the penlight I always carry with me."

She bent her head and tried to steady her breathing. When she felt she could speak again, she said, "Aim it away from me."

"Oh, yeah, sure. Your voice sounds funny. Kinda stiff. Are you okay?"

"I'm, uh, no big fan of storms."

"Scared of them?"

She so didn't want to get into this. But there didn't seem to be any way to avoid talk of it, as long as the lights remained out. "Uh. Yes. Dark."

"Why the hell didn't you tell me before now?"

"I, uh, thought I, uh, could keep things under control. That damned penlight. Threw me." Men and their toys.

"What can I do?"

Well, duh. "Turn it off."

The light went out. "Better? I'll just use it as needed. Need to save the battery anyhow."

"Talk."

"Okay?"

During storms … Sean would … read to me. Motocross … or racing. Subject … not important."

That little morsel of information filled in a few more gaps. Frightened little girls should have a mom or a dad to comfort them and soothe away their fears. At least Shae had her brother. Though motocross and racing were a far cry from dolls. "Interesting nursery tales."

"And … you?"

"I hid under my bed when storms really got bad. As for reading material, my parents were more into picture books. Two artists with a non-artistic son. I'd make up my own stories to go with the pictures."

"Start of … song writing?"

Her speech seemed to be on the mend, although it still sounded stilted. Funny how one could pick up on those things when in near darkness. "I was into music as far back as I can remember. Piano. Guitar. Singing. Song writing came later."

"Did you … want to be … megastar?"

He flicked on the penlight again, this time focused it on his face. "See this? No cocky smile. No dreamy expression. Just me being serious." He wanted her to know he hadn't gone into the business for the money. At least not then.

She didn't reply.

"I WANTED nothing more in my life than my music. Went to Europe right after college and indulged myself. No thought for the parents who'd struggled to pay my tuition. Nor the slightest notion I'd never see one of them again." Even now, as the words tumbled out, it hurt to admit what a jerk he'd been.

"Sure … they understood."

"That's the problem. They always understood. All they wanted was the best for me. I couldn't take it."

"You? Rebellious?"

Rebellious? He'd never thought of himself as such. More like thoughtless and unappreciative. "Not in the typical way—you know, drugs, alcohol, life in the fast lane. No, my poison was withdrawal. From them."

"Strange, isn't it? How I would have given nothing more than to have my dad notice me and you—"

"Shunned my parents' attention. I was a real turd. Didn't even make it back to see my dad in the hospital before he died." Probably the lowest time in his life. Or was that the day he left for California and had to face that brave look in his mother's eyes?

God, had he really said that? Out loud? He'd told her more than he ever intended. Seemed easy to do in the dark, where she couldn't see his expression, nor he hers. But that was enough. If he kept on, who knew? He might tell her more about the extent of his financial problems. Hell, he'd already revealed more than he should have.

He turned the penlight on his wrist. "Eight thirty. Seems later."

"Tired?"

"Yes. No. Hard to say. As much as I've enjoyed our game of 'Getting to Know You,' as I've sat here in the dark, I've lost my sense of equilibrium. I'm worn out compensating for loss of sight. I can still see, but just dark and less dark."

"I know what you mean," she added. "It's not like we can play cards."

"Or drink." Other than water.

"We can't even play a radio."

His stomach gurgled, reminded him one bite of a cracker sandwich and four cups of water did not a nutritious meal make. The cracker's hard, salty surface didn't mix with a throat on fire. He'd nearly gagged on that first bite. He considered offering Shae the rest, but he didn't want her to know the rain and cold had seized his throat again.

He was surprised she hadn't commented on the numerous cups of water he'd consumed. Soon, he'd have to use the throat spray tucked away in his valise. But he waited for the right time, when she wouldn't notice. Maybe after she was asleep. "I checked out the back room on one of my water runs. Just one small bed back there."

"This trailer is intended for one-person occupancy," she replied.

"Then you take the bed. I'll arrange some sort of nest out here."

"No, you take the bed. You've already been coughing. Let's not make it worse."

She had noticed. "I'll be fine." He lied.

"Forget the gentleman stuff. You take the bed."

"We could flip a coin. Though I'm not sure if we could find it or see it with just the penlight."

"We could, uh, share the bed?" she said tentatively.

Tempting solution. For a couple reasons. But not a wise idea. "Uh—"

"What I meant," she rushed to add, "you take one side, I'll take the other. If we can find enough blankets, we'll roll one up and place it down the center. I, uh, saw that done in a movie once."

He'd seen the same movie. The next scene showed the blanket on the floor and the couple wrapped in each other's arms. Had she forgotten? Or remembered?

CHAPTER 11

'll take the side closest to the door," Shae called over her shoulder to the shape behind her. She hobbled down the hall in her blanket casing like an ambulatory hotdog. Once she reached the back room, she groped along the side of the bed until she felt the soft surface of the pillow. She reached underneath, grabbed the top of the blankets and pulled them down far enough so she could sit on the edge and swing in.

This was such a bad idea. What had possessed her to offer to share? As she recalled, the bed was hardly big enough for her. How could two people share it without rolling on top of each other? Her insides percolated at the thought. Too late now. She'd said her Good Samaritan piece and he'd taken her up on it.

She knew Ned followed by the stream of expletives muttered as he bumped into things along the way.

"What's going on out there?" she called.

"This is an obstacle course."

She made out his form, darker against dark, when he reached the door. "The hall's no more than eight foot long and a straight shot. How could you possibly collide with anything?" she asked.

"You ever tried to walk a straight line in pitch black? Okay, you just did. I'd bow to your superior night eyes, except I'm afraid I'd knock into something else."

"Reach down. The bed starts about an arm's length inside the room. The bottom is about even with the middle of the door."

The mattress jolted. "Ah, damn!"

"I said reach down, not walk right into it."

"You should've told me you meant the length of your arm, not mine."

A heavy pressure crossed over her feet. "Okay, that's me under those blankets you've pummeled."

"Sorry. This isn't easy when I've only seen this room for all of a few seconds."

The mattress on the other side of the bed dipped under his weight. She clung to her edge, faced away from him. She had no idea how she'd react if their bodies inadvertently came in contact.

"I'll sleep on top of the blankets," he said from way too close.

"Won't you get cold?" Oh, God, the thought of his naked chest so close to her made her mouth go dry.

"In this steam bath? I doubt it. But just in case, I've got my trusty blanket to keep me warm. Since I doubt that's going to happen, I'll roll it up so we can use it for that virtue barrier you mentioned."

"Virtue barrier? Oh, right." That should keep things platonic. Not!

The next thing she knew, something soft batted her head. "What?"

"Sheesh, this bed is small! Sorry. That was the virtue wall under construction. Get ready. You'll probably feel this too."

And she did, as the malleable "wall" was inserted between them. Was he putting her on by following through on her dumb idea? True, it did set up a sort of quilted reminder to go no farther, although, when sound asleep, a mass of blankets had never stopped her from sprawling across her own bed. She doubted it would halt Ned either, once sleep overtook him.

They lay there in silence. Shae hugged her side of the bed, straight as a plumb wall. A cloud of masculine heat wafted her way, curled around her like a caress and tempted her to move toward it.

Breathe, dammit, Shae. With effort, she unclenched the hands she'd fisted as her nails cut into her skin.

The bed shook. Then shook again. Ned wasn't comfortable.

"How can you stand it under those blankets? I'm sweating up a storm."

Without further thought, she turned and stuck her arm across the wall of blanket. She placed her hand where she thought his head would be. "Do you have a fever?" His forehead was wet with perspiration, but it didn't feel hot to the touch.

"Well, nurse?"

"No fever. But, you're right. It is a little stuffy in here."

"That a window above the bed?"

"I think so. Why?"

"Wonder if it opens."

She removed her hand just in time. Once again, the mattress jiggled as he shifted his weight. The bed creaked as he appeared to pull himself up. A small shaft of light shot through at the same time she heard what sounded like a wooden slat shifted. The bed shook again as he must have attempted to open the window.

He slid back into sleeping position. "Success! Let me know if this gets to be too much, either the cool air or the sound of the storm."

"The rain won't come in, will it?"

"No. Wind's the other direction."

She could use some cool air about now. Every time Ned shifted position, let alone sat up, her body heat inched up another degree. Maybe she could remove the blanket over her lower body? She'd still be able to protect her modesty—as long as she remained under and Ned above the blankets.

But would they remain in those spots as they slept? Deep, deep down, would she not prefer they both be under the covers? Maybe, from the safety of her own bed when she was alone, she could fantasize about the possibility. But not when he lay so close to her.

What little air the open window allowed to seep into the room didn't help. She dismissed her concern that Ned might find his way under the blankets and opened the one wrapped around her. Much better. She stretched her legs as best she could while unable to move from side to side. She never slept in the nude. Something—panties or pajama bottoms—always covered her nether regions. This was delicious!

She released a tiny moan.

"Shae?"

"Huh? Oh. Just stretched my back. Felt so good, I forgot you were here."

"Uh, sure." Surely she wasn't … God, no! Not here. Not now. Not her. Still, that moan didn't sound like she'd relieved a back cramp. Now he'd heard it, the moan kept repeating itself in his brain. How was a guy supposed to sleep when the sound of a woman's— what? pleasure?—amplified itself to the point where his ears felt like the room screamed it.

Like most guys, it was the visual that turned him on—a woman's eyes, her smile. Okay, a well-endowed breast or a curvaceous, spank-me ass got to him just as readily, in half the time. But sounds? Those were the audio signals that told a guy he'd gotten to the lady, turned her on. The kind of thing that encouraged him to go faster, deeper.

He had to stop these thoughts. Focus on something else. If his brain replayed that moan much more, his fella wouldn't readily curl up and go to sleep. This wasn't the time or place to follow through on his body's hard attack. Painful as the notion was, he'd have to lie here this close to her and do nothing.

Exactly when had the woman next to him moved beyond builder status to object of desire? Before the moan. It had only solidified the thought. When she checked him for fever? When she'd suggested they share the bed? When she'd peeled away her underwear and wrapped that blanket around her legs?

No. If he was really truthful, it had been earlier in the day, when she'd burst into the tent to confront him about the revised order. Even though he'd caused her no end of embarrassment with her suppliers and subs, she'd worked with him to make things right. Stayed with him even as the storm approached, despite her fear of the damned things.

They were quite the pair, her with her need for approval from her father, him with his need to protect a mother who didn't need to be protected because he hadn't been there when she had needed protection. Shae tried to conceal her fear of storms from him, he pretended his throat was okay.

"Ned? Are you still awake?" Her voice sounded different. Less fearful but also less confident than usual.

"Yeah. Why? You need to talk some more?"

"That sound you heard earlier? It wasn't for the reason I said."

"Really?" What on earth had led her to confess?

"I'd, uh, just removed the blanket from around my legs. I, uh, thought you should know, in case you changed your mind during the night and moved under the blankets."

Was that a come-on? She wanted him to know she was half-naked, because …

"It's not like you think," she added, as if she'd read his mind.

"I'm not sure I know what to think."

"That I was, uh, you know … Please, Ned, don't make this any more embarrassing for me than it already is. This so-called blanket wall could no more hold you back if you rolled this direction than our clothes resisted all that rain earlier."

"Was that an invitation or a prediction?"

"Neither. I thought if I mentioned it now, we could avoid a potential misunderstanding later on. Go to sleep. Don't give it further thought."

He wanted to strangle her. *Don't give it further thought?* Unless by some miracle he'd fall asleep, that's all he'd be doing. Pretend his throat was fine. That his finances were sound. That he wasn't sharing a bed with and practically on top of a gorgeous though naïve naked woman who was within inches of his reach.

He groaned. Who could blame him?

"You okay over there?"

"What do you think, Shae? It's like you told me not to notice the elephant in the room."

She didn't reply immediately. Had he scared her? Well, fine. She never should've told him.

"You're right. It was a stupid thing to say. This whole idea to share the bed is dumb. But other than one of us on the floor, what else can we do?"

At least she'd finally realized what a dumb idea this was. Helped to know she was just as frustrated as he. "Maybe you just did. We already had an elephant in the room, sharing the bed. You had the guts to bring it up."

Movement on her side of the bed. She must have sat up. "Leaving?" he asked.

She chuckled. "Not that generous. Just propped my head on my elbow. I thought we should talk about it."

Women. Had to overanalyze everything. "Thought we just did."

"It's like this. At home I sleep in a queen-sized bed. I'm a night owl, and despite the darkness, it can't be more than nine or nine thirty right now. Usually the television blares to keep me company. I'm not accustomed to sharing my bed with anyone, let alone a superstar millionaire who happens to be my client. I am so uncomfortable, I could scream."

He thought she was done, but apparently she just caught her breath. "Tomorrow, I will heartily deny I told you any of this. It's not like me to open up so."

That was for sure. As much as she talked project and construction, everything he'd learned about her personal life had either come from others or from times like this, when circumstances forced her to talk about herself.

He owed her something in return. "I have a king-sized bed. I nod off fast and sleep tight, but somehow I manage to occupy most of the space at some point during the night. Right now, I feel like I've been nailed in a coffin with almost no air to breathe."

"So. We're both miserable." Brief silence. "What if we sing ourselves to sleep?"

"Uh—"

"Oops. Sorry. Forgot about your no-singing thing. Okay, I'll do it myself. I sing slightly off-key, but it's better than nothing." She started in on the chorus of a popular song, though not one of his.

She was right. She couldn't carry a tune worth a damn. But he let her try. Maybe boredom would knock him out, which after a few minutes, actually happened. In the far depths of his subconscious, the low hum of her voice droned on a bit longer, then faded away.

The next thing he knew, he'd set sail on a treacherous, never-ending river. He clung to the small raft as it hurtled over swells he couldn't control. His vessel shuddered and careened recklessly toward a wicked precipice. Beside him on the craft, Shae screamed.

The shriek brought him awake with a start only to realize the last part was real. Through streaks of light, which now flashed more frequently outside, he made out Shae's form huddled against the back of the bed

He pulled her into his arms without a thought to the consequences. "Shh, shh," he cooed, trying to calm her. The room felt cooler. Apparently the small opening in the window had done its job.

She dug her face into his chest, shook her head, all the while her body quivered. "Did … didn't you hear it?" She drew away from him. "That explosion. It was … so close."

He swiveled around to pull the window blind aside. Several hundred feet away, flames engulfed a tall oak. Even as he watched, though, the heavy downpour began to douse the fire.

"You're right. It was close. But it's over. The rain will prevent the spread."

"You're sure?" The voice was that of a scared little girl.

He stroked her hair, tangled now from sleep but still soft and silky. He lowered his lips to the top of her head. "Just one less tree to fell when we clear that spot. Everything's going to be okay." The hand that had touched her hair drifted down to the arm, which escaped from her blanket. "Just relax, sweetheart." Had he really said that?

Her body gave a tiny start. Yep, he'd really said it. Emerged as naturally as saying good morning. And she'd heard it.

She twisted to face him. Her breath lengthened, and in the fraction of the second in which the room lit up from the action outside, he could see her study him, as if to read his intentions.

Well, damn, what were his intentions? In this moment, there was no Just Past or About to Come. Only Now, endless, suspended. Near darkness. Only touch and smell and taste. Oh, hell! He bent and kissed her. Not like that miscued day in her office. This time was stronger, his action came from somewhere slightly to the left of Lust and a little bit shy of the Other L Word. He cared. Yeah. He cared.

Her lips reciprocated. Pressed harder, demanded more. Her arms went around his neck, pulled him closer.

This was crazy. There was only one way this would end, and like an out-of-control car that sped downhill, he knew there'd be no way to stop until it crashed at the bottom. Once they finished, things wouldn't be the same. Was he ready for such a change?

The longer his lips remained on hers, the more his better judgment drained away, the Now obscured everything else. He drew her closer, one hand strayed under the blanket, down her back, onto one naked buttock.

His penis came alive. His brain turned off.

A sharp, cutting pain slashed through his throat. He released her to grasp his throat with both hands.

"Ned? What's wrong?"

The pain was so severe he could only hold his throat. He felt rather than saw Shae hover over him.

"Your throat? How can I help?"

He couldn't talk. The most he could manage was to lean over his side of the bed and grope around until he found the throat spray. He thrust it her direction until it rammed into her chest.

"What's that?"

He'd also retrieved his penlight, which he pushed toward her now.

Shortly, the light came on, illuminated the bottle. "Throat spray," she said. "Okay, let me read the instructions first. Open your mouth." She held the light with the other hand and directed it so she could see his uvula. Then she sprayed the back of his mouth liberally.

A moment later, reassuring warmth covered his body. Shae must have straightened out his blanket, and from the added weight, unrolled the virtue wall and placed it over him too.

He closed his eyes and breathed with a little less effort. Within seconds, he drifted off.

SHAE DEBATED whether to let him continue to sleep or to wake him from time to time to check his condition. The storm appeared to have abated. The terror that had awakened her eased, and the moment of damn-the-torpedoes desire had flown. Ned's breathing lengthened, and in a bit, she heard soft snoring.

He was out. Not much she could do for him now. They both needed their rest to cope with whatever challenges the morning presented.

As she eased her way over to her side of the bed, she felt the coolness on her naked bottom. She lifted the two blankets and climbed back under. At first, she clung once again to the side of the bed, didn't dare get too close. Ned might be out for the night, but she wasn't. Despite the lethargy that approached, she was acutely aware of his body so close to hers. The body with which could have shared an ill-advised night of passion had his throat not intervened.

Shae relaxed as she listened to the soft exhalations beside her. Inch by inch, she gave in to both the overwhelming need to move closer to him and overpowering fatigue. Before long, she spooned him and enjoyed the delicious nearness of this incredible hunk.

Just for tonight. They hadn't indulged themselves physically. But she could indulge the heart that craved his presence, if only for this one night. She so wanted to be near him. If there was a toll to pay, she'd deal with it in the morning.

CHAPTER 12

The next morning, Ned massaged his temples, attempted to rub away the pounding that had plagued him ever since he opened his eyes and recalled what had almost happened in the middle of the night. Big mistake to sleep in the same bed with Shae. Even if they'd been total strangers, to know she was so close, naked from the waist down, to take in her delectable fragrance, he would have succumbed to temptation. But he did know her—all her foibles, idiosyncrasies, now even her fear of storms—which made it worse. The feelings that had clawed their way into his conscience for days, feelings he'd worked so hard to suppress, took over. He wanted her.

Still asleep, she was buried under the covers, although a sensuous cascade of auburn hair streamed over half her face and fell softly down that long, creamy neck and over her shoulders. One leg uncovered, the glimpse of skin was enough to make him envision the rest of her nude. He got hard just to watch her sleep.

It would be so easy to pick up where he left off before he conked out last night. Damn, he wanted to. His body was certainly primed. Underneath that brash exterior was a woman who waited to be awakened, not just this morning but for all the physical pleasure he could give her. He could tell by the way she'd halfway come on to him and then suddenly retreated. All she needed was coaxing and gentle persuasion.

Normally, he'd be happy to supply those, but not now. Not while Sullivan's Creek was in its infancy. Maybe never. Shae didn't appear to be the kind of woman who could enjoy the moment and move on once the ardor cooled. He didn't need a woman in his life who demanded commitment. Marriages didn't fare well in his world.

Pinpoints of sunshine penetrated the window covering and illuminated the opposite wall. Eventually, they intensified enough to trigger a reaction from Shae's one exposed eye through the curtain of hair that covered it. She blinked several times, arched her back and flexed her arms.

She felt wonderful. Sleep had been filled with lovely dreams of … what? She couldn't recall, but she couldn't shake the feeling of euphoria that streamed through her.

Then it hit her. This wasn't her bed.

She lay there to give her brain time to recharge. Something about water. Rain. The storm! That was it. She and—oh, God … Ned … stuck here. In the trailer. In this bed!

Some hidden sense of self-preservation kept her planted in bed rather than shooting from the mattress. She reached down and felt her naked bottom. Good grief. Surely they hadn't—no, she didn't think so. A harsh crack of lightning had struck a nearby tree, which made her freak. Ned held her. Comforted her. Kissed her. She'd kissed him back. Like her life depended on it. Then his throat intervened.

Wake up, Shae. After last night, today promises to be something special. All she had to do was reach over, touch a sleeping Ned and … No one there. Where was he? She hadn't felt the bed shift.

She rolled onto her back and sat. A few feet away, Ned leaned against a small chest of drawers snuggled in the corner, the room's only other piece of furniture. He stared at her, his eyes reflecting that unmistakable look every woman instinctively recognized. He was ready— and eager—to play out the scene of the night before.

"Good morning," she said. My, her voice was breathy.

While she debated what else to say, the look disappeared. He came to life, started to collect his things and made a production of folding and refolding the blankets he'd used.

What was going on? Just a few hours ago, he stroked her bare butt. Now, he couldn't get away from her fast enough.

Maybe he was still in pain. "How's your throat?"

"Seems fine. Thanks for helping with the throat spray. Really knocked me out. Slept like a baby." The words poured out almost as fast as the deluge hit the ground the night before.

He sounded nervous.

A hard object rammed into her back. The throat spray. "Looking for this?" she asked. She held out the container.

He shifted around to face her. "Yeah. Thanks." But as soon as he retrieved the bottle, he hightailed it out of the room so quickly he bumped into the doorjamb. "Ouch! Damn!"

Irritable, too.

What had changed since they'd nearly given in to what appeared to be mutual desire several hours earlier?

First things first—retrieve her clothes, whether they were still wet or not. That task completed, check the conditions outside. Inspect the storm's damage, although she seriously doubted they'd be able to resume work today. Maybe not even tomorrow.

Her shirt was barely back on when outside the trailer she heard a voice outside. "Shae? Ned? You in there?" Dave. Bless his heart. He'd come to rescue them, not only from the storm but from themselves as well.

"I CAN'T BELIEVE YOU TWO," Dave grumbled as they drove back to town in the company's all-terrain vehicle a few minutes later. "You stayed on-site long after I warned you to leave. That storm could've turned into a tornado and sent you knocking around in that rattletrap trailer like a bouncing ball."

"Storm came on faster than we estimated," Ned replied. "Made more sense to hang out in the trailer until the rain stopped than get our cars stuck in the mud. Had no idea we'd be trapped overnight."

"Scared the daylights out of me when I couldn't reach either of you this morning."

"Yeah, well, we'd tried to get hold of you last night, but Shae discovered she'd left her cell behind in the tent, and after we lost power, I couldn't recharge mine."

Dave continued to shake his head like a parent who'd bailed his two teenaged kids out of jail. Shae felt about as foolish as one. Sure, she shouldn't have stayed so long. Her, the one who not only hated storms but usually went to the basement with the first rumble of thunder. But yesterday she'd remained despite the warning signs, because she had to undo the damage Ned had caused when he meddled with the orders.

"You're mighty quiet back there, Shae," Dave said over his shoulder.

"She's feeling guilty for keeping me out here so long in the wind and rain, because my throat acted up again," Ned replied before she could say anything. "But it was my own stupid fault. I should've known better."

Dave shot him a quick glance. "We need to go to the ER?"

"I'm fine. Shae found my throat spray in time. I don't remember much after that because I passed out. From fatigue."

So that's why he'd cut into her response. Afraid she'd inadvertently tell Dave how they'd slept in the same bed. Now, informed their night had been no party, Dave would discourage any speculation on the crew's part as well.

Had Ned tried to save her reputation? Or his? Or was his self-image so fragile, the thought that anyone, even Dave, might see her as a potential bedmate for Mr. Big Time Entertainer had prompted him to set the record straight?

Conjecture about Ned's mood wasn't worth her time. She sank

further into her seat and turned her attention to the question of work resumption. Unpleasant as the delay might be, it was something she could get her mind around, easier than wondering what might have happened between her and Ned. One almost-kiss, one real one, one rebuffed on her part, and another one in which she'd been a willing participant until his throat cut things off. A pattern seemed to be emerging. Despite her good intentions and efforts to keep things professional, circumstances continued to tempt them to take things to a different level.

She'd almost succumbed to those temptations. How much more could she withstand?

NED FOCUSED on the road ahead as the ATV hurtled over ruts and dodged downed tree branches. Even though he'd chided them for remaining too long and not letting him know their whereabouts, Dave couldn't have arrived at a better time. Ned didn't know how much longer he could have continued to give Shae the cold shoulder. She'd looked so hurt and confused when he turned down her friendly over-tures. Dave's presence cut off any potential to change his mind.

His throat was under control, for now, but he'd give the doctor a call when he returned to Mike's. Damn! He hadn't experienced another attack since he'd been taken to the hospital. He'd come to believe the excruciating razor bite was gone. But it was still there. Why hadn't he healed? Would his throat condition deteriorate further? If it didn't get better fast, he stood to lose everything—not just his bank account and this development, but his career too.

"You awake over there?" Dave's question cut into Ned's thoughts.

"Huh? Oh, yeah. Sorry. Looks like the fields took quite a beating."

Dave scanned the surrounding countryside, returning his eyes to the wheel. "If the water doesn't recede fast, the plantings will drown." He paused, then went on, "I asked whether you'd like the name of my mechanic or if you already have someone who can tow your car back to town."

Hadn't given a thought to his car. His throat. Shae. Finances. Throbbing head. Those were enough to worry about. "Thanks, but Mike Woodley can help me."

"Oh. Okay, fine."

Shae hadn't said boo since she'd climbed in the backseat. What was going on with her? He shot a surreptitious glance over his shoulder. Still there. She stared straight ahead, expression unreadable.

Had she seen how excited she'd gotten his fella this morning? He thought he'd done a pretty good job keeping the tenting of his pants from her view. What did her silence mean? Thus far in his acquaintance with the woman, she hadn't been reticent to share her opinion whenever and wherever. Did she expect him to make the first move? *Can't allow myself to do that, lady.* He didn't want to hurt her.

If good for nothing else, the weather delay would send them in different directions. Even if there had been a spark in the air, it would fizzle after a day or two.

They should have exchanged jokes and reminiscences of their night as they waited out the storm, but neither he nor apparently Shae wanted to go there. The only place he wanted to go at the moment was to a hot shower. Better yet, a cold one.

Two hours later, shaved, showered and checked in with his doctor, Ned was ready to return to the countryside to reclaim his car. The front gate intercom buzzed just as he and Mike were about to go out the door.

"This is Zoe Johansen from the Verdant Prairie Bank. I'm here to see Ned Collier. I understand he's staying with you."

Ned shook his head no, but Mike either didn't see him or refused to. "Yes, he's staying here. What's this about?"

"I've been assigned to work with Mr. Collier on his housing project. I'd like to discuss it with him in person."

Ned swished his hands in front of him, like a referee calling no touchdown.

Mike ignored Ned's signals. "We were just about to leave. We can give you five minutes."

"I, uh, okay."

Mike released the intercom button and flipped the switch that opened the front gate. "Company," he announced. "You've got about sixty seconds to tell me what this is about."

Ned's stomach plunged. How had she tracked him down? Ten more minutes and he could have eluded the woman yet again and kept Mike unaware of the state of his finances. Had to think fast to discourage Mike from joining them. "She's with the bank. She's been helping me work out the details for the next phase of the project. You know, make sure the cash flow is there when needed."

"Great! I want to hear this, too."

"Well, uh, yeah, sure." Then inspiration struck. "I think you should meet her. You probably have a lot in common."

"What d'ya mean?"

"Okay, call me Cupid, but—" He deliberately let his sentence trail off and hoped Mike would pick it up from there.

"Not you, too? Your mom has been hinting I should meet her new artist. You know, the one whose showing you conned me into attending?"

That was news. "No kidding?" He didn't give himself time to wonder why his mother had now aimed her arrows at Mike instead of him. For once, a break. "An artist *and* a banker. Not bad. Form and function." Whatever that meant. Sounded good.

Mike hitched his shoulders. "I don't need your mother, you, or anyone else to arrange my social life. I can still find a date on my own whenever I want." He headed for the back of the house. "You're on your own with the woman. I'm going to enjoy a muffin. In the kitchen."

Mike disappeared just as the doorbell rang. Ned beat the house-keeper to answer it. "Ms. Johansen. Nice to see you again. Come in." He glanced at his watch. "But like my friend said, he and I were on our way out, so we'll have to keep this short."

He led Johansen, an attractive blonde in her late twenties, to the library. After he closed the door, he stepped around the massive desk but didn't sit. He gestured to one of the two leather club chairs that faced the desk.

As soon as she was seated, she pulled a folder from her oversized purse. "Since our time is limited, I'll be succinct. The bank is concerned about your equity stake. When you arranged financing with us several months ago, your assets and projected revenue were in excellent shape, which was the only reason the financing was approved. We've since learned you've cancelled all your personal engagements for the next several months, which will affect your projected income."

They were on to him. The possibility he'd dreaded and reason why he'd ignored this woman's messages had finally tracked him down. "I'm still quite solvent, although my assets have, uh, altered somewhat since my throat problems forced me to curtail my singing gigs." He massaged his throat column slightly to drive home the point. "However, I have various film scores to work on as well as my own compositions."

"We're aware of your throat problems, Mr. Collier, and we certainly hope this is just a temporary condition. But with the decline of your projected revenue, we want to assure your equity stake remains viable."

Ned leaned into the desk. "My payment schedule from these other, uh, sources, is somewhat different than my concert intake, which included up-front money. These are all as-completed ventures. They will show up soon."

"We appreciate these assurances, but they don't represent solid proof of your continuing financial health. The bank needs to see a considerable influx of income by the end of the month or we will be forced to call in your loan."

"The end of the month? That's not much more than two weeks away!"

In response, she removed a sealed envelope from her purse and handed it to him. "This is a courtesy copy of the document you will receive by messenger later today. It states the conditions I just mentioned." She rose, placed the strap of her purse over her shoulder, and started to leave. "I'm sorry it had to come to this, Mr. Collier. I've tried to contact you several times, because I hoped we could work out alternate arrangements."

Ned cut her off at the door. "*Alternate arrangements.* That's a great idea. Surely there's still time to discuss some other option? I can't believe the bank would do this to one of the town's more prominent citizens. I'm a hometown boy who's made good. I'm even building my own home here. Surely the bank wants to avoid the bad publicity that would be generated if I am forced to declare bankruptcy?"

She drew in her lips, paused, as if his threat made her rethink the bank's actions. "Actually, you're the one who can't afford such publicity, Mr. Collier. We tried to warn you about the volatility of the housing market and the unconventional nature of your financing, especially since you've never been a developer. That's why we built such strict provisions into your loan agreement."

He gripped the door handle. "Isn't there anything I can do to dissuade you?"

She stared at his hand until he removed it. "Find more money." She looked around the room. "This is a lovely home. I understand it's owned by Mr. Woodley or his family. You might start here." She took off for the front door before he could rebut her suggestion.

Damn! Why hadn't he returned her calls? It was never was a good idea to ignore one's problems, a lesson he learned too late years ago when he refused to see how his first fiancée had usurped the leadership of his band.

But the die was already cast. *Zoe Johansen and the bank have written you off. Say good-bye to Option One.* Other than going to Mike, which he still resisted, that left only one more option. He needed a backer.

"WHAT DID THAT BANKER REALLY WANT?" Mike asked as they made their way to the project site ten minutes later.

Ned pulled at a button on his polo shirt. "Gave her an update on the project. Told her excavation was underway until the weather intervened."

"C'mon, Ned. When a banker shows up at your door, it's not for a chat about foundations. What aren't you telling me? Not like you."

This was his chance. All he had to do was open up and tell Mike about the corner he'd painted himself into, and his money problems would disappear.

"It's no disgrace to admit you weren't cut out to be a financial genius. That's why you've got me," Mike said before Ned relented.

"I've told you before, I have to be totally in charge of this project to make sure Grandpa Jake's dream comes true exactly like he imagined it."

"I know all that," Mike said. "But if you've got problems with the bank or can't understand your financial picture, you could at least let me check things over for you."

"Do you realize how patronizing you sound?"

"Patronizing? Since when did you get so sensitive about anything I say?"

"Since you've treated me like an imbecile."

Mike's palm hit the top of the steering wheel. "I just want to help, man."

"You want to help? Then do this for me. I need to make a quick trip to the coast. Just overnight. I want to be back in town by the time we resume digging. Could you fly me out and back?"

Mike raised a brow. "Guess so. What's up? Surely you're not singing again? I'm not going to enable you to totally wreck your voice."

Mike claimed he didn't want his own family. Too bad. He made such a good parent, albeit an authoritarian one. But Ned kept his tone casual, non-defensive. "No singing. Even with my thick head, I learned my lesson. Have some unfinished business to attend to."

"I thought I dealt with all your business."

Ned thought fast, tried to manufacture a business deal Mike wouldn't usually handle. His house. He flinched mentally as he considered what he was about to propose. But with that Johansen woman on his tail, he needed to liquidate as many of his assets as he could as fast as he could. The effort wouldn't meet the bank's deadline, but it would demonstrate good faith. "I want to sell my house in Brentwood."

"Why? It's a good investment. Bad time to sell. If nothing else, rent it."

"I want to make a statement to my investors here in Iowa. Something that demonstrates my commitment to Sullivan's Creek. Besides building a home in the development, I plan to make it my permanent headquarters."

Mike shook his head. "If you're hell-bent to sell, at least let me take care of it for you. I know several topnotch realtors. But I still think it's a big mistake."

Ned pretended to consider Mike's offer. "I suppose you're right. What if we split the task? You deal with the sale part and I'll make arrangements to either ship my belongings back to Iowa or dispose of them. I'm not crazy about the furnishings anyhow."

"You really want to relocate? I thought this was all just temporary."

"I've started to rethink some things as a result of this throat business. What I really want from life. For some reason, I want to be back among my roots." He surprised himself with his words. But the more he thought about it, maybe he believed what he'd said.

CHAPTER 13

"Great view, don'tcha think?" Irv Farley swirled the ice in his glass of primo whiskey. For someone atop such a massive fortune, the guy still needed validation. Lots of it.

Although Ned hated to kiss up—he'd done more than his share in the early days of his career—he was prepared to pucker up today. He needed the guy's money now more than ever. "Probably the best view I've seen out here in Malibu, Irv." They were seated in lounge chairs along Farley's pool deck, which faced the ocean.

"Glad you think so. Didn't just fall into my lap, y'know. No sirree. Had to work long and hard for every inch of beach." He did a sweeping motion with his hands, then set his empty whisky glass on the small table between them. He continued to stare out at the Pacific, bluer than ever today. "I don't give handouts to just anyone with some 'high concept' moneymaking scheme."

"I'm not here for a handout, Irv. This is a genuine business opportunity for you."

The rotund businessman, dressed in Hawaiian print swim trunks and a baggy orange shirt, turned to face Ned. His eyes had narrowed, the earlier smile gone. "Tell me again how I'd benefit."

Ned ran through his proposal again. "Minimum risk, maximum potential," he concluded.

Farley reclined in his chair, made a show of scratching his chin. "Hey, Wallingford," he called. "Bring me another." Back to Ned. "You want more water, Jake. Too bad your docs won't let you drink these days."

"No, thanks. I don't mind the no-alcohol thing. I feel much healthier."

"Yeah, well, I heard the voice is on ice, so to speak, for some time to come? The concerts have dried up. That why you're trolling for money?"

Though he'd prepared himself to respond to cutting remarks like this, Ned's stomach roiled at the cavalier way Farley addressed his tenuous career situation. He gripped his thighs just enough to keep his eye on the prize. "This *thing* with my throat is just a minor setback. But to be on the safe side, I've voluntarily taken myself out of the limelight for a bit. While the revenue from other projects realigns itself, I need a little cushion."

Farley continued to rub his chin, but didn't say anything. Wallingford, his houseman, arrived with his new drink and removed the empty glass, then quickly disappeared. "I like the idea, Jake. But the return you propose is, well, since I'm a polite gentleman, let's just call it naïve."

Naïve? Polite gentleman, my ass! You're lowballing my proposition. "C'mon Irv. This is more than doing a friend a favor. I've offered a significant return on your investment." He'd bluffed, angled for the best deal he could get. The other man probably knew as much, but Farley expected him to do a little negotiating.

They traded proposals for the next several minutes; neither shifted his position. At length, as he guzzled the rest of his drink and shook the remains of the ice cubes as a reminder he was the one who called the shots, Farley rose and sauntered to the edge of his pool, which lay between them and the ocean view. Ned debated whether to follow but stayed where he was. He sensed any change in body position might signal concession.

Farley turned back to him, a hint of a smile played across his face. "For an entertainer, Jake, you drive a hard bargain."

How amateur does he think I am? Over the years, Ned developed a sixth sense when it came to false praise from people trying to screw him. His alarm system was fired up now. "Do we have a deal?"

Farley's expression morphed into one Ned remembered from a childhood storybook, a cartoon of the Wolf as he attempted to convince the Three Little Pigs to come out of their house.

"There might be a way for us to reach a win-win agreement."

The guy actually sounded slimy, like the stereotypical car salesman. Ned chose his next words carefully, as he led Farley to believe he was taking the bait without realizing the cost. "Yeah? Tell me more."

"I've recently established interests in several businesses in the Midwest. Construction-related businesses." He actually lifted his brows should Ned not have caught his meaning.

"I've already got my people signed on, Irv."

"For the life of the project?"

The deals he and Shae had worked out with their vendors and subs were tenuous at best and none of Farley's business. He had no desire to face the wrath of a controlled but pissed off Shae again. They'd reached some kind of truce during the storm. He didn't want to rock the boat now. "Most of our contracts and purchase orders are for specific aspects of the project. But I won't pay double or triple the price for supplies or services."

The other man cocked his head, the Big Bad Wolf expression deepened. "Wouldn't necessarily be the case with what I propose."

It was like he had to find his way through a minefield, all the while aware his chances of survival were zero or less. But Ned heard him out.

"Here's the deal," Farley said, any hint of a smile gone. He stated his terms, which if Ned agreed, would reduce profits considerably. "Haven't quite sealed the deal with my new businesses yet, but once they're in place, I'll get back with you to solidify our agreement."

～

THREE DAYS AFTER THE STORM, Shae drove out to the site to oversee the resumption of work. After two full nights' sleep in her own bed, she actually caught herself humming during the trip. In the past two days, she and Dave had studied and realigned their work schedule to recover lost time as quickly as possible. She was anxious to put their plan in place.

Dave approached as she alighted from her vehicle. "I thought I'd beaten you here for once. It's barely six thirty," she said.

He sipped coffee. "Didn't sleep much last night. Wife threw me out early this morning so she could go back to bed in peace."

"You worried about something? I thought we'd rearranged things enough that we'd be back on track again within a few days."

"I wasn't able to discuss the schedule changes with Ned."

"He didn't return your call?"

"Called right back, but he was out on the coast."

"Really?" First she'd heard of this. As anxious as he'd been to get back to work? Maybe there was someone out there he wanted to see, which might explain his changed attitude the day Dave picked them up. "Couldn't you have emailed him the new schedule?"

"Offered, but he told me to wait until he got back."

Interesting. "Did he say when that would be?" She didn't really care, of course. In fact, after his foray into revised bids and then their awkward parting, things would run a lot smoother if he stayed away. As long as he agreed to the schedule changes they'd worked out.

Dave shrugged. "Maybe today. Or tomorrow. Wasn't sure when."

An involuntary sigh escaped her. She'd been so up this morning as she anticipated a fresh start on the project. Now, thanks to Ned's disappearance, their hands were tied. She wanted to hit something, but her SUV didn't need any more dents. The delay in dealing with Ned wasn't so bad, but sooner or later they'd have to get past the discomfort they felt around each other.

She hadn't taken much time to survey the storm's damage two days earlier when Dave brought her to pick up her vehicle. Today, as they walked onto the site, she took a closer look. Although tree branches and leaves littered the property, other than the one tree that had been struck by lightning, no others had gone down. The ground was still spongy, though miraculously, not of bog proportions after so much moisture.

Ned's tent lay abandoned on the ground, a testament to the storm's fury. Like a shroud, the canvas covered the collapsed folding table and what must have been the two chairs. What would Ned do now—attempt to reconstruct his former office or bully his way into using their trailer?

She didn't have long to find out. The missing developer showed up a few minutes later with a huge black and tan RV that made the trailer look like a poor cousin. Should have known. Hollywood types like Ned needed their luxury—the trailer had probably proved too primitive.

Her throat went dry, yet her hands started to perspire. He was back! Now they could get down to business. Damn, he was back. She'd have to face him again. She had about ten seconds to get her head together.

He emerged from the passenger side of the RV and swaggered over to them sporting a broad smile. "What do you think?" he asked Dave. He gestured behind him. "Saw my tent was pretty much done for when I came out to get my car the other day, so I made other arrangements."

"I'll say." Dave moved closer to inspect the RV. "Pretty fancy vehicle for a construction site. You gonna drive it back and forth each day?"

"Nah. Gas is too expensive. I'll leave it out here as long as it isn't in your way."

Dave shook his head. "Sure. You can hook up to our power supply, if you want." He waited a beat. "Glad you're back. Shae and I need to go over that revised schedule with you."

"Right." Ned drew out the word, finally dragged his attention to Shae.

She struggled to breathe normally after they exchanged looks. What was going on? One minute he was a little boy who bragged about his new toy to the other admiring little boy. The next minute, his eyes bored into hers like a very big boy. Then, as fast as it had shown up, the look disappeared to be replaced with one of total disinterest. In her at least.

She didn't like this now-he's-interested-now-he's not business one bit. Just because her feelings about him waffled didn't mean he could do the same. It was disconcerting.

"I printed the revised schedule after I returned to town last night and read it over this morning. Got a few questions before I agree." He looked directly at her. "Can we go over them now?" This was the first time he'd talked to her since they climbed into the ATV three days ago.

"Crew's starting to arrive," Dave said. "I need to speak with them. If all goes well, we should be able to finish the footings, pans and rebar today. I'll be around, if you need me, Shae." He squashed his coffee container, threw it back into his truck, then promptly headed off to the temporary work sheds across the way, where members of the crew gathered.

Ned motioned for Shae to follow him.

"Where are we going?"

"Don't you want a tour of my new digs? We can catch up on the revised schedule at the same time."

"Oh. Okay." It was like their night in the trailer never happened.

Once inside, Ned came to an abrupt halt at the door, just inches away from her, barred her way. "Look, uh, before we get down to business, I want to apologize for the other day."

She grabbed hold of the door latch behind her to keep her knees from buckling. He was going to acknowledge that night after all. Now she wasn't sure she wanted to get into it. She assumed her most nonchalant air. "For what?"

He glanced from one side to the next, sighed, and then looked her in the eye. "You know. That kiss. Kisses. You woke up so scared, and out of reflex, I took you into my arms to comfort you. Kissed your hair. That led to more kissing. Had my throat not gone haywire—"

He paused. Was she supposed to respond?

But he continued before she could speak. "Even though it was spontaneous and well meant, I shouldn't have crossed the line. Any kind of relationship between us other than professional while we're working on this project would be inappropriate. It won't happen again."

"Oh." So that was how he wanted to play it. She may not have had much experience with men, but she knew instinctively those few minutes of foreplay had been more than reflex. He'd been turned on. She knew it. He knew she knew it. So why paint it like he was now? Why rub it in by hovering so close she could see the light growth of whiskers that speckled his chin?

"I don't want to jeopardize our business relationship," he said.

She averted her gaze afraid her eyes would betray her. Although, at the moment, she wasn't sure what he would have seen there. She was just as confused about what she wanted as she was prior to his arrival. Didn't want to jeopardize their *business relationship*? If she'd been one of those hotties he must surely squire around Hollywood without the least hesitation, he would have trampled their so-called *business rela-tionship* the minute his libido kicked in. She just wasn't hot enough.

No way would she acknowledge she'd read more into things. She stuck out her hand to shake on it. Not the wisest of moves, but she had to do something rather than just stand there and look stupid, though the contact was brutal on her already-wobbly knees. "Apology accepted. But not necessary. My fear of storms unnerved me. I'm sorry about the throat thing, but I guess it kept us from tempting fate."

"I got the throat checked out. No setback, but I have to watch it closer. No more rainstorms or other foul weather."

"Good to hear, although I don't know what you'll do come winter."

"Yeah, well, I'll deal with the snow and cold when the time comes. Probably hide out in this vehicle." His mood switched back to genial host. "So, c'mon, let me show you around."

As he pointed out the small kitchen/seating area, the question that had plagued her since his arrival wouldn't go away. "Are you renting this thing? Surely you didn't buy it given what you told me the other day?"

"Ah, that." He waved away her question. "Mike Woodley loaned it to me. Pretty nice, huh?"

"Uh, *nice*, yes." She was no expert on RVs, but this vehicle appeared to be a fairly high- ticket item. But then, even she, social ignoramus that she was, knew about the Woodley family wealth. They'd probably travel in nothing less.

His apology rankled. Her fingernails cut into her thumb pads. She had to get away from him as soon as she could brief him and gain his signature on the revised schedule. He may have stuck with her as his general contractor, but it was clear she wasn't good enough for him on a personal basis. She'd been such a fool.

Ned appeared oblivious to her self-recriminations as he continued to point out the overgrown bus's features. "Thought I'd set up my computer here on the banquette." The small table was anchored in the middle of a U-shaped padded bench. "You can sit on the other side whenever you stop by to correct my construction faux pas."

He was totally unaware of her mood. *Snap out of it, Shae.* She made a show of measuring the distance across the table surface with her arms. "I don't know, Ned. Pretty close quarters here, so close I can breathe down your neck. You may want to rethink your invitation."

"Ah, but once you sit down over there, observe the tight fit. There's no way you'll be able to spring up and lean across the table to brow-beat me."

He viewed her as a *pest?*

Ned moved farther into the RV. "Of course, other guests may avail themselves of these two club chairs. He shifted to the other side of the room. "Or use the couch here, which, unlike the less comfy set-up in your trailer, unfolds to become a second bed." He rubbed his neck. "Too bad this wasn't here the other night."

"Too bad," she repeated mechanically as she realized yet again how much he'd disliked their night together.

HER TONE MADE him pivot to face her. She wasn't smiling or appearing to enjoy their banter. She looked like he'd struck her. But he kept on, not sure what was with the woman. Hoped she'd snap out of it. He edged toward the back of the vehicle. "Down here, you'll note, like your trailer, we also have a small closet. Actually, two. I made sure to stock it with plenty of sheets, blankets and clean clothes before I set off this morning."

"Um. Good."

What was with her? He'd already told her he'd borrowed the RV from Mike. No added cost, other than the gas to get it here. Hadn't even bought the groceries. Instead, he'd *borrowed* those from the Woodley larder also.

This had been a great idea, if he did say so himself, even though he only said it to himself. After he'd convinced Mike he didn't need his money but did need transportation to California and help selling his house, he'd come up with the idea to use the Woodley RV as his field office. Brilliant afterthought. Caught Mike at his most receptive state when the guy had practically begged him to accept help.

"You're okay with this set-up, aren't you? Dave seemed fine with it."

She didn't reply at first.

"Shae? Tell me this was a good idea."

"It certainly beats that muddy, crumpled piece of canvas you called a tent."

Progress. Of sorts. "I, uh, thought you'd be relieved. This will keep me out of your hair, and yet I can be close enough to oversee things the way I want to."

Shae opened the second closet, stuck her head in briefly and just as fast withdrew it.

He couldn't help himself. "What's going on?"

"You just don't get it, do you?"

Get it? What was there to get, other than the lady was obviously in some sort of snit. Even after he'd apologized. God, he'd agreed to Farley's terms just to keep this project afloat, which turned his world upside down. Even though she wasn't aware of what he'd done, his situation was much more world-shattering than whatever bothered her. "No, I guess I don't. Enlighten me."

Rather than shed light on her mood, though, she immediately

morphed into her general contractor mode, returned to the front of the RV, ponytail swinging all the way. When she reached the banquette, she paused. "Nice vehicle. Thanks for the tour. I'm glad you'll be more comfortable. But let's get back to the schedule changes so we can resume this project."

He approached, not yet willing to assume his developer role. "Fine. We'll talk about the schedule in just a minute. But first, I want to know why you act like you can't stand to be around me. I thought we shook on my apology?"

"You know everything, you tell me." Her eyes blazed with blue-green fire.

He raised his palms in surrender. "I wouldn't keep pushing you, if I knew."

"Your decision to bring this fancy RV here is like saying to me, 'See how much better I can do than that rundown trailer of yours? See how much better I can do than you.'"

If she'd slugged him in the gut, he couldn't feel more sucker-punched. What on earth was she talking about?

"I know I'm nothing like the glamour girls that usually surround you. But to rub my face in that fact—"

"Rub your face?"

After a brief knock, Zoe Johansen stuck her head in. "There you are," she said seeing Ned. "They told me I could find you here."

Could her timing be worse? He needed to follow up on Shae's strange comments, but he also didn't want Shae anywhere near the woman who could so easily let it be known how close he'd come to bankruptcy.

"Uh, hi." He turned back to Shae. "I need to take care of this, but then you and I have to talk."

Shae blinked, like she couldn't believe he'd dismissed her. She studied the other woman. "Sure. I couldn't have made my point better."

As soon as the banker made her way into the RV, Shae dashed out, slamming the door.

"Sorry, I didn't mean to interrupt," Zoe said.

Ned shrugged. Too late now. He'd catch up with Shae later and attempt to figure out what was on her mind. The woman had more moods than Mike had wardrobe. "My general contractor. The storm put us behind schedule, so we were working out new dates. What brings you all the way out here? You want to check if there's an actual project?"

"Oh, I—the bank, never doubted that, Mr. Bonneville, er, Collier."

"Just joking."

She appeared to relax slightly. "Your financial situation seems to have improved with an influx of new revenue yesterday. I'm glad you were able to keep things going. For now, the bank is satisfied with the status of your equity stake."

They'd certainly better be. He'd sold his soul to keep this project alive. But she didn't need to know. No one did. "Glad to hear that. As I told you the other day, I just needed time for my finances to realign."

She turned to leave. "Uh, yes. I'm glad it worked out. By the way, it's beautiful out here. I'm intrigued to see how things develop."

Ned followed her outside. Not like he was anxious for her to leave, although he was. It was bad enough Shae had seen her. He didn't want anyone else to know who she was or why she was there. "It's still pretty primitive, or I'd give you a tour."

"Another time, perhaps."

She made her way back to her car, a yellow sports number. A bit jaunty for a banker.

He breathed a sigh of relief after she drove off. Was this what he had to look forward to in the months ahead? His new *best friend* from the bank making surprise visits.

CHAPTER 14

Shae stomped out of the RV ready to spit nails. Fortunately for her mouth, and anyone with the bad luck to be near her, the arrival of those supplies was still a few weeks away. Who was that woman? Why had she tracked Ned here to the site?

A blonde. Should have known. Hair color had to have come from a bottle, but then, it was probably the *look* Ned was accustomed to in L.A. Had he brought her back with him after his recent trip? Or had she followed him here because she couldn't stand to be away from him?

Didn't matter. The woman was here. Any hope something might still happen between herself and Ned totally disappeared with the other woman's arrival.

While Dave was off with the troops, the trailer provided refuge. This was the first she'd been inside the vehicle since the morning after the storm. Her eyes took in the stacks of office supplies, boxes and other clutter. Who would have thought just a few days ago this was almost the scene of what might have been a torrid night of passion?

She scrutinized her surroundings. Functional. Met their needs. But compared to today's new kid on the block, it truly was a dump.

As if a magnetic field had ensnared her, she drifted to the side window, which gave her a direct view of the RV. Nothing really to see. What had she expected—the trailer rocking back and forth?

To her surprise, the woman emerged, in a hot pink pantsuit, no less. Who wore that kind of get-up to a construction site? Ned exited right behind her. They exchanged a few words, and then the woman pivoted and sashayed away. Parting so soon? Must've made plans to hook up later. In the distance, Shae spied a canary-colored convertible. Must belong to the hot pink glamour girl.

Shortly thereafter, a flash of yellow shot down the road toward town. Good riddance. Shae released her hands from the hammerlock with which she gripped them.

The best thing she could do for herself was keep her distance from Ned the rest of the day—and however long it took her to calm down. Now that he'd made his lack of interest in her known, she couldn't afford to be around him at the risk she'd give away her feelings. She remained in the trailer the better part of the day and let Dave obtain Ned's approval of the revised work schedule.

Around five, she called it a day. Dave and the crew had already left. She opened the trailer door to head out only to discover Ned there. "Oh, hi."

"Talk about timing." He glanced at her handbag and briefcase.

"I'm on my way out. Can whatever you're here to talk about wait until tomorrow?'

"I need a ride."

She angled her head. "Oh?"

"I was so intent on getting the rig here this morning, it totally escaped me I'd have to find another way back to town. Must've missed Dave, because the only vehicle still parked here is yours."

"I, uh, lost track of time."

"Works to my benefit, if you don't mind a passenger?"

Had he totally missed her mood earlier in the day? Shae twisted around to assure the door had locked behind her while she bought time to figure out how to handle this. Couldn't refuse his request for a ride and leave him out here on his own, tempting as the thought might be. But to share a confined space with him again unnerved her. "Okay, sure." She thrust the load she carried into his chest. "Here, make your-self useful." She took off, left him in her wake.

He caught up with her. "You make all your clients lug around your office?"

"Cost of bumming a ride."

"Yeah. Guess beggars can't … you know."

She opened the door of her SUV. He stuck her stuff on the backseat, then settled into the passenger seat.

Shae concentrated on the road, fearful what would come out of her mouth if she initiated conversation.

"Sorry about this morning."

So, he hadn't forgotten. Best to play dumb. "What about this morning?"

"We didn't finish the tour of the motor coach."

Or maybe he had forgotten. "Oh. That. Guess there'll be plenty of time in the weeks ahead for me to see the last three feet of the interior."

"And the sarcasm is back. What's the deal, Shae?"

Shouldn't have opened her mouth. He had her dead to rights. Best to make light of it. "RV envy."

"Huh?"

"Don't you think we'd like a classier mobile office ourselves?"

He had the grace to shift position. "Uh—"

"Remember that bare bones estimate we agreed to in order to keep your contract?"

"Well, hell, Shae. Why didn't you say so? There's room in there for you, if you want. Dave can have the trailer to himself."

He was being too considerate. But then, the RV hadn't really been the problem. Just a convenient red herring to avoid having to delve into her deeper feelings. "A minute before you arrived, Dave and I said the last rites over the remains of your tent, wondered how you'd get by, and the next minute, you charged up with that monster RV."

"So? We're okay now?"

Please don't make me go there. "Uh, sure. Once you tell me who that woman was." Damn! The sentence just slipped out.

"Woman? Oh. Her. That was Zoe Johansen. My banker."

She blinked. "Your banker? They make house calls? Why come all the way out here? There's not much to see yet."

"I told her about the same thing. Invited her back a few months down the road."

His banker? A blonde in a notice-me pantsuit with a yellow sports car? Too ludicrous not to be true. Her hands slid down the steering wheel as her heart beat slowed.

He slapped the dash. "You didn't think … My God, Shae. That's rich."

"Rich? She wore a hot pink get-up to a construction site three days after a major storm left the place a near quagmire. All the bankers I know wear funereal black."

"So you assumed she had to be some babe come for a booty call?"

"I didn't assume anything. Other than suddenly my presence wasn't needed or wanted when she showed up."

He sank back in the seat and ran a hand through his hair. "I should've introduced you."

"But anything to do with your finances is confidential, right?"

"Actually, I'm in better shape moneywise today than the day in the tent. That was my reason for going to the coast." He turned his head to gaze out the window.

"You must be relieved." As was she, if he wasn't out there to visit some woman. But then, he hadn't clarified his statement about her assumption. He'd brought up the banker instead.

"Hey! Wasn't that our turn?"

She snapped out of her speculations. He was right. "Shoot. Oh, well, there's another turnoff in just a mile or two."

"Isn't there a mom-and-pop diner along this route—Susie's?"

She scanned the road until she spotted the blue and yellow neon sign for the famous eatery. "Right ahead. Why?"

"Turn in. I have a hankering for a tenderloin. You hungry?"

Hungry? When had she last eaten? "I, uh, guess so. Memories of their ill-fated business meeting a few weeks earlier flooded back. She couldn't very well get out of eating with him now. "But how 'bout we take our food to my place?" she asked before she had time to consider the implications. "Well, my dad's place. I'm not much at housekeeping, so lower your expectations, but the kitchen is in pretty good shape." Why had she done that? It made much better sense to grab a quick meal with him here in public than to be alone with him at her dad's place.

As soon as they arrived at the Harriman house, she went to the kitchen, where she grabbed a few plates. Meanwhile, Ned checked out the first floor—living room, dining room, which she and her dad both used more as an office, bathroom and bedroom. "This is where you grew up?" he asked as he entered the kitchen. "Interesting place."

"That's what people say when they can't think of anything nice to say about something."

"A surprise, that's all. I would've expected a more modern layout. Different furnishings. Did he even build this?"

She chuckled. "Ever heard of the cobbler's children who had no shoes? All Dad's money goes right back into the business."

Ned seated himself at the kitchen table. "Have you lived here all these years?"

Shae bit into her sandwich and swallowed. "I had my own place since the first year out of college. I was on my way out of town when Dad was admitted to the hospital, so my previous digs had already been rented to someone else. I'm back here at the old homestead on a temporary basis. Slept on the davenport the first week, because I was sure I'd be off to Dallas any day."

"How much longer will your dad be in rehab?"

"Is that your poorly veiled attempt to find out how much longer I'll be in charge?"

He set down his cold drink. "Actually, I wondered what you'll do when he's back here. He won't be able to return to work immediately, will he? Or will he work from home? Either way, that might prove, uh, problematic for you. Maybe cramp your style, if you're used to living on your own?"

His question surprised her. "Hadn't considered that. It's been all I can do to stay one day ahead of the crews ... and you."

"Guess I've made your life somewhat difficult. But you understand now why?"

She put her tenderloin aside. "Let me count the ways." She held up a finger. "One, you have very little idea what a project manager does."

He started to protest, but she cut him off, raised a second finger.

"Two, you have control issues. You want to call all the shots." Third finger. "Three, you don't trust my lack of experience, so you doublecheck everything I do."

"Geez, you don't have to—"

"Four, you may not want to admit it, but you get some kind of wicked kick out of hassling me."

"That's your imagination."

She stared him down.

"Okay, I admit I get a certain amount of pleasure from seeing you torqued off. But not all the time. Like now. Despite all this talk about my hassling you, we've gotten along pretty well. Even after your outburst over using preformed walls for the foundations, you were willing to help me rectify my mistakes. But since that night in the trailer, you've held back." He removed a pickle from his sandwich and placed it on the wrapper. "Want to talk?"

Certainly an open invitation, but the very last thing she wanted to do was tell him she felt rejected when he didn't follow through on the sexual overtures that night. "It's just I have so much riding on your project, and I don't always know how to deal with your, uh, need for such involvement. I should stand up to you even more than I have, but I'm …" Here was the tricky part; she wanted to articulate her thoughts, but she didn't want to offend him—he could still break the contract— or let him get too close to her actual feelings, whatever those were. "I'm not that good with people things. I'm an engineer. I deal in facts and numbers."

He gazed directly in her eyes. "I'd say you've stood up to me pretty well."

"Thanks, but the longer we work together, the better I get to know you. Like a friend." Okay, more than a friend, but she didn't want to go there. "I was able to renegotiate with some of our suppliers and subs, because I didn't know them. But to tell a friend no or that he's full of horse manure is different."

"I've experienced similar dilemmas with some of the booking agents I've worked with over the years. That's why I have Mike, my buffer, when I need to say no or ask for more money.'

"Maybe I should have Dave step in for me. Except, that wouldn't be the job my dad gave me to do. I only have this one chance to make good."

"Your dad's that unforgiving?"

She sipped her cold drink while she figured out how to phrase her response. "Not so much unforgiving as fearful. For me."

"Explain."

She ran a nail down the paper cup, debated how much to say. "My dad always planned my brother would someday run the company. But Sean wanted to join the motocross circuit and race his bike. He'd cut out early every time he thought he could get by with it. The day of the accident, he was miles away from town when a storm hit. He didn't want Dad to catch on, so he tried to outrun the downpour."

"And didn't make it."

She gave an involuntary sigh and nodded. "Dad's always referred to Sean's death as an industrial accident, even though Sean was nowhere near the site." She swallowed with difficulty. Sean's death was still painful to talk about. "Funny how I'm the one afraid of storms, yet Sean's the one who suffered from one."

"Sounds like your dad hasn't yet come to grips with your brother's death."

His comment cut right to the heart of the matter. "Perhaps. Dad has never acknowledged Sean's discontent. Instead, he's built up this picture in his head that no one can ever replace Sean. Including me."

"And you wouldn't be in your position now, if your dad hadn't been so desperate for you to stay."

"Blunt but correct. Like I told you, after Sean's death, I thought if I switched my major to civil engineering I could take Sean's place. It was as much to honor Sean's memory as to help my dad. But Dad hasn't wanted me anywhere near construction sites, because he doesn't want to lose his only living child to an actual on-site incident."

He took a last few bites of his sandwich, as if chewing over her story as well. "Isn't that, uh, somewhat far-fetched? If he really feared for your safety, why didn't he take you under his wing and teach you accident avoidance techniques?"

"Exactly!"

"Grief can do strange things to a mind." He stared at the wall of cabinets behind her as if the subject of grief held its own blade over him.

"Guess I'm not the only one who carries a heavy family obligation on her shoulders." Then she realized what she'd said. His father had been gone about the same amount of time as Sean. "Sorry. That was a misery loves company statement if there ever was one."

He cleared his throat. "Sometimes the memories sneak under the radar and grab you when you least expect."

She reached across the table and took his hand in hers. When it dawned on her what she'd done, she quickly withdrew. Though her gesture had been offered in sympathy, the contact triggered vibes she'd fought so hard to repress. No, not now. She'd held back her feelings this long, surely she could keep them in check a little longer. How could she be all sympathy one minute and the next all stimulated?

He rose, scraped the chair on the floor. "I, uh, should be going. Confession may be good for the soul, but it can also be tiring. We both need our rest."

She rose, too, her eyes bored into his. Now or never. "No. Stay."

CHAPTER 15

The invitation just slipped out. But once offered, she knew this was exactly what she wanted, despite all the arguments she'd given herself.

A muscle twitched on Ned's on his jaw. Probably involuntary, but the movement shot ripples of pleasure throughout her body. Yes, this was what she wanted, all right, discretion be damned.

"I've got to know," she whispered hoarsely.

His eyes narrowed into a blur of gray curiosity. "Know?"

"What it's like. Making love with you."

He stepped back. "I … uh, where did that come from?"

She removed her hand from his arm. "Left field, I guess."

He eyed her, probably to figure out how to rebuff her advances gently. But she'd put herself so far out there that anything he said or did other than drag her off to bed would be a rejection. Why had she set herself up like this?

"That's quite an offer," he said finally.

Was he considering or stalling for time? If he was the least bit interested, she had to push him over the brink. As if she'd always known what she had to do next, she moved into him, pulled his face to hers and kissed him. Out of pure improvisation, she added tongue.

Ned willingly participated, slid his tongue along hers, augmented her moves as they went. Suddenly, he pulled back. "You sure about this?"

One last chance to change her mind. "Yes, I'm sure. But what about you? You've accused me of running away from confrontations. Said I wasn't tough enough to tango. I'm ready to prove you wrong."

He took her hand in his, rubbed his thumb against her palm. "Okay, then. Let the dance begin." He folded her into his arms and kissed her back, ignited a fire within her that burned its way from her throat to her toes.

She had no idea how she could stand upright and be kissed like this. Her body had gone limp in his embrace. Paradoxically, it came alive.

At length, he drew away. "I'm not into long-term relationships. Can you deal with that?"

She'd expected as much. Her passion cooled but not enough to renege. She was too far gone to stop. "Then we're two of a kind." Liar.

NED KNEW BETTER. But the look in her eyes drilled into his resolve. Molten blue-green fire consumed his free will, beckoned him to jump in. His swollen cock urged him on as well. Hell. He'd fantasized about screwing her since the first day they'd met. No turning back now.

He tipped her chin up to stare right into her soul. "No regrets?"

"No regrets."

Understanding established, he couldn't get her to bed fast enough. He picked her up and rushed up the stairs.

In her bedroom, she paused long enough to turn on a small light on a bedside table. "My room's a mess."

He didn't care what the place looked like as long as the bed was clear. "You're all I'm seeing." He laid her on her bed and climbed in beside her. Though he wanted to rip off her clothes immediately, he forced himself to slow down, like a kid on Christmas morning who wanted to savor every last minute with his new gifts. He leaned into her hair and nuzzled her neck just behind her ear to breathe in the fragrance of citrus. "I love the way you smell. Fresh. Clean."

"Do that some more. It feels so good."

"I aim to please." He massaged the area behind her other ear.

Her chest jutted forward, her hips almost came off the bed. His restraint would last only so much longer. He slid his hand from behind her ear to the small of her back, brought her into him. He cooed and made lazy spirals along her spine. "Easy does it. Relax." She tensed, tried to fold into him.

His hand roamed south, covered the curve of her buttocks and squeezed ever so lightly.

Her approval emerged as a moan. "Oh. Oh …"

"Like that?"

Her breathing grew raspy, disjointed. "I can … barely … stand it." But she still demanded more.

She wasn't the only one about to lose it. "You're wearing too many clothes."

"Then remove them."

Couldn't resist that invitation. Her work shirt came first. "I've wanted to remove this since that meeting at my mom's gallery."

"Nothing sexier than a work shirt."

He lifted an eyebrow. The lady hadn't completely lost her sarcastic edge. Good. A little sauciness added spice. "Works for me."

As he slipped the garment from her shoulders and pitched it on the floor, goose pimples immediately dotted her arms. He eyed the result of his efforts. Didn't expect this. The woman wore a lacy lavender bra, one of those low-cut, push-up jobs that produced incredible mounds above the top edge. "Had I known you wore such fancy lingerie …" He licked his lips rather than finish the statement.

"Recent purchase." Her words were sluggish, as if she were on drugs.

She'd been lingerie shopping? Had she planned this? Never mind. They were here together now, a near naked Shae before him. He didn't care how it happened. He'd take it from here. He placed a finger on the curving landscape. "Smooth."

"I, uh, thanks."

He finger-walked down the front of her bra until he reached her smooth abdomen. The lady got her exercise. "Firm abs." He spread his palm, swirled it in a slow, clockwise motion. Gradually, he slid his hand up, continued the circular movement. Though she jerked as the tip of his thumb reached the bottom of her bra, she pushed into him, apparently wanted him to increase the pressure as his hand swept to the right, circled the tip of one breast.

"Oh, Ned. I-I—"

"Shh. Don't talk. Just feel. I want you to enjoy this. Are you?"

"God, yes! More."

Though he'd grown so hard he could barely move his legs, he took his time with her breasts, blew through the lacy fabric but swiftly shifted to kissing. His mouth worked its way around the tip of one breast, covered every inch of lace.

"Umm," she murmured.

"You ain't seen nothin' yet, lady."

In one swift motion, he reached behind her, undid the bra and threw it over his shoulder.

She blinked in response to his boldness, then lifted cloudy eyes to his, as if to check his reaction.

"God, you're beautiful!" He had to remind himself to take a breath. As much as he wanted to plow into her, those gorgeous breasts couldn't be ignored. "No wonder you wear those body-covering shirts. If your crew had any idea these beauties lay beneath, you'd need a bodyguard round the clock." He grabbed one in each hand, began to fondle.

Before his blood completely flowed south, he had to taste those goodies. He placed his mouth over one and suckled. His mind melded with every creature from the beginning of time that had engaged in the sex act. Unrestrained euphoria.

Her pelvis arched inches off the bed. "Oh. Oh. Oh."

You got that right, babe. His dick was close to exploding, but he couldn't leave this feast just yet. He licked around the engorged nipple, leaving a trail of moisture. The nubbin had grown so taut he tongued it back and forth just to see if it would grow larger.

Beneath him, Shae squirmed, urged him to move on. But first, he had to kiss that glorious mouth. He crushed his own against it, deepened the kiss. His tongue sought then danced with hers. He couldn't bring himself to break away, like he'd been awakened from a long dream. Her mouth was his reality.

The realization made him shudder. What was with him? This was sex. Sex with an incredible, willing woman but sex just the same. *Get on with it, man.*

He tore his mouth from hers, reached down, undid and removed her jeans. She lay there, clothed in only silky black panties, which hardly shielded the delights beneath from his gaze. He tongued the flimsy fabric, inhaled the inviting scent of her sex. Shit! Enough of the preliminaries. Nipping the elastic waistband in his teeth, he pulled down the garment to reveal her mound.

Throughout his ministrations, Shae lay there, her body so stimulated, she could barely move, pleasure like she'd never known coursed through her. All she could do was open herself—literally—to experience every nuance, and let Ned take her to places she didn't know existed. Was he affected the same way? Was there more to this than two consenting adults who enjoyed each other's bodies? Was this making love?

Ned abruptly ended the kiss and moved lower, which negated her conjectures. No, this was sex, with all its flaming, demanding, incredible sensations. This was what she'd asked for and Ned was giving it to her. With a vengeance. Though somewhere deep within her a soulful prayer begged for there to be more than now, that would never happen.

His fingers edged their way into her private region, stroked her repeatedly. She'd long ago gotten past the embarrassment of her wetness. He seemed to revel in it. The next several minutes were a blur, as Ned did things with his mouth that sent her whirling into a dreamlike stupor. She heard herself gasp, but she couldn't do anything to stop it, like she'd entered a parallel universe where only feeling existed. Wonderful, powerful sensations so intense she thought she might pass out gripped her.

Just when she felt she could absorb no more of this excruciating ecstasy, he peeled off his pants and briefs. Unbelievable! Ned was a man endowed, and at the moment, swollen - with passion. Enormously swollen.

She nearly fainted at the thought of him inside her body. Not from fear. From sheer anticipation. She wanted this, him. Now.

In a croaky entreaty, she told him as much.

His eyes had grown dark and smoky, unfocused when he glanced up. But he got the message. He moved on top of her.

Such demanding power about to overcome her should have scared her silly, but instead, she warmed to the idea of having her own power over him.

But even in the throes of heated passion, she realized this wasn't about power at all. This was about her offer of herself to him, and even if she didn't give him the gift of her love, at least she gave the gift of pleasure. All she wanted now was to please him, one night stand or not. "Now, Ned. I want you now."

He didn't argue. From nowhere, he produced protection, deftly slipped it on and entered her. Nothing had prepared her for intimacy. Such swift connection with another human being was a kind of cosmic connection she hadn't known existed.

He moved in and out, agonizingly slow at first, then with increasing speed. Her mews crescendoed as his thrusts grew stronger. She screamed his name, grabbed his hair and grasped her pillow to hold onto her sanity.

She didn't think it could get any better and then, in a cataclysmic burst of fireworks, she was proved wrong. Her world exploded. The embers that remained of her ardor engulfed her. She lay there gasping, tried to catch her breath while she congratulated herself for her wanton behavior. Gradually, her body stilled, her breathing calmed.

Unbidden tears filled her eyes as the totality of the experience overwhelmed her.

Ned collapsed next to her and lay there dazed.

"That was fantastic."

He didn't reply. Chalk it up to post-coital fatigue. She'd wait. But he remained silent longer than she thought necessary. "You okay?" she asked.

"Yeah. Just, uh, regrouping."

"Want to do it again?"

He sat up abruptly. "No!" Then, apparently when he noted the shock on her face, he added, "That is, not right now."

"Okay. I'm pretty blown away myself." But she probed for more of a response. "Help me here, Ned. I'm pretty green at these things. Do you take a shower and leave? Do we nap a bit? Or do you stay the night?"

He took his time replying. "What do you want from me, Shae?" he asked finally.

"I want for you not to feel threatened."

"Threatened?"

"I may not have much experience at this, and I may not be very good at reading people, but even I can tell the temperature has gone down about twenty degrees since we finished and reality returned."

"Picked up on that, huh?"

"One minute you're snorting like a horse on the backstretch and the next, it's like you're pawing at the fence trying to escape."

He released a deep sigh. "Thought we agreed this was just a physical thing before we hit the mattress?"

She offered a shy smile. "I remember. I didn't realize I'd feel quite so, like this, afterwards. But a deal's a deal." She licked her lips. "I feel delicious. Happy with the world. Not a care, thanks to you. So how do I play this so you feel okay, too?"

"I'm fine. Don't worry about me."

His expression changed as she downplayed the sex they'd just enjoyed. Easier than she thought it would be. Were all men this gullible? All he'd needed to hear was she wouldn't hold him to anything, and he'd relaxed to the point of sleep. He already snored softly.

She allowed herself a few minutes to gaze, admire the way his nose curled up every so often, how his tight pecs twitched from time to time, and *be truthful, Shae,* how his cock, no longer quite so much like a stallion's, was still magnificent. The media would pay thousands for just one picture of this. Women around the world would pay just to lie where she was now. And she had him all to herself.

Correction, she had him all to herself for the fleeting present.

Some deeply ingrained feminine insight told her to make light of their coupling and let Ned think he was off the hook. She'd told him how great it was, which was true, but this also appealed to his ego. She'd given him several options to end the night.

But she'd lied. He'd been pretty clear he didn't expect anything to come from their time in bed. Her brain told her it was for the best. But her heart, yes, her heart, now fully engaged despite their this-is-only-sex agreement, wanted more.

She had no idea how she could get it unless she broke her word, which would only wreak havoc on both their careers and the project.

Now, more than any time since she was a little girl, she wished she had a mother to turn to for advice. Though there was still her father, how could she tell the person who'd entrusted her with a multimillion-dollar deal she'd screwed the client?

Shae found a quilt and covered said spent client. Then she dragged herself to her shower to dispense with the only remaining evidence of intercourse with that glorious creature.

As she turned on the shower, an unbidden tear trickled down her cheek.

CHAPTER 16

"You're at it pretty early," Mike observed the next morning as he lifted one of Ned's earphones.

Ned turned off the playback on his keyboard and pulled down the other side of his headpiece. "Got inspired and didn't want to lose it."

"Yeah? Good to hear. What was that? Didn't recognize it."

"One of my own."

"Good idea. No need to sit around waiting for the next project. Have something warming up in the bull pen."

Mike meant well. Though misguided, his comments were intended as support. Nonetheless, Ned couldn't resist unsettling his friend's world. "Actually, this is something to promote Sullivan's Creek once it's done."

Mike angled his head, narrowed his eyes. "Really? How?"

"Not sure. I've heard these arpeggios and chords in my head as we've progressed through the various stages. Hey, why don't you take that part—figure out how to use it?"

"Me? I'm no PR type."

Ned shrugged. "Just a thought. Never mind. I'll find someone else."

Mike held up a hand. "Not so fast. I didn't say no. Sounds intriguing. Might expand my horizons."

Like Mike's *horizons* weren't already stretched beyond capacity with his family's business, his consulting business and managing Ned's career. But now the idea was out there, it appealed to him as well. One of those *bones* he could throw Mike to keep him out of his finances.

"Can I hear it?"

"When it's done."

"And that will be …"

Ned threw up his hands. "Beats me. But a while yet. I need to live through the rest of the construction phase first."

"That's what it's about? Building houses?"

Ned considered. "More than that. It's the excitement of what I'm doing. The fear and anxiety and hope that I've captured Gramps' vision as well as my feelings about the land."

Mike placed a hand on Ned's shoulder. "Okay, okay. I didn't realize so much was going on in that composer's brain of yours." He stepped back and studied him. "It's really important to you."

"Uh, yeah. But like I said, it's just a concept in its infancy right now."

"Well, keep it up. I want to hear it as soon as you've got something." Mike turned to leave. Then he stopped just before he reached the door and came back. "You apparently were out on the town most of the night."

His second mother must've heard him return to the house in the wee hours of the morning. "Didn't know I had a curfew."

"Of course not. But since you've been back in Des Moines, you've rarely been out past ten. Found it odd, that's all."

"Should I call the next time? Get it cleared with you first?" His sarcasm would only urge Mike on with his inquisition. But Ned couldn't help it. He was a grown man of thirty-five, who should be able to come and go as he pleased.

Mike gazed at him again. "Mighty touchy this morning. Did the lady say no? Nah, you would've been back sooner, if that were the case. What happened? She kicked you out as soon as ... well, you know."

"You want to go fishing, there's gear in the garage and Grey's Lake awaits."

"How come so close-mouthed? Not your usual MO." He appeared to turn the question over in his mind. "Wait a minute. Not that general contractor?" Ned didn't answer.

Mike slapped his forehead. "Are you out of your mind? You know better than to mix business with pleasure. How many times has that backfired for you in the past?"

As much as he resented Mike's interference in his personal life, he couldn't defend himself against his friend's admonition. Had Fiancée Number One, Gillian, his untrustworthy band manager, not tied them up in Europe, he could've gotten back to see his dad before he passed away. Hooking up with Shae was a dumb idea. He'd told himself as much ever since he met her. Why hadn't he listened?

Mike shook his head repeatedly, like he couldn't believe what had gone down. "You've changed, man. You never threw caution to the wind, took such chances before."

"Did I say I'd been with her?"

"Didn't have to. Your denial confirms my suspicion."

Ned pushed away from his keyboard. "If I had, what would be so wrong with that? She's a decent person."

"I didn't attack her character. Just reminded you that you are paying her to do a job for you, a construction job. If you share the same bed, what will you do if her company doesn't follow through on its obligations?"

Ned considered Mike's question. "Fire their asses, I guess."

"You guess?" Mike's voice rose. "Not the words of someone who's made this multimillion-dollar investment."

"Hey, I'm still the guy in charge, the one who pays the bills. She knows that."

Mike released a long sigh and held up his hands in surrender. "That's my say. Whenever I voice my concerns about something, you dig in more. So I'm done."

"For now," Ned added once Mike was out of the room.

Good thing he'd turned the recorder on while he composed, because he had no idea what he'd put together. He'd told Mike a bunch of crap to keep his friend from questioning the heavy metal chords and high volume of his frustrations. Funny thing, though. His ideas, disconnected as they were at the moment, made sense, despite the complicated reasons he'd sought out the music room.

He'd returned to Mike's in the middle of the night after he woke to discover he once again shared a bed with Shae. Only this time, they were both under the covers and he was buck-naked. Last night had been no escape-to-the-trailer, only-one-bed-available kind of thing. No, last night they'd both deliberately chosen to share the bed.

Back at the Mansion after a shower—a cold one— he'd tried to sleep, with little success. The memory of that blue-green gaze that had induced him to stay and make love to her wouldn't go away. Once those eyes fixed him with their resolve, free will had flown out the door and left only raw physical need in its wake. The CIA should have such a weapon.

It had been great. Hell, it was the best sex he'd had in ages, if ever. Shae had been great, not just her body, or her participation, but her take on the whole experience. No strings, no regrets. Yeah, she'd cuddled afterwards, a female thing that spoiled most of his other booty calls, but she'd backed off when he hadn't responded in kind. Fell asleep, actually. His guys hadn't been up for a second go round. When he'd come to several hours later, she was on her side of the bed, her back to him.

Why did he vacillate between the memory of something pretty damn toe-curling and something else akin to what—guilt? Nah, couldn't be. He'd done nothing wrong. Hadn't pushed, merely responded to her invitation. Been the perfect lover. Lingered over certain areas to give her pleasure to the point where he thought he would implode.

After sleep had evaded him for two hours, he'd resorted to his music. Mike had turned over what the family euphemistically called their music room to him. It contained no musical instruments except

Ned's keyboard, which had only recently taken up residence. However, in deference to, or in defense of, the period in high school when Mike thought he might join Ned's band, the Woodleys had soundproofed the walls.

He'd gone into free-fall, let his feelings emerge in his music. Other than the mansion's gym, this was his only option to let it all hang out. Only after every confusing emotion had expressed itself on his recorder would he stand a chance of deciphering what the hell he'd gotten himself into the night before.

NED WAS GONE by the time Shae awoke the next morning. No surprise. She hadn't expected him to stick around. Still, it cut that what she considered a pretty spectacular night of passion ended without fanfare.

She dressed with little thought to her wardrobe and made herself eat a bowl of cereal even though she wasn't hungry.

She was about to leave for the site when her phone rang. "Ms. Harriman? This is Cheryl Park, your dad's case manager at Blackhawk Hills. Could you come over right away? Your father has packed his bag and is ready to leave."

"Leave? I thought he still had a few more weeks of rehab time with you."

"Correct. But he doesn't agree."

"I'll be right there." She threw her things together and ran for the SUV.

Her father had taken up residence in one of the lobby chairs by the time she arrived, his bag on his lap, his expression locked in permanent disgust. "Dad? What's this all about?"

"I told them not to call you. I'm still a competent adult who can make his own decisions."

She pulled over another chair. "Of course, you can make your own decisions. Apparently the latest is to leave. But why? Did something happen?"

He inhaled deeply, then blew it out in a huff. "That's just it. Nothing's happened."

"You mean your heart's not doing better? I've heard otherwise."

"I meant me. I'm doing nothing. The ticker's getting all the attention. I just sit here, lie here, day after day, the highlight of my agenda when they take my vitals."

Should have known. Should have anticipated this and prepared the staff. But her mind had been elsewhere the last several days, what with the storm and the revised work schedule. And Ned.

Cheryl Park, whom Shae had met the day her father checked in, came up to greet her. "Good morning, Ms. Harriman. Your father and I were just discussing his progress. It's been remarkable, considering the shape he was in when he arrived."

Tim Harriman crossed his arms in front of him. "If it's so remarkable, why can't I go home?"

The case manager shifted her attention to her client. "Because your body still has a way to go to repair itself. That will happen much faster if you remain here where we have the equipment and expertise to help you."

"My dad is bored. What can we do to help him?"

"Bored? Then why have you turned me down, Mr. Harriman, every time I've suggested an activity? The only time I've seen you up and about was the day you played checkers with your daughter." His case worker wasn't one to back down.

Shae's father scowled. "Let's put it this way, I'm not into needlepoint, Bingo, zumba—whatever that is— ceramics, and God forbid, certainly not Mah Jongg."

"Check," Cheryl acknowledged. "You've got me, Mr. Harriman. What I should have done was ask you what you wanted to do."

"Leave. But that doesn't seem to count."

Park had the grace to smile. "What else?"

He glanced back at Shae. "I want to be back running my company."

"We've talked about that. It's what got you here in the first place," Park said.

He tightened up again. The case manager meant well, but she

didn't seem to realize the pro she was up against when it came to hard heads. Shae needed to think fast and come up with something to appease him. "He's allowed to read, isn't he?" she asked.

"Yes, of course. There's a fairly well-stocked library on the premises, and anything we don't have we can get from local libraries."

"How about technical stuff?"

The case manager considered. "Depends. Would it get him riled up?"

"More likely put him to sleep. He could review the various permits we've obtained for our construction project."

"Hello? *He's* still here. And *he'd* like a say in this."

Both women turned to Shae's father, eyebrows raised.

"That all?"

"For now," Shae replied. "We'll make it a test to gauge how much you can handle. Not your brain. I know that's loaded for bear. But your stress level."

"What do you say, Mr. Harriman?" Cheryl Park asked. "Your daughter's come up with a great idea."

"I'll ask Dave to bring some over this afternoon," Shae told her dad.

"Why not one of the guys? I miss 'em."

"Let me check with your doctor," the other woman said. "We'll start with one at a time. Accompanied by Mr. Hale."

Shae's dad grimaced, but behind his expression, Shae detected a look of triumph.

Eruption averted. At least for today. But Shae didn't fool herself. Her dad's acquiescence would last only so long. Needed to plan now for how she would counter the next move. It was almost cathartic to deal with her father. Took her mind off the previous night. At least for a while.

"How's your dad?" Dave asked once she was back at the site.

"The old Tim Harriman is fighting to take control of the new, healthier version. He was packed and ready to leave when I got there."

Her superintendent glanced behind her. "Don't see him. You must've won this round."

"Barely. Agreed to send him that stack of permits to review. We've put them off."

Dave gave her a thumbs-up. "Good thinking."

"Hello?" an older female voice called from behind them as they headed to the trailer.

Dave recognized her first. "You're Ned's mom, right?"

"That's right. Janice Collier. You both attended the meeting at my gallery a while back."

Shae extended her hand. "Mrs. Collier. Nice to see you again, although I'm not sure Ned's here yet."

"He's not. I've just come from what he now calls his mobile office. No one's there."

Had he slept late after his busy night?

"Ned suggested I wait to come out here until my house was framed, but my curiosity got the better of me." She surveyed her surroundings. "I grew up out here, you know. Already looks a lot different from the landscape I knew." Her tone had assumed a wistful quality.

"Right now, all you'll see are these holes for the foundations with nothing more than the footings, rebar and pans inside them. The rough-in plumbing will go in today. But I think you'll like the results, once we're done," Shae said.

"I'm looking forward to living here. It will please Ned."

Interesting insight into their mother-son relationship. This whole development began when Ned wanted to do something for his mother, and apparently she'd agreed to move here for his benefit.

"I wish I could tell you when Ned will show up, but his schedule's somewhat unpredictable."

Janice Collier patted Shae's hand and chuckled. "I'm quite used to his sporadic comings and goings. I'll head back to town and wait until construction is a little further along. Do you have time to walk me back to my car? I had another reason to visit here today."

Dave said good-bye and made tracks for the trailer. What did the woman want? Surely his mother hadn't learned Ned spent the night and had come to warn Shae off? No, she wouldn't be so friendly.

"I'd like to invite you to a showing at my gallery next week," Janice said, as she picked her way over the rough ground.

And there it was. "A showing?" Shae repeated as she attempted to buy time to frame a polite refusal.

"I've come across a wonderful new landscape artist I want to feature. I've invited the usual suspects, but I also want to include some people who may not frequent art galleries but have some interest in the land. Like you."

"Me?"

The older woman pulled up and focused her smile on Shae. "Why, yes. You work with the land every day."

"True, but I, uh, don't buy art. For me or our properties."

Janice Collier waved a hand. "Don't worry about that. That *usual suspect* group I mentioned will do the buying. Provided we pique their interest. Me, or people like you, whose opinions may carry more weight."

Shae scrunched her face. "Why would they listen to me? I'm only the acting general contractor, while my father recuperates. I'm a civil engineer by training. Civil engineers aren't typically known for their appreciation of art."

"Maybe." She leaned in to Shae. "You're also very attractive. Even though I'm sure as modern-day women we reject the idea that sex sells, we're also both realists who would privately agree it does."

Now she had Shae's interest. "Are you saying you want me there as … what do they call it—eye candy?"

"Call me Janice. May I call you Shae? I grew up at the time feminism came into its own. I wouldn't do anything to jeopardize the gains women have made since then. Those gains have made it possible for me to run my own business."

Why her? There were a lot more attractive women in town who could more readily drum up business for the gallery. "Thank you for the invitation, Janice. But I have to beg off."

Janice frowned. "Oh? That's a disappointment. Are you sure you won't reconsider?"

By now, they'd reached Janice's car, an older model sedan. The woman was so nice. Shae was almost sorry to turn down the invite. "I, uh, I'm not very good at things like your showing."

Janice cocked her head to appraise her. "Really? Have you ever attended one?"

She had her there. "No, but I meant events like your showing, where people get all dressed up and stand around and make small talk."

"Uh-huh. What part don't you feel comfortable with, since you're making small talk with me right now? If you're concerned about wardrobe, I'd love to go shopping with you. Just name the day."

She'd neatly dispensed with both Shae's excuses. Only one other card remained. Shae pretended to give in. "Okay, you got me on both counts. You've forced me to admit I don't know anyone I could bring as my guest."

"That's the easiest part to fix. I've already conned my son into attending. I'm sure he'd be happy to bring you as his date, which should make this ordeal more palatable for both of you."

She'd been had. Janice had manipulated her into a corner. "You're good, Janice."

The older woman offered a shy smile. "I've been told that. Is it a deal?" Shae let her shoulders sag. "When? I may already have plans for that night."

Janice gave her the date. Of course, she was free. She groaned inwardly. And she thought her business dinner with Ned had been a challenge.

CHAPTER 17

Ned threw down his cell. "Damn!" He'd thought Shae was different. But as it turned out, she was just like all the other women he'd ever slept with, who told him one thing—she wasn't interested in a relationship—and did just the opposite—got herself invited as his date to his mother's showing. Going through his mother to get to him was a cheap shot. A huge disappointment in her credibility.

When he charged out of the RV in search of her, he spotted her near one of the excavated sites. The sub she talked with moved off. Perfect time to confront her. No, he couldn't. He told his mom he'd escort the general contractor to the showing, although she was not to set him up again.

"I hear we're going to my mom's showing together," he said as he approached.

She took a step back, obviously hadn't expected to see him again so soon after the previous night. "Yes. Earlier, she made the trip out here to view the progress on her house, but she left since you weren't around."

"She told me. I got involved composing a new piece and lost track of time." Maybe if he'd been here, he could've impeded Shae's machinations. Too late now.

"This was her first time here, wasn't it?"

"Yeah. Wish she'd called first, but those things happen."

Shae turned to leave.

"About the showing?" he said.

"Yes?"

"I'll pick you up at seven."

She flicked her head, her ponytail swishing behind. "That's okay. You're off the hook. It was your mother's idea for you to escort me. I tried to get out of it, but she cut me off at the pass."

Just plain low, attributing the invite to his mom, and now offering to release him from the obligation. "She's really looking forward to this event. Let's not disappoint her."

She shrugged. "Okay. Your call. I've got to check on another site. See you." She took off.

She was going to play it like it didn't matter the least to her. Women. Why couldn't they be up front with a guy?

At least he'd broken the ice from the previous evening. Hadn't known what he'd say to her after he'd slipped out in the middle of the night. She hadn't even mentioned last night. She was so playing him. Just like Gillian and Julie, his backstabbing, moneygrubbing ex-fiancées.

She'd gone behind his back to his mother. How would she like it if the tables were turned and he sought out her dad's participation in his life? Interesting thought. While he digested how to best use it, he'd give her wide berth.

He spied Dave at a lot down the road from the first group of excavations. He'd get an update on the project from him rather than Shae.

"How soon do you plan to dig that one?" he asked as he sidled up to the superintendent.

Dave swiveled. "Hi there, Ned. Haven't seen much of you today."

"Spent some time on my music. You didn't need me, did you?"

Like Shae, Dave mentioned the visit from his mother. "Admitted she hadn't called first, but she was disappointed you weren't here."

"Yeah, well, I would've been around if I'd known she was going to drop by. Wasn't much for her to see yet anyway." He glanced at the lot in front of him. "When do we get started on this one? Who owns this one?" Hadn't studied the site map for a while.

"Your architects, Lacey Rogers and Scott Dalton. Their wedding's coming up in a month or so."

"Right. This project brought them together. First time I've ever played Cupid. Geez, that was over a year ago."

"Understand his parents have since decided to build here also. Quite the little neighborhood you're putting together." Dave snuck a look at his watch. "Did you, uh, want something in particular?"

"Got a question. Why can't we dig everything at once? That'd reduce both the down time between each new section as well as the cost to bring back the equipment for each successive dig."

"We can only handle so many housing starts at a time, because we can only accommodate so much heavy equipment in one place. That's why we stagger the digs. Once we've framed this first group, we'll move on to the next section while the finish carpenters move inside the first group."

"What do we do in the meantime?"

"Shae and I have a few other projects pending. You've got your music, right? Or something out on the coast?"

In other words, they didn't need him.

Dave shuffled his feet, tamped down a stray clump of mud. After a minute, like Shae, he produced some other task that required his attention and excused himself.

Ned returned to his car, but he didn't start it. He sat there, as the message from Dave sank deeper. He wasn't needed. Even though he was the underwriter of this entire project and he was supposedly project manager, he didn't have a thing to do at the moment.

His fingers drummed the steering wheel. He hated this hurry-up-and-wait part of construction. Reminded him too much of recording or television production. Why couldn't they just keep on with the excavations? It had to cost more to bring the excavating crews out to the site intermittently rather than just do everything at once. They were probably already scheduled to work someplace else the next few days. But it wouldn't hurt to check. After all, he was the project manager.

He grabbed for his cell.

THE NEXT DAY, as Shae examined the newly dug foundations, she heard a rumbling sound in the background. Excavation equipment rolled off the carriers headed for the sites scheduled to be dug later. What the…?

She sought out Dave to learn what he knew about the heavy equipment, but one of the crew told her he'd gone into town to check on a permit.

Across the way, Old Man Todd directed his crew where to lay out the stakes. She ran over to him. "What's going on, Todd? Thought you'd finished up here for now."

He returned an intense scowl. "Like you don't know."

She crossed her arms and stood legs apart. "What's that supposed to mean?"

"Someone from your outfit called my assistant yesterday and insisted my whole crew return today to dig several more foundations."

"I don't know anything about that. Dave Hale is away from the site at the moment. But he would have told me if he'd changed the plans." As she spoke those last words, a sudden, horrifying thought crossed her mind. The previous day, Dave had mentioned how Ned wanted to know why they couldn't dig all the foundations at once to save money. *Oh, dear God!*

"Hold off for a bit. Let me check on this."

"It'll cost you, you know, if you cancel. We're running on the clock."

Like he had to remind her.

She hurried to the mobile office to call Dave. "We've got problems," she told him without preliminaries. She related her recent exchange with Old Man Todd.

"You think Ned set this up?" Dave asked.

"If you didn't and I didn't, who else?"

"Maybe it's just some misunderstanding with his schedulers?"

She told him how Todd had said someone called his assistant the day before. "I can't believe Ned did this," Dave said. "I thought he was just making small talk when he asked about the next lots to be dug. I had no idea he'd take it upon himself to change the schedule."

"Yeah, well, he's dangerous that way. Just be forewarned for the future. Our only options are to let them dig a few more foundations and then postpone the rest, or refuse service. I'm going to do some fast calculations to compare the financial implications of both options, but I can't help but think we should call off today's work."

"I'm with you there. Call if I need to return and support you when you tell Todd. He's not one to take changes to his schedule lightly."

As if she hadn't already experienced Todd's wrath. She thanked Dave and hung up. Where was Ned? Probably hiding out until this latest exertion of his so-called authority blew over.

She made herself take several cleansing breaths. The first item of business was to do the cost comparisons she'd mentioned to Dave. For accuracy, they required a cool head. But once she verified her assumptions and dealt with Old Man Todd, their penny-pinching client was her next item of business.

"THEY TOLD me I'd find you here. Are you up for company?" Ned asked Tim Harriman from the door of the sunroom in the Blackhawk Hills rehab facility. Harriman occupied a chintz-covered easy chair, stacks of paper and folders around him. Two small tables were apparently set up as his impromptu office.

The older man twisted around. "Collier? Your throat acting up again, so they ostracized you here, too?"

"Call me Ned, like we established when we worked on my project a while back."

"Ned, then. Is this a visit, or was I right about you being sentenced here, too?"

Ned wandered into the room, sighted an empty chair not being utilized by the builder, and pushed it closer. "Visit. Overdue, for which I apologize."

Harriman took a few seconds to study his visitor, his eyes narrowed, as if he waited for another shoe to fall. "How's it going— working with my daughter?"

Loaded question. As much as he wanted to show Shae he could meddle in her family issues just as readily as she could interfere in his, he had to be truthful about how hard she'd worked on the project. "I'm reasonably happy with progress."

"Reasonably? That your way of saying things could be better?"

Heart attack or not, the guy's mind hadn't been impaired. "I'm an impatient guy. I tend to have several balls in the air at once to keep me occupied. I find the construction business full of waiting periods."

"You sound a lot like me, young man. My doctors have kept me in this prison for my own good. I'm bored out of my mind. So, tell me, why are you really here?"

"Brought you something." Ned reached inside his windbreaker and removed a paper sack. "Don't want to be accused of being an enabler but thought you might have grown tired of the food here." He handed the sack over to Harriman.

"Bribe?"

"Definitely. But can you resist triple chocolate ripple ice cream? It's just a bar. Didn't think you'd have your own fridge to stow away a pint."

Harriman reached inside and pulled out the ice cream treat. "Where's yours?"

"Ate it on the way."

The older man pulled away the paper and licked the top of the bar. "Good stuff. You must want something really bad."

Ned settled into his chair, leaned forward. "Are you aware that I'm serving as Sullivan's Creek's project manager?"

Harriman momentarily ceased his attack on his ice cream bar. A sort of growl emerged from his throat. "Found out recently. They keep shielding me from information they think will send me over the top again. Not crazy about the idea." He looked directly at Ned. "You're a fool, you know? You may have gained more control of the project, but it'll cost you the expertise and experience a professional project manager would have brought to the table."

"So I've been told."

"That's beside the point now. What's on your mind?"

"I changed the date for the second round of excavations yesterday. Moved it up to today. Couldn't let things just sit there while we waited for the first holes to settle."

Harriman raised a hand to halt Ned's discourse. "Let me get this straight. You used your position as project manager to call our sub and tell them we'd changed the dig date for the next section?"

"Right."

"You did this on your own without the approval by my daughter or Dave Hale? You didn't even consult them?"

"Correct as well."

Harriman shook his head. "So, you're here on this *courtesy call* to convince me to cover your behind with her?"

The old guy could sure cut to the chase. "I can protect my own ass, but I thought I'd better check my facts before I went to the boards to defend it."

"You are one hell of a fool, Collier, going behind my daughter's back like that. She may be new at running my company, but she knows her stuff. Plus, she's got Dave Hale keeping her on track. I hope she read you the riot act. I certainly would have, if it weren't for this fool ticker."

"That what you're doing now?"

"I'm certainly not congratulating you on your good sense. You want to check your facts? Okay, by preempting the dig schedule you'd better be prepared to add more crew, which is gonna cost. All so you won't have to sit around and twiddle your thumbs for a few days. What's the payoff for the added expense?"

Ned relaxed. He'd anticipated such an outburst, although milder than what he'd observed when he'd worked directly with Harriman. Was the guy on tranquilizers? "The sooner these subscribed houses are finished and the owners take possession, the sooner we'll get our money. I'm betting I can absorb these added costs down the line, if we put the extra effort in now."

Harriman eyed him. "You've bet a lot on that assumption, boy. Not just your own money, but the reputation of my company as well as the livelihoods of my people."

"I'm well aware of that, Tim. To put my butt on the line is one thing, but I won't do that to you and your folks. I may not be able to perform right now, sing at least, but I have some new ventures that should help me underwrite the additional costs."

The other man studied him, as if to decide whether to believe him. "You're fortunate I'm bored out of my mind and hankering to be involved in real matters concerning my company," he said at length. "Not just kid stuff reviewing contracts. If you're prepared to pay for this, then I'll back you up. This time. Only this time. Don't undercut my daughter again."

Ned couldn't believe what he'd heard. "Uh, great."

Harriman looked at his watch. "It's just ten. By now, Todd and his crew will have arrived—grousing all the way, I'd guess—unloaded their equipment, and begun to dig. I'll call my old pal and tell him you have my approval."

His exit cue. Harriman was letting him get by with this. Shae would be so pissed.

"Time to return to the scene of the crime." He stood and made ready to leave.

"Hey, I like this ice cream," Harriman called from behind him. "Next time, save yours so you can eat it with me." A beat went by. "And next time, just come to visit. I like checkers."

"Hey, Shae, baby."

"Dad? Did you get your phone back?" Surely someone at Blackhawk Hills would have let her know her dad could communicate with the outside world again. No one mentioned it when she was there the day before.

"Not to panic, Sarge. The General, otherwise known as Cheryl Park, let me use hers for this call. And the other I just made."

He'd made another call? She cringed.

"Had an interesting visit with our client a while ago. He wanted me to know he'd moved up the dig schedule and why."

Her mouth went dry. She could barely get her next words out. "Ned came to see you?"

"It's not like we're strangers. We worked for months on the infrastructure."

"I, uh, just learned about the schedule change this morning, when Old Man Todd showed up. I've, uh, been going over estimates of the increased costs this change will cause. I was about to go find him and cancel."

"Don't."

"No? Why?"

"I told Collier it was okay."

"You what?"

"Since Todd was already on the scene, no point to waste their time or ours."

Had she heard him correctly? "Old Man Todd will detonate when I tell him to go ahead and dig."

"Todd already knows. That was the other call I made. Thought I could spare you the inevitable diatribes. Everything's all set. And thanks for those permits. I'm almost done with them. Can't wait for your next assignment."

She hung up and shook her head. Her dad had sounded more alive than he had in weeks. Well, of course, he'd been delighted to intervene and steal her thunder. Was this the beginning of the end? Her dad was starting to reclaim his job.

And who'd helped him reach that point? None other than her favorite client. Less than two days ago, they'd made hot, passionate love in her bed. Now, she wanted to kill him, with her words if nothing else.

CHAPTER 18

Ned had found the one way he could end-run her by going to her father. So much for cost comparisons, now that her dad had given Old Man Todd the green light.

The sound of heavy breathing reverberated through the small office. Surprise, it was her. Two disembodied hands shook like an earthquake had hit the trailer. Her also.

She erupted from the seat, unable to remain in her chair; her pad of figures flew to the floor in her rush. Her arm swiped across the desk and sent the contents all directions. Felt good. She tried to pace but bumped into a filing cabinet, sure to cause a bruise on her rear. That didn't feel so good, but who cared? No one would see her naked butt for a while anyhow. If ever.

She was about to blow. Time to get out of here.

Before she got to the door, though, Dave opened it first. As he caught sight of her, he stepped back. "You don't look so good. Did you get into it with Todd?"

"No chance."

"Ned?"

"Nope. Dad. Can you believe it?"

Dave stared at her. He pulled the door tight behind him and leaned against it. He noted the clutter. "Maybe I should come back after you've finished redecorating." He didn't wait for an answer before he retrieved the items strewn over the floor and placed them on her desk.

"How could he do this, Dave?"

"Your dad or our client?"

She slammed the back of her chair. "Both. Dad was probably so anxious to remind us he's still in charge, he agreed to something he would've laughed down otherwise."

"And Ned?"

She shook her head. "Who knows? There's more behind his control issues than he's let on. But that's no excuse to cut us out of major decisions."

"Agreed. But how about you give yourself time to, uh, cool down before you have it out with him?"

"I have every right to be angry. So do you."

"True, but Ned's not a sub you can rebuke whenever he doesn't deliver. He's our client. If we continue to attack his actions, he might decide to be his own general contractor, whether it's a wise move or not."

Shae froze in place. Such a possibility hadn't occurred to her. "No, surely he's not that foolhardy?" Even with the possibility of his going it alone facing her, she had to set him straight. She grabbed her calculations and charged toward the door.

"Where you goin'?"

"To visit Ned."

Dave slid in front of her. "You sure you want to see him now?"

She pulled back her shoulders. "No time like the present, while these numbers are fresh in my mind."

Dave didn't budge. "What numbers?"

"Those that compare our way of digging versus his."

"They support our way, right?"

"Of course. Never any doubt." She attempted to slip around him.

"I'd like to see them first."

Since when had Dave gotten this involved in the numbers? Since he'd decided to be her one-man think-better-of-it squad to help her calm down. Bless his heart, but damn, she didn't want to cool her jets. Ned Collier deserved every bit of wrath she still felt. "I know what you're doing. I'll share these with you later. Right now, I have to see our client."

Dave pursed his lips, as if to decide whether to stand his ground. "Count to a hundred first. Okay?"

"Ten."

He frowned. "All right, ten."

She did as he asked. "Nine … ten. Happy now?"

He nodded, though he still didn't appear particularly supportive.

"Maybe you could stop by and see Dad on your way home tonight?" she said, to placate him. "Make sure he's okay? Don't bring up this situation unless he mentions it. He's probably done cartwheels in the corridors, or the heart patient equivalent of them, delighted to out-maneuver us. But I want to be sure he's okay."

"Sure. I'll be happy to talk with Ned, too, if you'll let me."

The guy didn't give up readily. "Thanks, but I'll deal with him."

~

NED COULDN'T BELIEVE his luck in convincing Tim Harriman to go along with the schedule change. Should've thought to appeal to the old man sooner. Instead, he'd stuck by Shae, despite her inexperience. Then she'd used his mother to get to him.

She wouldn't take this turn of events lightly. She'd feel honor-bound to ream him up one side and down the other, just to make sure he understood the significance of his actions. Since he couldn't escape her ire, might as well determine the setting for his tongue-lashing. His RV, of course. His territory.

Once he reached the project site, it didn't take long to notice the heavy excavation equipment was still there. He went directly to his mobile office to await the inevitable confrontation and flopped on the couch across from the banquette, so she'd have to stand. She'd really be frosted when she was forced to look down on his relaxed frame. The thought appealed more than it should have. Not very professional, but a hell of a lot of fun.

He dug out the score he'd brought with him. His wait only lasted ten minutes. A quick knock announced her arrival, and then she was in the door. She stood over him, hands on hips. "We need to talk."

"Really? What's up?"

"You changed the dig schedule without checking with either Dave or me, and then, to back you up, you got my dad involved. Do you have any idea how many poor decisions that makes?"

He liked the way her chest heaved in and out in her chambray shirt, as he remembered all too well the curvaceous body beneath. *Cool it, boys. Playtime's over for now.* "None, as far as I'm concerned."

"You overstepped your authority as project manager, Ned. Just like you did when you replaced the pans with preformed walls for the foundations. Project managers help things move smoothly on a job, relieve the superintendent and general contractor of that type of operational detail. They don't make independent decisions without the knowledge of the super and GC. I know you're the client and you tend to get impatient to get things done, but you can't change such major items before you consult with us."

"I consulted your father."

"I'm in charge right now. Not my dad. You knew he couldn't take the stress while he recovers. But did that stop you? Not only do I resent you for going over my head, but I'm furious with you for taking my father's health so lightly."

"C'mon, Shae. Your dad was pleased to be consulted. I didn't do anything to upset him."

She blinked, like a thought had just occurred to her. "You didn't … Oh, God, you didn't tell him you're acting as your own project manager, did you?" Her eyes went wide, like an animal caught in a trap.

Any other time, he might have backed off the topic. But not today. "Didn't have to. He already knew. Thought you'd told him days ago."

"No, I didn't." Her voice had gone soft.

"Better watch your back, then, because someone else got to him."

She didn't speak at first, apparently unwilling to admit to holes in her organization. "Whether he knew or not doesn't justify going behind my back," she said eventually.

"But it's okay to go around me to get invited to my mother's showing?"

She blinked. "Is that what this is about?"

Yeah, but he wouldn't admit it. "No, of course not. This is about *my* keeping *my* project on schedule. Your dig-a-few-holes-then-wait-then-dig-a-few-more-holes philosophy didn't make sense. So, I did something about it."

"Do you recall any of our discussion after the near disaster when you took it upon yourself to decide how the foundations would be built?"

"Of course, I do."

She stuck a document she brought with her under his nose. "I thought you told me you wanted—needed—to cut costs. These figures show the financial impact of messing with the dig schedule."

Explained why he hadn't heard from her sooner. She'd been busy with her calculator.

"You upped the initial excavation costs fifty percent."

She'd gotten too big a charge from dropping this little bomb. Time to defuse it. "If I get the subscribed houses underway as soon as possible, I can realize a return on my investment earlier than anticipated."

She removed her hands from her hips, and her breathing seemed to stabilize. Her eyes scrunched as if to consider his reasoning. "Just how bad are your financial problems?"

He flinched. Direct shot. "Much better since we talked in my tent. I've found a backer to augment my finances while my other sources of income realign themselves."

"A backer? Who?"

"Sorry, that's private."

"You have a partner? We'll have to work with a second party?"

"Not to fear. You still will only have to contend with me. This is a background person who saw a great investment opportunity with this project. The party has no intention of becoming directly involved."

No, Farley just planned to force them to use his businesses when the time came. Wait 'til she learned about that. He'd probably burned his one get-out-of-jail-free card with her father with his dig decision. He'd have to find another way to defend his further dealings with his asshole of an investor.

She attempted to stare him down, as if she dared him to tell her more about Farley. "I hope you're right," she said when he didn't. "This project is already unusual in so many respects, we can't afford any more extraordinary measures." She didn't give him a chance to reply before she turned on her heel and rushed out the door, letting it slam behind her.

Even though she'd had the last word, he got the win. Win? Perhaps a bit optimistic, since he really had increased his costs. For the moment. Nor would he characterize Farley's money as his salvation. There was still the piper to pay there, whatever it turned out to be.

He probably shouldn't have involved Tim Harriman. The guy's health was still on the line, as she'd pointed out. Had he really gone to her father in retaliation for her involvement with his mom? Or was he just spoiling for a fight? If that was the case, why? Somehow his business dealings with Shae had strayed over the line and gone into personal territory. Maybe that explained why, even though he'd won the extra digs, he felt he'd lost something in his relationship with Shae.

Shae flounced into their mobile office. The door slammed.

"Ned still alive?" Dave asked.

"Yes. Now it's your turn to face the firing line."

Dave glanced up, eyes crinkled in confusion. "Excuse me?"

"Even though Ned saw fit to tell Dad he's been serving as his own project manager, Dad already knew."

Dave shifted his attention to his desk.

"You told him, didn't you?"

He drew in his lips as if he debated how to respond. "You knew I visited him almost every day. Did you think the subject would never come up? You should've told him yourself long ago."

She started to reply but couldn't. He was right. She'd excused not reporting to her dad Ned's acting as his own project manager as protecting her father from too much stress too soon. Was that really the case? Or had she feared he would relieve her of her duties if he found out? "What did he say when you told him?"

"You should ask him yourself."

So, his role as middleman only went one way. Shouldn't surprise her. Dave had been loyal to her dad for years. Her dad had told her as much when he offered her the temporary job.

"Okay, I will. Todd should've cooled off by now, so I'll leave him to you for a while."

Although she marched off to her SUV, determined to get this straightened out with her dad, by the time she arrived at his room at Blackhawk Hills, her steps had slowed. This could be it, the day he pulled the rug out from under her. Contract renewed, it was no longer necessary to keep a Harriman at the helm. Dave could take over. Ned would be delighted.

Her dad glanced up from his magazine as she entered his room. "Just talked to you on the phone. Need more help with Old Man Todd?"

She slipped into the room's only visitor chair. "Uh, no. Need to bail myself out of a hole I dug myself." Couldn't really blame either Ned or Dave for this.

That got his attention. He cocked his head.

A succession of implosions wracked her stomach as she considered his possible reaction. "It's time—past time—to tell you Ned Collier has assumed the role of project manager."

"Wondered when you'd get around to that minor detail."

No explosion yet. But it was sure to come. "I didn't tell you at first, because I didn't want to worry you," she attempted to explain. "Then, as time passed, I hoped it would work itself out before you heard."

He threw the magazine aside. "Why in hell would you agree to such an asinine idea?"

"Didn't Dave tell you why? He seems to have briefed you about everything else."

"Don't blame Dave. He's only done his job. Plus, he's a loyal friend."

Loyal to you. "It seemed to be the only way we could keep the contract. Ned, uh, Collier, threatened to go to one of our competitors when he learned I'd been made temporary head of the company. Despite my education, I couldn't convince him I knew what I was doing. He'd only stay with us if he could have ongoing, direct involvement."

He leaned back against his pillows, his eyebrows formed a V. "You had such an exaggerated opinion of your talents you thought you could override his lack of knowledge about construction?"

"I knew it wasn't a good idea. But we needed this project to keep the company afloat." Oh, God, she hadn't meant to go there.

Her dad seemed to jerk. "You know about that?"

She sucked on her lower lip. "A little. Mostly it's suspicion of what I don't know. You've refused to share the company books with me, despite the fact I'm currently in charge."

He lowered his eyes. "Yeah, uh, s'pose that wasn't such a good idea. Just didn't want to scare you."

"Scare me?" Her voice rose. "Like I haven't been frightened to death to be unaware of the company's actual financial picture? Or to receive the opportunity of a lifetime to run the company but have little experience to draw from and a crew that questioned my every move?"

He continued to focus elsewhere. "You seem to have survived all that. So far."

Huge admission from her father. He seemed to accept the project manager thing. Didn't like it. Nor did she. But so far, he hadn't canned her. So maybe she should share a little about Ned's finances. "Did Ned, uh, Collier, explain why he wanted to be so involved with his project?

"Nope. He brought me an ice cream bar and got me to approve the extra digs and left. Why?"

She related how anticipated revenue sources from upcoming concerts and other personal appearances had dried up for Ned, at least until his throat recovered. "Ironic? Isn't it? Your recuperation gave me the chance to step up and lead the company. And at almost the same time, Ned's recuperation has challenged me every step of the way."

"Already told him he was a fool to make himself project manager, but you want me to talk to him again?"

She had to laugh. Nerves. But she'd gotten this far by her own wits. She wasn't caving now. "Thanks, but no. I've worked things out with him," she bluffed. "I'm banking on his losing interest once he can sing again." She held her breath, prayed her dad wouldn't ask how much longer that would be, since she figured at least four more months.

"The man who visited me today didn't appear bored with his new job. You got your hands full, kiddo. Keep on top of him."

Been there, done that, Dad. Wasn't such a great idea.

TWO DAYS LATER, Shae found herself back at the department store where she'd searched in vain for a dress to wear to her dinner meeting with Ned. Only this time she wasn't alone. Two racks of dresses over, Janice Collier examined cocktail frocks.

"Given your eye and hair colors, I think you'd look good in jewel tones," Janice told her.

"Jewel tones?"

"Blues, greens, some reds, possibly pink."

"I thought brown."

Janice glanced up with a start. "You're not serious?"

Apparently not. But she liked the color. It was so no-nonsense. "Black?"

"Black's fine. Very sophisticated. I just, uh, pictured you in something more vivid."

Shae moved closer to prevent onlookers from hearing. "But you said black's sophisticated. Isn't that what you want for your showing?"

Janice nodded. "True. But most of the other women there will probably think the same thing and wear black. I want you to stand out."

Shae's stomach turned over. *Standing out* in a crowd wasn't her thing. "Uh, Janice. I don't know. Just my agreement to be there is a huge step for me."

Ned's mother patted her arm. "I appreciate your effort. But ..." she raised wide, plaintive eyes in Shae's direction, "it would please me so much if you would consider augmenting your wardrobe."

"What did you have in mind?"

Janice flipped through several hangers that displayed a rainbow of colors. "How about this one?" She removed a blood red sheath and held it out to Shae."

"Red?"

"This darker tone will look great with your hair and pale skin."

With auburn hair, she'd rarely, if ever, worn red. Okay, she'd try it on, although she'd never worn anything as flashy in her life. She scanned her other options. "As long as I can try on this one as well." Her choice was navy blue.

Twenty minutes later, while Janice studied her from a chair near the three-way mirror outside the dressing rooms, Shae pirouetted for the older woman to see her from all sides. "Okay. You win. The navy was nice. But this one," she twisted around to see the back, "makes me look sensational. I've never felt so, uh—"

"Hot?"

In the mirror in front of her, Shae saw her cheeks color. Not quite the same shade as the dress, but to hear Ned's mother echo her thoughts out loud threw her. Again, she wondered if the woman suspected she and Ned had been intimate. "Well, yes."

"Congratulations, then. It's about time you experienced that feeling."

"What makes you think it's so new?"

"Your face. You're glowing, like this is all a big surprise."

Shae glanced once more in the mirror to check Janice's statement. "I've, uh, never known what clothes to wear. My mother died when I was a little girl, and I don't have any female relatives."

"Surely you had girlfriends?"

Girlfriends? "I was kind of a loner. I certainly wasn't part of a group of girls who lived for shopping at the mall."

Janice eyed her as if about to say something more, but quickly shifted her attention to another clothing rack. "Maybe I should take some of my own advice. Buy myself something new for this affair."

"What do you usually wear?"

"I have one outfit I bring out for every event, a fancier version of my hippie costume."

"Costume?"

Janice removed a long black velvet hostess skirt from the rack. "You don't think I actually mean to look like a refugee from the seventies, do you? I've played a part all these years." She swayed her hips enough to swirl her skirt and checked her image in a nearby mirror. "When my husband was alive, I was the behind-the-scenes person at the gallery. He was the gregarious one. After his death, when I was on my own, I adopted this modern-day hippie persona. Thought it would appeal to patrons."

More than likely, the *costume* had provided something for her to hide behind while she greeted customers. "The get-up must have worked. I've heard nothing but good things about Serenity."

Janice continued to inspect her reflection. "Maybe it's time for a change."

"You could keep the lines, you know, long skirt like that one, and an overblouse but swankier fabrics."

Janice screwed up her eyes. "Hmmm. I see what you mean."

After another half hour, they'd selected the black velvet skirt and a silver lamé top for Janice and strappy heels for both of them. And, of course, the red number. As they carried their bags to Shae's SUV, her cell rang. She gazed at the caller ID and frowned. "Gotta take this. My dad."

They climbed inside the vehicle, where Shae answered her call. "What's up, Dad? Uh-huh. No. That's all the permits until next week. No, I can't think of anything else at the moment, but I'll check with Dave. Okay. Bye." Her dad had done enough for a few days.

"That was short and sweet."

"Short, yes. Sweet, not so much. I knew this would happen as soon as Dad got the least bit re-involved with the company." She explained how she'd kept her dad from leaving the rehab facility by giving him some actual work to do. "It's like I'm pulling a loose string on a sweater. The more I yank, the faster the sweater unwinds. The more I give my dad to work on, the more he wants. He can't overdo. That's what started his problems in the first place. Then Ned got involved."

"Ned?"

Shouldn't go there. "He went to my dad about something he'd already done without consulting me. He knew I'd never approve it. My dad probably wouldn't have stood for it, either, if he'd been back in the saddle. But I think he was so excited to have someone come to him for help, he went soft and let Ned get by with it."

"Ned can be a bit, uh, driven at times. He's the one who decided I need a new house to retire in, you know."

Her dad had told her some of the story of Ned's "hush-hush" project when he first approached the architectural firm that came up with the design concept. He'd insisted on anonymity, because he hadn't wanted his mother to know what he was up to until it was a done deal. Even though she'd gotten wind of his plans before he told her, apparently even Janice wasn't safe from Ned's take-charge tactics.

"Why did you give in to him?"

Janice seemed to run the question through her mind. She didn't reply at once. "He agreed to build his own home in Sullivan's Creek if I accepted his gift."

"Has he always been so, uh, strong-minded?"

Janice didn't answer. Instead, she asked a question of her own. "Has the subject of his broken engagements ever come up?"

"Yes. Briefly."

"Both fiancées took advantage of him. Different reasons, but they each disappointed him in their own way. He doesn't like to have his opinion challenged. Especially by a woman." She turned to Shae. "I'm explaining. Not defending." She stopped, as if to consider her next words. "I'm not suggesting you've done that, though. In fact, I applaud you for not letting him walk all over you."

Although he had, and now she had to be constantly on guard. She really liked this woman. "While we're on the subject of hard-headed men, what if I visit your dad and get him interested in painting?" Janice added before she had a chance to say as much.

Shae's grip on the steering wheel tightened. Brave woman. Or foolish? "Thank you, but—"

"I know, your dad isn't into that sort of thing."

"He'd see painting as some female pursuit to be avoided at all costs." They pulled into a parking place in front of the gallery. "You're welcome to try. Just don't let him hurt your feelings."

"I've really enjoyed myself today, Shae," Janice said as Shae prepared to leave. "I can't wait to see everyone's reaction to you in that red dress."

"And you in your new duds."

"I'm looking forward to this event more than ever. It should be quite a night."

CHAPTER 19

Though not the least bit uneasy or nervous about returning to the scene of the crime just days after the amazing night he'd spent with Shae, Ned still managed to drop his keys just after he rang the doorbell. He was still bent over when the door opened. "Ready for my mom's big show?" he asked, rising.

His voice dropped as he took in the vision before him. Brownish-red hair, aquamarine eyes. Yeah, it was Shae. But other than those tell-tale physical traits, the woman who stood before him in a body-hugging red dress hardly resembled the contractor whose daily uniform consisted of shirts and jeans or even the gothic creature of the ill-fated business dinner.

This woman was a knockout. His tongue collided with his teeth as he stammered over his words. "You look, uh, great."

"Thanks. C'mon in. I have to grab my wrap and purse."

"I'll, uh, wait here." With the way she was dressed, the further away he stayed from the kitchen where she propositioned him and the bedroom where they … Coward! No—wise. A wise man who didn't need this complication in his life. Whether she'd wheedled this date with him through his mother or this was truly his mother's idea didn't seem to matter as much now as he continued to gaze at this gorgeous dark red flower. "Ready." Shae breezed past him.

His nose took in the heady fragrance of spices she left in her wake. Her ass swayed rhythmically from side to side as she made her way to his car, the motion now augmented by black patent stilettos. God, the dress hugged her like the cummerbunds he was forced to wear to formal events.

She stopped a few feet short of his ride and turned back to him. "Coming?"

Dangerous term. *Snap out of it. You've been around your share of glamorous women. Don't let this one get to you.*

He sprinted to the car and arrived just in time to open her door for her. "I know you'd rather do this yourself, but tonight you'll have to let me show off my gentlemanly ways."

She tilted her head in his direction and smiled. "Actually, I kinda like this custom."

Once her door was closed and he was seated on his side of the car, he stole another glance at her. "No ponytail tonight?"

She brought a hand to her coiffure, preened like any other female. "Like it? I haven't been to a salon in … uh, well, I don't remember how long."

"New dress, too. You must really be up for this showing."

"I wanted to do your mother proud."

Sounded ominous. "Didn't think you knew her well enough."

"We talked a bit the day she came to the site looking for you." She straightened her skirt and repositioned her wrap and purse. Apparently she didn't want to discuss his mother.

"Ever been to one of these things?" he asked, at length, as the silence got to him.

"No."

"Nervous?"

"Should I be?"

She gripped her hands tightly in her lap. Yep, she was nervous. Why couldn't she just admit it? "Not at all. Especially something my mom puts on. She's pretty laid back. You walk around and admire the artist's pieces. At some point, you meet the artist and gush over their work. I think this is some woman Mom got excited about after running into her at the grocery store. There'll be wine and hors d'oeuvres. Hope you ate before coming, because you can't fill up on that stuff."

"I'll keep that in mind."

"She'll expect me to stick around. The celebrity bit, you know."

"Actually, she asked me to do something similar. Not as a celeb, of course. More like window dressing."

"Mom said that?" Not his mom. Janice Collier didn't pay attention to appearances.

"Not in those words. If I mingle, fine. But mainly, just be there and look good."

Hence, the dress. Leave it to his mom to see the potential beauty in Shae. Not that he himself had been unaware of Shae's attributes but more from an unclothed aspect than gussied up like this. No doubt about it, though, she really looked great tonight.

Their arrival caused a bit of a stir. Heads turned in their direction and nodded, and the general buzz in the room receded a notch. Ned was used to it. Even expected it, truth be told. But Shae was another matter.

Instinctively, she drew closer to him.

He leaned into her ear. "Smile."

She did, and the nods and smiles continued.

"This will be over shortly. It goes with the territory."

"There you are," his mother said as she floated over to them. She immediately grabbed Shae's hands.

"You look ravishing, Shae."

"So do you," Shae returned.

Ned took a step back. "She's right, Mom. What have you been up to? I haven't seen you dress up like this since I was kid."

Janice seemed to glow in the light of his attention. "Thank you. I decided to put the, uh, costume aside for the evening. Get with the glamour myself."

He didn't know what to say, other than to repeat how nice she looked. "You cut your hair, too," he remarked as he took in her full appearance. Didn't usually notice women's hairstyles, but tonight both Shae and his mother really surprised him.

His mother twirled around for them to better see her new do. "Not real short, but the braid is gone." She noticed Shae's hair then. "And you did something, too."

"I still need the ponytail for workdays, but for tonight, I let the hairdresser have her way."

When had all this feminine bonding happened? Just as he'd begun to believe Shae's contention his mother initiated the invitation to this affair, this little gabfest made him wonder anew what Shae had been up to with his parent. "Uh, you probably should attend to your other guests," he suggested to his mother, then he steered Shae in the other direction, toward the refreshment table.

"Stick around. We'll talk more later," Janice called as she approached a rather dour-looking older man.

"Hi, Ned. Ms. Harriman." The petite blonde architect, Lacey Rogers, had come up behind them. "Your mom is so tickled you were able to attend this showing. That's all she could talk about when I went with her to get her hair done today." She shifted her attention to Shae. "And, you, Ms. Harriman … Shae. You accomplished what I've attempted to do for months, you got her out of that dowdy hippie garb. She looks incredible tonight."

Shae could only nod at the unexpected compliment.

"You convinced Mom to change up her wardrobe?" Ned asked, an incredulous note in his tone.

"I must have caught her when she was susceptible to the idea. She helped me pick this dress and got sucked into the fashion thing more than she realized." She glanced over her shoulder to pick out the gallery owner. "She even went for shoes. With heels."

Ned eyed her with an expression that said he couldn't believe she'd downplayed what must have been a tremendous achievement. He put a grateful arm around Lacey's shoulders and gave her a hug. "Thanks. To both of you. I may be building her a house, but you've probably given her an experience equally as thrilling."

On Lacey's arm, Scott Dalton, her fiancé and partner on the project, had remained silent until the women finished their pleasantries. "I hear ours is ahead of schedule," he offered.

SHAE BIT A LIP, forced a smile but let Ned talk. She wasn't about to take credit for something she would have vetoed, had she been consulted. Besides, she'd promised herself she'd steer clear of their recent difficulties while she was with Ned tonight.

Ned explained how he'd added more houses to the initial dig to the two architects. Scott nodded, apparently not alarmed. Lacey turned to Shae. "Ned is indirectly responsible for Scott and me getting together."

"Ned, a matchmaker?" Shae responded, surprised.

Lacey continued with the story. "Ned's initial idea was to make Sullivan's Creek a retirement area for baby boomers. Scott and I were assigned the design concept, but neither of us had much experience with that generation, nor did either of us really want to work with the other. Once we found our way to a truce, for our research we taught a Salsa class, where Janice was a member, although we had no idea she was Ned's mother."

"Nor that Ned was our client until the design concept was almost finished," Scott added.

The three of them laughed as they reminisced.

"Well, uh, your mother probably wants to introduce you around," Lacey said eventually. "We're here to pick out something for our new home, a wedding gift from your mom. See you later."

"Rather than let my mom show me off, let's give the guests a gander at you," Ned told Shae once Lacey and Scott had wandered off.

She studied him briefly. "You're sincere, aren't you?"

"Yeah. Why would you doubt me?"

"The last few days. We've certainly had our highs and lows."

Ned steered her to an unoccupied corner of the room. "How 'bout we borrow a page from the happy couple over there? Call a truce. On the project. Personally."

A truce? Must have run out of ways to make her life miserable for the time being. But she could use a little peace. Not have to worry about what he'd come up with next. "Good idea. We don't have to sign anything in blood, though, do we? I don't do well around my own blood."

"Pinky swear instead?"

"Okay. Sean used to make me do that so I wouldn't rat him out to Dad."

They latched little fingers and tugged.

Mike joined them. "What's this?"

"We've just agreed to a truce," Ned said.

Mike narrowed his eyes. "Uh, yeah. Sure. Whatever. Only you'd better mix it up with the guests. They all caught that little show with the fingers. Folks now wonder what's with the two of you. Including your mom, who's salivating even as she convinces that old geezer over there to part with ten thou."

"You mean your dad? Glad he was able to attend while he blew in for a few days. We watched a baseball game together last night while you were out."

"Slipped in around eight," Mike said. "You two seemed so cozy in the den, I hid out in the music room."

"Wouldn't have killed you to spend a few hours with your dad. What were you doing in the music room anyhow? You'd better not have listened to my playback."

Mike's neck turned almost the color of Shae's dress. "No. I watched the game on a set I snuck in for just such occasions. Those soundproof walls can shut out more than your music."

"Every so often, your dad would check his watch and stare at the door."

"You've got no room to talk. You avoid your mom whenever you can get away with it."

Ned gave Mike a quick guy-type nudge, punched Mike's arm as a follow-up. "If you can't tell he's here because he misses you, you're just blind," he said, through a forced smile. "And you'd better not have listened to my new piece. I told you, I wasn't ready yet for you to hear it."

Not to be outdone, Mike knuckled Ned's arm. "He wants me back in the company full time. As for your piece, you really shouldn't tell me not to do something, because you know what that does to me."

Ned elbowed Mike back with even more force. "Did you … like it?" he asked, his voice going soft.

Mike leaned into Ned and pushed. "Yeah, I did. It's different than anything you've done before. Really powerful."

As Ned reared back to return Mike's shove, Shae slipped in between them. "Stop! Whether this is brotherly love or the beginning of a duel, this isn't the time or place. Both of you, turn and smile at those two very concerned faces over there."

To her surprise and relief, they did.

"Okay, Mike. Get yourself over there and talk to your father. That appears to be what he wants." She pivoted back to Ned. "We need to circulate and make nice with everyone and encourage them to spend lots of money on this new artist we have yet to meet."

Mike drew in a huge breath, released it as he squared his shoulders. "Ned's right about you being a ball buster," he said before he marched off.

"I never said that! Exactly," Ned replied while she was still in shock.

She was about to respond when she remembered their truce. If she cross-examined him about what he'd actually called her, that discussion would probably fall outside the realm of permissible topics. "They actually have a music room?" she asked instead. "A room devoted only to music and Mike's private TV viewing?"

Ned nodded as he guided her to the refreshment table. "Yep. I thought they never used it, so I moved my keyboard in and set up shop. Had no idea about Mike's secret television."

She had to get herself invited to the Woodley mansion. The idea of a special room just for music staggered the brain. "What's this about your new piece?"

"It's like when people keep a journal to record their lives. Only I do it through music."

"What have you journaled?"

"The project," he said. She raised a brow. "The Iowa countryside. You know, the rolling hills, the smell of the fertile earth, the changing seasons?"

Why had that last part sounded so forced?

"White or white?" he asked, shifting subjects.

"Huh?"

"Mom only serves white wine at these things. Easier to clean, if someone spills."

"What will you have?"

He grabbed an empty wine glass, opened a bottle of water, and poured. "This. I'm supposed to stay away from alcohol while my throat heals."

"Then make mine the same." She tried to remember how much wine he'd consumed at their business dinner meeting and recalled he'd only taken a sip.

He gave her a curious glance but didn't say anything further.

"Ready?" she asked. "Oh, wait. "Any lipstick on my teeth?"

He checked. "No. Do you want me to tell you about the dirt mark on your forehead?"

"What? Where's a mirror? How did I get that?"

She'd gone several steps down the back hallway before he caught her. "You're fine. I couldn't resist. Didn't realize you'd take me at my word."

She rolled her eyes. "I thought we just pinkie swore to a truce."

"I didn't swear not to tease. You're much too serious about things, Ms. Harriman. Gotta shake you up every so often."

Like you haven't every day for the last six weeks? "I am not that serious."

"Right. Okay, show me. Let's see the non-serious Shae Harriman hit the handshaking trail."

"I know what you're doing, Ned. You think I'm nervous, and this is your way to help me

get through it."

"Are you nervous?"

She wet her lips. Sean had delighted in hassling her as well, but not quite this way.

Was this Ned attempting to keep things light between them? "Forget it. Let's go."

For the next few minutes, she smiled, shook hands, and made ferocious small talk. "Nice to meet you," "Love your dress," "Thank you, no, this isn't couture." She was surprised she even knew what they meant. Throughout this discourse, she got to listen to, "Jake Bonneville, didn't expect to see such a megastar here," "So you're Janice Collier's son?" "Jake, good to see you up and about, how's the throat?" "When will you be able to sing again?"

Ned morphed into Jake Bonneville before her eyes. His posture became more fluid, with-it. He walked with a little more swagger. And his face—though the Ned Collier she knew might be a control freak, his facial expressions were usually relaxed, approachable. This guy's face, Jake Bonneville's, seemed molded to appear perfect, remote. She became so engrossed watching his act she forgot to perform her own charm thing.

Janice slipped in beside her and drew near her ear. "It's a bit intimidating at first, isn't it? I thought of warning you, but I was sure you could hold your own," she told Shae.

"I don't know what to say, how to act, when people go into fan mode."

"Let him handle it. Just smile, nod whenever it's called for. My sales increase every time someone discovers my connection to Ned. I hate it, but I'm a business woman."

Once she'd imparted her wisdom, the gallery owner drifted off to yet another guest. Shortly after that, Shae and Ned reached the guest of honor. "Ned Collier, Miss Williams. This is my guest, Shae Harriman."

A woman slightly shorter than Shae's five-foot nine stature finished her good-byes with a middle-aged couple and turned her full attention on Ned and Shae.

Where Shae was curvy, this woman was slim, athletic looking. Straight black hair hung slightly below her shoulders. But her most striking feature was her eyes, a dark violet with gold flecks.

As she reached for Shae's hand, Darren Williams showed off ripped arms in her sleeveless black sheath. "Ms. Harriman, the builder. May I call you Shae? I've heard so much about you from Janice."

"Really?" Shae replied, surprised at the recognition. "I've only gotten to know her recently, although I met her several weeks ago when I first took over for my dad."

"You made quite an impression."

Ned gave her a curious sideways glance but then turned back to the artist. "I'd say the same for you, Darren. She doesn't do showings for just anyone."

"I know. I'm honored to be here."

"We've admired your pieces as we've worked the crowd," Shae said. "My favorite so far is 'Pink Dawn'. The subject area looks familiar, but I can't place it."

"There's an overlook along Highway 59 near Cherokee. I caught it just as the sun was coming up."

"I knew I recognized it," Shae replied. "We used to take that road on our way to see family in Ida Grove. I've always loved the view, but you brought it to life."

"Thank you. You have a good eye. Guess that comes with the territory for builders."

"Are all your landscapes of Iowa?" Ned asked.

"I've done a few other places as well. Seascapes. Mainly on vacations. Only my Iowa pieces are here tonight."

"Somewhat limited, wouldn't you say?" Mike observed as he suddenly appeared from nowhere.

Darren rolled her shoulders. "For an all-Iowa crowd? I don't think so."

Mike edged slightly in front of Ned. "Your landscapes are striking, but folks here travel more than you think. They want to decorate their walls with more than fields and other rural scenes."

"And you?" she said, Shae and Ned seemingly forgotten. "What are you looking for?"

Mike actually raised a lewd brow. "Depends." Pause. "I've already picked out a scene from Greenwood Park to take with me to my condo in Malibu. But when I stay here in Des Moines, I'd like something to remind me of the Pacific."

"I see." She leaned toward the small table behind her and retrieved a business card. "Here. Stop by my studio, and I'll be happy to show you my ocean and beach series."

Her responsiveness seemed to throw Mike, because he almost dropped the card. "Uh, sure. Didn't realize it would be so easy."

"I aim to please." Throughout this exchange, she kept her smile intact while Shae and Ned looked on fascinated.

Mike accepted the card and backed away quickly, nearly knocking into one of the catering people.

Once they'd said good-bye to Darren, Shae and Ned exchanged looks as they walked away. "What was that about?" Shae asked under her breath.

"Beats me. He wasn't excited to attend this deal tonight, but he acted like he had an ax to grind with our artist friend. It's not like him to take it out on innocent parties. I'm more his preferred target."

"Guess he's left that honor to me."

"You still angry about the other day?"

"Not tonight. Even though the color's right, I don't want to bloody my dress."

NED SMILED at Shae's sense of humor after she excused herself to powder her nose. He stood on the sidelines, where for the next few minutes, he observed the other guests and returned an occasional wave to those who sought to catch his eye.

"Mr. Bonneville. Good to see you again."

What was Zoe Johansen doing here?

"Quite a nice turnout tonight. Your mother must be very pleased."

"You know my mother?"

"No, just about her. My boss, one of her regular clients, couldn't attend and asked me to stand in for him."

"I hope he gave you carte blanche to purchase whatever appealed to you." Just a pleasantry, but he wanted to keep things light around this woman.

She took him seriously. "Not so much, although I am taking notes."

"Ah, I see." He didn't know what else to say, although she remained planted in front of him, as if she expected him to keep up the conversation.

The silence became awkward. "I'm glad you were able to solve your financial issues for now," she said finally. "That quarter-million-dollar installment from your new backer was just the shot of adrenalin you needed for your equity stake."

"Financial issues?" Ned heard from behind him. "What's this about a new backer and a quarter of a million dollars?"

Zoe Johansen's complexion turned a horrible mottled color. "My apologies. I thought we were out of earshot of everyone. I, uh, should be going." She almost ran from the gallery.

Of all the rotten timing. There was no way he could deny his money problems with Mike now that Johansen had blabbed about his backer. He attempted to think of a reasonable response.

"She was the one who came to see you a while back. You acted like you were attempting to set me up with her. Should've known it was to get me out of the room," Mike said.

Ned continued to stare at him as he struggled for an excuse like a kid caught passing notes in class.

Mike watched the banker leave, a less than friendly expression on his face. "You might want to consider a change in bankers at the same time you change friends. She doesn't appear to be one to keep things to herself. You needed a quarter of a million?"

Ned skipped over the reference to his financial needs, much more concerned about Mike's other statement. "Change friends? What do you mean?"

"Isn't it obvious? You didn't—wouldn't—come to me for money, despite the number of times I asked if you needed help. 'I'm fine, Mike. No need to worry.' A quarter of a million. My God, man!"

"I can explain."

"Really? Give it a try. Where did you get the money? Who's your backer?"

How to answer? Mike knew about Farley, but after Ned's disastrous benefit appearance for the guy, Mike had assumed the deal was over and hadn't been afraid to share his delight.

"Farley!" He guessed before Ned could reply. "You went back to that scum and made a deal of some sort."

"He's a legitimate businessman."

"My eye! What pound of flesh did he demand?"

No way would he divulge the details of his business with Farley to Mike. Although he himself wasn't happy about what he'd agreed to, Mike would go ballistic if he learned what Farley had demanded.

"Not going to share? Doesn't surprise me. You've been pretty close-mouthed these last weeks."

"C'mon, Mike. Let's not go into this here."

"If we go back to my place, you'll come clean?"

Ah, hell! Why couldn't Mike leave it alone?

"My place won't work either, huh? Well, *friend*, you don't leave me much choice."

"Huh?"

"I stuck around town because I thought you could use my advice, since you have absolutely no construction experience. But since you apparently don't want my money or my support, I might as well go back to the coast. I'll leave tomorrow. Don't worry, my house is yours as long as you need it. But I can't stick around and watch this insanity."

"C'mon, Mike. That's not what … Oh, hell, go then."

Mike turned on his heel and stalked out.

He'll be back. He's just hurt. Trying to make a statement. Surely their friendship wasn't over.

CHAPTER 20

ike slammed past Shae and Janice as he exited the gallery. "Leaving so soon?" Shae called.

Mike pulled up by Janice. "Thanks for the invite, Mrs. C. Send the bill for my purchase tonight to my California address. I'm headed west tomorrow."

"He's all yours. See if you can save his bacon," he said to Shae.

"All mine?" Shae repeated.

"You and Ned may enjoy playing at being builders, but one of these days the reality will catch up with you. When it does, you'd better be ready to help him survive."

Janice placed a hand on Mike's sleeve jacket. "What's going on between you and Ned? I've never heard you talk that way or intentionally be rude to one of our friends."

"Friend? I can't account for your tastes, Mrs. Collier. But this woman is no general contractor. Ned's so smitten with her, he can't see it."

He threw up his hands and backed off, as if he wanted nothing more to do with them, and shot out the door.

Ned appeared just as Mike left. "What was that about?"

Shae stood there stunned.

Janice took over for her. "Mike's upset with something to do with your building project." She gazed at Shae. "And with Shae."

Through the gallery windows, Ned glimpsed Mike blast off in his car. He'd try to meet up with his friend later, after the showing was over. "He's, uh, not happy with the way I'm running things." Damn Mike to have involved his mother and Shae.

"He seems to have little confidence in either you or me," Shae told him. "He said we were 'playing at' being builders."

Mike thought they were amateurs. He certainly was. He'd only done this to save money. But the guy was out of line to paint Shae with the same brush.

"Go after him," Shae said. "I can find a ride home with someone else."

"I'll take you, dear," his mother volunteered. "As for you, Ned, go make things right with Mike before he leaves town."

"I doubt I can change anything, but I'll give it a try." He attempted an apologetic smile for Shae. "Thanks for understanding."

Ned returned to the Woodley mansion to find Mike in his suite, packing. "Why'd you leave the showing? Your mom's gonna be disappointed," Mike said, not looking at him.

"She's the one who told me to come after you. I wanted to let you stew."

Mike pulled his best summer sports jacket from his closet and rammed it in his bag. "I'm not stewing. Just getting out of your hair."

Ned moved a couple pairs of shoes on the corner of the bed and settled there. "I know you've got my back."

"Really? So why won't you let me defend it?"

Why couldn't Mike drop this? Ned couldn't admit how deep over his head he was. Not now. Things had gone too far. "Is your life so boring you need mine to keep you busy?"

Mike started, dropped a knit pullover. "That's a damned cruel thing to say."

"You called me an amateur builder. That cut, man."

"Friends tell each other the truth. I can't sit around and watch you self-destroy."

Maybe Mike should leave for a while. The longer the guy stuck around, the more their friendship would disintegrate. "When you coming back?"

"Don't know. I need a change of scene."

"Your dad behind this trip?" Mike had talked with his dad at the showing after Shae had goaded him into it.

"He may have planted the idea, but it was hearing about Farley's involvement that decided me."

"I'll take you to the airport."

"I'll catch ride share."

He wouldn't push. Mike sometimes needed a wide berth when he was riled.

"Like I said, stay here as long as you want. The housekeeper remains whether anyone's around or not. You'll give her something to do. Keep the RV as long as you need it, too."

Ned rose and made his way to the door.

"You want me to check on the sale of your house and belongings?" Mike called.

"Still willing?"

"Hell, it's probably the one thing you'll let me do."

"Yeah. Right. Take care, bud." Ned closed the door and fled. He and Mike might bicker from time to time, but this disagreement was more serious. His head, his whole body ached, like they'd actually mixed it up with their fists. Mike was right to worry. But this wasn't his friend's problem. He couldn't involve Mike any more than he already had. He would not come between Mike and his family again.

"THANK you so much for tonight, Janice," Darren said. She shook the gallery owner's hand as she prepared to leave. "I could never have generated this much attention on my own."

"Of course, you could," Janice returned as she hugged her. "Talent will out, one way or another. I just pushed things along. I'll send you a list of the purchased acquisitions tomorrow, but I already know of ten pieces you sold. That's incredible for a new name."

"Just a few more minutes, Shae, while they pack up the food," Janice said as soon as Darren departed. "Hope you don't mind if we stop long enough to drop off the extra hors d'oeuvres at the mission? I know it sounds frivolous, but even the homeless like an occasional treat."

"Will someone be there to receive them this time of night? Meal hours must be long over."

Janice nodded. "I notified my contact there earlier today to give him a heads-up. I'll let him know when we're on our way."

"I never thought I'd say it, but the showing was actually fun," Shae said once they were in Janice's car. "You put on quite a party, Janice. You appear to have impeccable taste in artisans."

"Thanks. I credit a couple of those sales to you. Your small talk and observations about the lay of the land were just what a few of our more hesitant buyers needed to hear."

They drove in silence the next few minutes. The mission was located on the edge of downtown. Though this part of town that wasn't exactly a crime magnet, at this hour of the evening with most surrounding businesses closed, traffic was minimal. Shae watched the sidewalks, storefronts and driveways for questionable onlookers.

Janice noted Shae's not so subtle scrutiny of the area. "Not to worry. I've done this numerous times after showings and other festivities. But if it makes you feel better, I'll ask my friend to come out to the car." At that, she made her call.

As Janice predicted, all went well with the drop-off. Her friend, a hefty older male of about fifty, sprinted out to the parked car, pulled the two boxes of goodies from the back seat, thanked Janice for her continuing generosity and returned to the mission within ninety seconds.

Once they were on the freeway again, Shae turned to her driver. "You're a very generous, caring woman, Janice. I'm sorry I doubted our safety."

Janice waved away the apology. "Perfectly natural. Most people are a little leery to go there after dark. My son, in particular. Must be his L.A. perspective. He worries about the mission, the gallery's location, even our family home."

For some reason, Shae felt compelled to defend Ned's concerns. "The crime rate in Iowa may be lower than L.A., but we do have our share of problems. Especially in these difficult economic times."

"True. Even I had a brush with the criminal element. A little over a year ago, I was out one night and returned home to find signs of an attempted break-in. That's what fired up Ned's determination to follow through with his grandfather's development plan."

"Attempted?"

"Ned was in California. I didn't tell him, but one of my well-meaning friends mentioned it the next time he was home. I think she wanted to guilt him into returning more often. So here I am, soon to move back to the land where I grew up, now called Sullivan's Creek. Not that I don't want to, but by the time Ned learned of the incident, I'd already installed a new security system. I could have remained safe for the rest of my days in my current home."

"You'd rather not have a new house?"

"Oh, no. This isn't a complaint. This building project has brought Ned home again. At least, for a while."

"If you've got a new security system in place, why did he push you to move?"

Janice gave a sigh. "I think the security issue is a cover for something else." She continued to focus on the road ahead, exited the freeway and moved onto one of the town's main thoroughfares that would eventually take her to the Harriman home. "You've heard of survivor's guilt, haven't you? It's usually ascribed to those who make it out of an airplane crash, but there are other types of catastrophes people survive as well. In Ned's case, his father died and within the same year his career took off. But in order to make that happen, he had to walk away from me."

"Interesting theory. Have you ever confronted him about it?"

"Considered it, but there's something else as well. He hasn't been himself for months. Since his throat problems developed. Mike noticed it, too, although neither of us can identify what it is."

"He's a very driven person," Shae observed as she recalled Ned's fixation on cutting costs. But this didn't seem like the time to share the information with his mother.

"That's what concerns me. None of this is necessary. He doesn't have to prove anything to me." Her voice appeared to crack on the last part.

Time to change the topic.

Before she could, though, Janice introduced her own subject. "How far off base was Mike when he said Ned is smitten with you?"

"Smitten? I don't think so, not the way we've argued over so many details about the project."

"You didn't appear to argue tonight."

"Called a truce for your sake."

Janice chuckled. "Very thoughtful. I hope it wasn't too much of a strain."

Was she joking or probing? Whichever, Shae didn't want to discuss this topic, either. Whatever had happened between her and Ned seemed to have fizzled out, as it probably should, given their work relationship. "We both enjoyed the evening. As for our truce, only time will tell."

NED ARRIVED at the GC's mobile office the day after the showing to find only Dave there. A very frustrated Dave.

"All right. If that's the best you can do, let's leave it like that for now," Dave told someone on the phone. "But this won't go over well with my boss."

Ned slipped into the visitor chair and waited for Dave to acknowledge him.

Dave clicked off his cell and slammed a hand on top of the desk. "Damn!"

Really odd behavior for Dave, usually the calmest member of the crew. "Safe to ask what's up?"

"That was the sub who's supposed to pour the foundations tomorrow. We have to wait until next week now, because they're still tied up with a government project downtown."

"Can they do that? I thought we had a contract with all the subs."

"Handshake on scheduling. We've used Reuben Triggs and his crew for years. This has only happened once before that I recall. When Tim pissed him off about something."

Great. "Can we get someone else?"

Dave rubbed his jaw, considered. "Maybe. I could get on the horn and call one or two others who can handle this size job. But I don't know their work as well. I'll check with Shae. Have you seen her this morning?"

"Uh, no. I thought she might be visiting other sites, if she wasn't in here with you."

Dave picked up his cell and hit a button. "Shae? Just heard from Reuben Triggs." He relayed what he'd told Ned. When he hung up, he gave Ned a grim smile. "She's gonna call him. What d'ya think? Will she be able to change his mind?"

"She'll certainly give it a try."

Ten minutes later, Shae burst through the door. "Good. You're here, too," she said, noting Ned. "Dave's brought you up to speed on the concrete situation?"

Ned nodded. "Did you get hold of Triggs?"

"I started to call him, and then it occurred to me if he's behind on his current project, and you said it's with the government, a heated call from me probably won't accelerate things. But maybe if we sweeten the pot, we'll get his attention."

Who was this person? When had she started to go after her prey with molasses instead of vinegar? "How … Wait…what's with the look?"

"Well, Mr. Mega Entertainer, I think it's time to scatter some of that stardust surrounding you."

"Huh?" Dave said, baffled.

But Ned caught her drift. "You think I should hand out free CDs and hold an autograph session for his crew, concrete-studded arms and all?"

"Bingo! Maybe not that exactly, but something they won't get if they don't make it here until next week."

"Too bad I can't sing yet," he said, for a lot more reasons than simply to charm a concrete crew. "That might help."

"We treated our folks to a free lunch when things didn't go well for me at our first staff meeting. What if we offered Triggs and company something similar, only made it free hotdogs and beer after work for not only them but also their families?"

A cash register ka-chinged in his head. Lunches cost money. His money. On the other hand, a casual wienie roast would cost far less than to wait another few days on the foundations. "Call him. Let's get those foundations poured."

She went to work, used catch phrases from his book on the uncooperative sub. "That's right, Reuben, the offer's only good for tonight. Jake may have to leave for the coast soon and can only guarantee his presence for the next few days."

She hung up and beamed. "We're back on schedule."

"What do you know?" Ned observed. "I think you passed the second lesson in Leadership 101."

"Second lesson? What was the first?"

"Always give the client what he wants."

CHAPTER 21

The day after the impromptu hotdog bash, Ned stood with Shae and Dave to the side of his mother's lot and watch musty-smelling concrete rain down the chute. Reuben Triggs' crew guided the stuff over the footings that would form the basement floor and into the pans that would form the basement walls. Since they'd managed to keep Triggs and crew on the original schedule, his adrenaline rush had diminished, and left in its wake a restless impatience. "So now we play the waiting game again while the concrete cures," he groused.

"Three weeks at least, Ned," a patient Dave explained.

"There's nothing we can do in the meantime? How 'bout the schedule for the subs after the framing?"

Dave spun around as he made his way toward the trailer. "All lined up and double-checked."

"Why don't you go back to the coast for a bit?" Shae suggested. "Check in with your friend, Mike. I heard he returned to L.A. right after the showing at your mom's gallery."

Though she'd been a knockout in that red dress at the event, Ned was relieved she was back in her jeans and shirt. His testosterone flowed just a little slower when he saw her in work clothes. Just a little, but he needed the edge, so he wouldn't fantasize about what lay beneath. His obligation to escort her to the showing now met, he was free of all further non-work interactions with the woman. Free. Right. As long as he kept his libido in check.

As for her suggestion, she had no idea how much he wanted to make things right with Mike, but he didn't intend to set her straight. "We argued. Probably too soon to approach him."

"Mike seemed upset about your new backer. Is he the one you told me about but wouldn't name? Is there a problem with the guy?"

"Mike doesn't like him, that's all."

"How come?"

She probably had a right to wonder about the continuing health of his finances, but he didn't want to get into this with her any more than with Mike. Half the story. He'd give her that and hope it would be enough to reassure her. "I collapsed on stage at a benefit for Irv Farley. He'd placed me outside on the beach in the cool night air instead of inside the house, as he promised. Since I'd already been experiencing problems with my throat, Mike didn't want me to risk it, but I wouldn't listen."

"What else is new?"

He let her comment slide. "Didn't want to anger the guy and jeopardize my chance to gain his buy-in on the project, in case I needed it at some later time. Which is what happened. Remembering that night still sends ice through my veins."

"Oh." She didn't say more.

Had she bought it? "I doubt I'll go west right now. There's a piece of music that's really got me excited."

"Good. Go work on your music. There's no more to see or do around here for a while."

Could she be any more obvious in her efforts to get rid of him? He went about ten feet, then stopped and returned. "You want to hear it, once I've got a little more done?"

She returned a broad smile. "I'd love to!"

He rarely got to see those blue-greens light up like that. Still, why had he made the offer? He rarely showcased his work until every last measure was perfect. Not even for his mother.

EVEN THOUGH THE company still had smaller projects to oversee while they waited to frame the houses in Sullivan's Creek, Shae had more free time during this period to visit her father. Ever since Ned took it upon himself to drop in on the man, she'd made it a point to stay in closer touch with her dad, though trips to Blackhawk Hills challenged her at times.

She was about to enter the sunroom on one of the mornings of her temporary respite, when she noticed her father wasn't alone. Janice Collier had apparently made good on her offer to visit.

Shae held back. Didn't want her father to think Janice's visit was something the two of them had cooked up. Although they had.

Janice approached the patient. "Mr. Harriman?"

"That's me. Who are you, another of the counselors that Park woman foists on me?"

Before she answered, Janice pulled up a nearby ottoman and settled in front of him. She clasped her hands in her lap and leaned forward. "You have something against counseling?"

"A counseling-type question, if I ever heard one."

Shae started into the room to rescue her new friend before her father scared her off but jerked to a stop and backed up behind the door as she heard Janice hold her own.

"My approach to small talk." She held out her hand. "I'm Janice Collier, Ned's mother."

Shae's father seemed to consider the information but still followed through on the handshake. "Your son send you? Figure he was no longer in my good graces?"

"Ned isn't aware of this visit. I met your daughter recently, and she told me you were here. I thought you might like some company." Janice took in the rest of the sunroom. "This place is almost a resort. I like how the morning sun streams through the windows. And that huge flat screen TV. I could easily spend a few days in residence here myself."

Shae's father harrumphed. "Few days, maybe. Not weeks, like it's been for me. I'd prefer to be home."

"I detect frustration."

"Oh, you're definitely a counselor, lady. That last statement was a dead giveaway. Reflective, they call it. I've picked up on their happy talk."

"Believe what you will."

He stretched his shoulders, rubbed the back of his neck. "So? What's the story? Why are you here?"

"I came to ask a favor."

"Now you sound like your son."

She gave him a curious look but didn't follow up on his comment. "Actually, I own an art gallery and I'm doing a series of classes for men. It's not been easy to convince men to sign up or stick with it."

He shot from his chair. "You want me to paint pictures of fruit?"

Shae stepped from her hiding place. Time to referee.

But Janice wasn't to be deterred. "Heavens, no! I need your advice. Tell me what I'm doing wrong to attract, well, to keep, male students."

"Advise you? Forget it. I'm not about to rope in some unsuspecting guy to take your fruity class." Nonetheless, he settled back into his chair.

"My class covers more than still life, although painting pictures of fruit isn't as easy as some might think."

"C'mon. An apple's an apple. A circle with a lot of red and a little black."

"Really?" She gazed at his pile of papers. "Any blank pages in there?"

He thumbed through the stack, removed one. "Here. Sketch your heart out."

"Not me. You." She flipped open her bag and quickly removed what from Shae's vantage point appeared to be felt tip markers.

"I know what you're up to, lady. You're attempting to get me to draw."

"No way. I just want to show you it's not as easy as you think to draw an apple."

What was Janice up to? Shae hadn't bargained for her dad to get into art.

Though he muttered, Tim Harriman uncapped one of the markers Janice held out to him and started to scribble. "See," he pronounced within seconds. He handed Janice the sheet of paper.

She examined his work. "Uh-huh. Interesting."

"Interesting? That's an apple. Anyone could recognize it."

"It does resemble an apple though not a real-life one."

"You're nuts. Of course, it looks like one."

She scrunched her eyes, as she sought the right word to reply. "Okay, we'll call it an apple. So, how did you feel as you drew that piece of fruit?"

He slapped his thighs. "Feel? Must everything around here be connected to feelings?"

"I don't know about here, but you just experienced the first lesson in my class. You reacted about the same as my students. Insulted. Contentious. Ready to walk. Only half showed up the next week."

"And you wonder why?"

"Seemed like a good way to get my point across. What did I do wrong?"

Not the helpless female routine, Janice. He'll see right through it.

"You think you have to talk about *feelings*, make them feel good about themselves," he said.

"I didn't expect perfect products. I just wanted them to realize that painting still life wasn't easy."

"Then find a way to do it without shredding their egos."

She paused, appeared to think through his statement. "How?"

Shae held her breath, waited for the anticipated outburst from her dad.

It didn't materialize. "Get rid of the damned markers," he said instead. "Have them use brushes, the real thing. Give 'em each an apple to work from, something to use as a reference, not just loosygoosy ideas. Don't you check their work and give them that snooty nose. Have them judge each other's work."

Janice tapped her index finger against her chin. "Good suggestions, although I didn't mean to sound snooty."

"Then don't. The worst thing you can do is talk down to them. Talk *like* them."

"I was married for over twenty years and raised a son. You make it sound like I didn't learn a thing about men."

He shrugged. "Not how to talk to 'em." He eyed her. "Sure not how to dress for a man."

Shae winced at her dad's reference to the shirred floral skirt and yellow overblouse Janice wore today. The "real" Tim Harriman, the blunt, no-nonsense one, had shown up for this discussion.

Janice chuckled. "I'd be insulted if you weren't right. I recently decided a wardrobe makeover was in order. Just haven't gotten to it yet."

"Time's ticking."

Could her dad be more insensitive?

"Right. Which reminds me." She glanced at her watch. "Time to go. Thanks for the advice."

She pivoted away from him. "Hey, uh, Janice. My comments about your clothes didn't chase you away, did they? That's just me. You have trouble talking to men. I guess the same goes for me. With women."

Her dad had actually apologized to a woman?

Janice swiveled back to Shae's dad. "No offense taken. I have another appointment and need to get back to the gallery."

"If you want, come back again sometime and run the rest of that lesson by me. I'll critique it."

"Tomorrow soon enough? The class is Friday night."

"Guess I can work you in. And it's Tim."

Shae ducked into a nearby room before Janice left the sunroom. Didn't want either her dad or Janice to discover she'd eavesdropped. If she hadn't witnessed the scene with her own eyes, she wouldn't have believed it. Her dad had done his best to drive off Janice, but in the end he'd apologized for his gruff manner.

What did Janice know that she didn't?

Shae slipped away from the rehab facility and didn't return for two more days. When she did come back, the scene before her defied belief. She found her father seated in front of an easel in the sunroom, paintbrush in hand. He had created what appeared to be a red ball.

"Don't say it. I've expanded my horizons, whether I want to or not," he told her.

Thank you, Janice. I didn't think you could do it.

She leaned in to examine his work. "An apple, right?"

"Well, duh. What else would it be?"

"Nothing, I guess. What kind? Macintosh? Red Delicious?"

He withdrew the brush, swiveled his head in her direction. "Who knows? Who cares? Why are you here in the middle of the day anyhow?"

"Have a little more time than usual while the foundations settle."

"The doc called, didn't he?"

He had her dead to rights. An hour earlier, she'd learned from his physician her dad could be released from the rehab facility in a few days. Even though she'd known her dad could finish the rest of his recuperation at home sooner or later, the information still caught her up short. She assumed her most cheerful tone. "I talked to him this morning. Good news, isn't it?"

"S'pose he gave you the list of everything I'm not allowed to do yet? Or eat?"

She settled next to the easel, so she could attempt to read his expressions. "Yeah. He emailed me."

"Might as well stay here, for all the freedom I'll have."

"You'll be on your own, for the most part."

"You gonna continue to stay there?"

"I guess. If you're okay with that."

"What about your apartment?"

"Long gone. I was on my way out of town when you went to the hospital, remember? I can probably find other temporary housing, if you'd prefer."

For the first time, he gazed directly at her. "No, stay. I could use the company."

"You won't be totally on your own. A physical therapist is supposed to stop by twice a week and a home health nurse once a week."

"Oh, goody. Fool wouldn't tell me when I can go back to work. Visitors limited to two at a time, which includes that woman you sent to harass me. Janice Something."

He didn't sound all that upset about Janice. Nor had he forgotten her name, as he made out. "Collier. She's Ned's mother. She runs the Serenity Art Gallery."

"Collier, yeah, that's it. She asked for my help with an art class."

"Really?" How Janice had pulled off such a feat, she had no idea. "You've agreed to teach? Tell me more."

"Me, a teacher?" he harrumphed. "No way. I'm her *consultant*." He told her how Janice had asked him to act as a guinea pig, try out the week's lesson in advance of her students, so he could give her the male viewpoint.

Never underestimate Janice Collier. To get Tim Harriman to paint still life was brave. To get him to be the pre-class tester was absolutely brilliant.

"I heard about your wienie roast," he said out of the blue.

Should have known. The Dave Hale Gazette had struck again. If Janice could slough off his attitude, maybe she could, too. "You mean the hotdog bribe to get Triggs and his crew out to the site on time? Crazy, huh? But it was the best I could come up with on short notice. Ned didn't want to wait any longer."

"Not bad," he replied, to her surprise. "I'd never have done it, but I can holler a lot better than you."

"About that—"

"Hollering? God, I hope you haven't followed your old man's tricks."

He knew about that incident too. "Tried to. At first. I didn't have much practice at supervising people, let alone running the whole operation. I went with what I knew, which was what I'd learned from you, and that was, uh, to shout."

"How'd that work for you?"

"How do you think? They stormed out of the meeting." He didn't push for details. Of course, he knew. "No surprise there, right? Your information pipeline beats the evening news."

"You got 'em back, though."

"Dave got them back while I sat there and kept my mouth shut."

"Not so easy, is it?"

"How would you know? You issue orders and expect people to fall in line. You've never had to sit back and let someone else save your bacon."

"If only."

That stopped her. "You've had to eat your words at some point?"

"Of course, I have, girlie. Although maybe not so much recently, since I've built a reputation that encourages folks not to talk back. Besides, you're a girl. Even though you've grown up in this business, you should've known the guys would be out to test you."

She pulled back, stared at him. "You threw me into all that with no preparation. Did you expect me to fail?"

He set the brush down, wiped it on a rag, avoided her gaze.

"Dad?"

"Yeah, I heard you. I could say the drugs they had me on at the time wiped out my good sense. Maybe on some level I wanted you to flop. That way, I'd at least given you a chance to prove yourself."

Shae gripped the seat of her chair. Her surroundings seemed unfocused, not quite there. He hadn't wanted her to succeed. He'd set her up to crash and burn. His honesty blindsided her. Though she'd suspected his intentions all along, she hadn't been able to let herself believe he'd really do that to his own flesh and blood.

She wanted to run, but her body rebelled, her stomach roiled. She bit her lips, determined not to let the tears loose.

He reached over and patted her knee, then quickly withdrew his hand. "Hold onto the waterworks. I didn't finish. Things worked out differently than I expected."

She tried to ask how, but her mouth felt like she'd swallowed one of his paint rags.

"You surprised me. And Dave. The whole crew, from what I hear. You hung in there. Took your licks when the crew deserted you. Listened to our client's advice about how to get 'em back. Despite Collier's unorthodox involvement in the project, you've managed to retain him as our client and still keep the project on track."

He'd actually praised her.

"Thought you'd like to know before I return to work."

Her stomach lurched, like she'd suddenly braked her car for a squirrel that ran in front. This moment had arrived sooner than she anticipated. She'd told him when she agreed to take the job she wanted to be his partner when he recuperated. He'd never replied. Hadn't stopped her hopes and dreams of what could be.

"I promised the doc I'd be good for a while yet. Don't tell these fools here, but I actually feel better than I have in years."

She didn't think she could widen her eyes any more than she already had, but his statement made them pop open even more.

"I'm glad to hear you say that, Dad."

"Big admission, I know. But the doc says if I don't stick with the program, my recovery's at risk. As much as you're probably ready to turn things over to me, you're gonna have to stick around a while longer. At least until the homes in the first phase of the project are done."

She blinked. "Done? That's still weeks, months, off." He believed in her enough to let her stay through that period. Or was this an act, to convince her he was ready to come home?

"Yeah, well, doesn't mean I won't get more involved, but you're still in charge, kid, as long as things continue as they have."

As long as things continue as they have. What a catch phrase. And what a challenge.

CHAPTER 22

S hae's dad glanced up from his crossword puzzle as she breezed into the house. "Need a four-letter word for 'slightly open', as with a door. Whatcha got?"

"Let me think. How about *ajar*?" Shae replied. These word games had become the norm since her dad had returned home a few days before. Although not a crossword enthusiast, she'd gone along with him, because it gave them something to talk about other than progress on the site. Unbeknownst to him, and she had no intention of telling him, she'd been driven to install a couple crossword cheater apps on her phone to keep up with him.

"Works. Hey, thanks." He pulled his head up from the newspaper. "What you doing home in the middle of the day?"

"Lunch."

"You drove all the way back to town for a sandwich? You're gonna have to come up with better excuses than that to check on the old man, kiddo."

She set her purse on the couch and sank in across from him in his recliner. "My days aren't as long right now. Thought you wouldn't mind if I played hooky, as long as I did it with you."

His eyes narrowed, but he set his newspaper aside. "Interesting ploy. Include me, so I won't get on your case if I discover you've taken time off to enjoy yourself."

"Saw right through me. Okay, here's what I've got in mind. Thought you might like to go for a drive."

He raised a brow. "A drive? Anywhere in particular? Like out to the Sullivan's Creek site?"

"Actually, it's on the way, so sure, we can stop there. As long as you promise not to stay too long or let anything that's been done or not done to your satisfaction get to you. Could you do that?"

"Tall order, but okay. Wait. You said it's on the way. Where are we headed?"

"Picked right up on that, did you?" She tried to keep this light, because she wasn't sure how he'd react. "We didn't take flowers to Sean's grave on the anniversary of his passing this year, because you were at Blackhawk Hills. I thought we could do that today but also go check out the spot where it happened." She held her breath. It was high time, overdue, actually, for her father to move past his grief. But that didn't mean he would agree to this idea.

He grabbed his newspaper again, as if he'd dismissed her idea. At length, though, he set it aside once more. "How far away is this place?"

He knew the distance as well as she did. In the days after Sean's death, when her dad had roamed the house at all times of the day, he'd spent hours on the autopsy and accident reports, then consulted a map. "About an hour. I figured we could make an afternoon of it, have lunch first, pick up flowers and then stop by the Sullivan's Creek site before we visit the scene of the accident."

"Okay. Gotta change my clothes first."

Okay? He wanted to switch to a different outfit than the duds he'd worn. Good sign. She hadn't expected this degree of cooperation. Actually, she hadn't known what to expect.

Lunch went well, once she convinced him he had to stick to the diet the nutritionist had sent him. He grumbled through the salad and chicken, but he ate. Heartily.

They delivered the flowers to the cemetery with little ceremony.

They actually found tulips, Sean's favorite, still available at this time of year.

Even her father's first glimpse of Sullivan's Creek in weeks, his first glimpse of the excavated sites and poured foundations, went off without a hitch. No one was around. One good thing. He got out of the SUV at the future site of Janice Collier's home, walked around a bit. Then he got back in and told her they could leave. Didn't even want to check out the trailer.

"You're ready to go? So soon?" *Don't push it, Shae.*

"If I stay much longer, I'll start to get involved. Promised you I'd be good."

Wow. Who was this man? But she counted her blessings and immediately took off.

The site of Sean's accident was at the bottom of a hill that curved near the end. In the rain, he'd apparently overestimated the speed at which he could descend, lost traction and skidded in front of an oncoming car that had no way to stop in time. Today, in early summer, aside from a small cross crew members had placed there a month after the incident, there was no other sign that something horrific happened here a few years back.

Shae parked her SUV well off the road, so they could view the spot from inside the car. "I thought we could stay here in the vehicle and have a minute of silence. That okay?"

Her dad stared straight ahead, his body tense, like he was holding back, so he wouldn't break down. Maybe this hadn't been such a good idea. Yes, it was time for him to move on, but maybe he wasn't as recovered physically as the doctors had led her to believe.

"Dad? You okay?"

He nodded quickly. "Had to get my bearings." His voice emerged as a hoarse whisper.

"Okay. Take your time. But if this place is too much for you, just tell me. We'll leave."

"Gimme another minute."

She waited, prayed she'd done the right thing.

After a few beats, he seemed to come out of his reverie, and for the first time since they arrived, turned to face her. "I'd like to get out and go over to that cross."

"Okay. Sure." She started to open the door.

"Alone, if you don't mind?"

"You sure?"

"Yeah. I want to do this."

She let him go. Only after he'd reached the cross some fifty feet away did she swipe at her eyes. Had to get rid of these tears. Her dad wasn't one for emotional scenes.

He stood at the cross a few minutes, then pivoted and marched straight back to the vehicle and got in. Once again, he stared ahead. "Let's go."

She didn't reply, just turned on the ignition.

They didn't speak on the drive back to his house.

She considered the radio but changed her mind. He seemed to need this time alone with his thoughts with no distractions.

After she parked, they both alighted simultaneously. As they went into the house, he put a hand on her shoulder, briefly, but long enough for her to know she hadn't imagined it. "Good idea, kiddo. Thanks. Now, if you don't mind, I'm going to my room for a bit."

She obliged. Might have picked up fast food for dinner but was afraid to leave him totally alone.

About an hour later, he returned to the living room. "Where's dinner? My god, girl, just because you played hooky doesn't get you out of dinner prep." She smiled inwardly. He was back.

"Got a spare hour or two?" Ned asked Shae over the phone.

It had been almost a week since she'd seen or heard from him. The sound of his voice curled her toes. His call should have put her on immediate alert. Instead, she reacted like a teenage girl. Could she be any more naïve? Or foolhardy? She attempted to keep her tone cautious. "Maybe. For what?"

"How'd you like to critique my work for once? I could use some feedback on the piece I've composed."

He wanted her opinion? "I'm no music expert."

"You know what you like, don't you? That's all I ask."

For some reason, her breathing had grown ragged, and her hands perspired while she did a quick mental run through of her day's schedule. "I suppose I could help. Where?"

"You at the office? Meet me outside in fifteen minutes."

She arrived at the appointed spot in fourteen minutes. She could have made it sooner except she took time to change to the new pink and navy striped work shirt she'd bought on her lunch break. Even before his call. Was she psychic or just hopeful? What had possessed her to choose pink? Tailored, no less.

He charged around the car to open the door for her, but not before he halted long enough to take in her outfit. "Hi."

"Hi, yourself," she gulped, mesmerized by his smile. To see him again was like she'd walked into a concrete wall. God, he looked good.

His fingertips barely touched the small of her back as he helped her into the car, but the brief contact was enough to send a blast of fire down her spine.

Memories of the night in her bedroom flooded back. As much as she'd craved more personal time with him, she'd sworn not to push their relationship further, because she'd agreed to no strings. But now? She felt raw, vulnerable to his charm. How was she supposed to get through the next hour when all she wanted to do was jump his bones?

Big mistake to agree to this impromptu concert. She didn't feel any more at ease in his small sports car today than she had the first time she'd ridden in it, when they went to inspect the property. Yet again, that same woodsy scent from his aftershave permeated the interior. Intoxicating. The fragrance made her brain spin and every joint in her body wobbly.

"How're things going?"

"Things?" Her voice reflected how she felt. Disoriented. "You mean our other projects? Fine." Could she sound more inane?

"How about you?"

Relax, Shae. Keep it light. Find a safe topic. "Did you know your mom visited my dad the other day?"

"No kidding? She hasn't mentioned anything about it to me."

She related the scene she'd observed between their parents. "I should've let them know I was there. But the way your mother handled him fascinated me. He was still his gruff old self, mind you, but she wasn't fazed by him at all."

"That's my mom. She's made more than one sale at the gallery with that attitude."

They rode in silence for a bit, although now that they'd chatted about their parents, she relaxed somewhat. A couple times she caught him glancing in her direction as if to check her mood.

Suddenly, she noticed they were within a block of the Woodley Mansion. "We're going to Mike's house? Are you sure it's okay for me to be there?"

"He gave me the run of the place while he's out of town. You're my guest."

Alone together in this huge house? Such a bad idea. She couldn't wait to get there.

As they alighted from the car, he seemed to sense her thoughts. "Do you want a short tour first? No one's here except the housekeeper."

The housekeeper. Good. They wouldn't be completely alone. She couldn't trust herself to be alone with him.

After a brief glimpse of the rooms on first floor, he led her downstairs. "This is what I use as my music room," he said as he opened a door to a massive area surrounding a keyboard. He left her long enough to retrieve a chair and seated her about five feet away.

"This started out as just random feelings about the property," he said before he began. "I've added to it as construction got underway."

For the next several minutes, music filled the room. She closed her eyes, hoped he'd assume she'd shut out everything else to experience the sound rather than pick up on her spiking hormones. When she did open her eyes, she couldn't take them off the figure seated before her, especially his hands. She'd never noticed how large they were. Not just large, but dexterous and commanding as they ripped across the keys or coaxed a tender melody from the instrument. It was one thing to observe Jake Bonneville work the crowd at his mother's gallery showing, but this was the musician Jake Bonneville, someone she'd only now met. No wonder he boasted so many lady fans. His playing was hypnotic.

She attempted to focus on the music, but all she could see was Ned bent over the keyboard, his long legs at the pedals, his glorious hands caressing the keys, his eyes intent on producing a sound just for her. The thought of being the lone recipient of his efforts overwhelmed her.

At one point, she discovered his eyes on her. Not like he gauged her reaction to the music. He watched her for some other reason.

She let the piece carry her away to a new world of sound. A world rich and melodic. It reminded her of something Ned had told her about his grandfather the day he first drove her out to the property. Something about his grandfather's desire to preserve the pristine quality of the prairie, even as it was consumed by modern day technology. Ned had really captured that sense of yearning in this piece.

She clapped like a maniac when he finished. "That was gorgeous. It swept me away to places I've never been."

"Yeah?" He pulled her into a bear hug. "I hoped you'd like it."

In his arms, her resolve disintegrated like an ice cube melting in a glass of lemonade on a hot summer day. So much for her pep talk to herself. Those same hands that a minute before had created such musical magic now held her under their spell. She floated in his tight embrace. "Uncle!" she finally said.

He set her on her feet and stepped back. "Sorry, didn't realize how much I wanted someone else's approval." He gazed into her eyes, his own eyes had gone limpid and cloudy. "Especially yours."

That look, his croaky voice were all it took to ignite the sexual tension she'd repressed for so long. "Play it again."

He studied her briefly, like he'd expected her to say or do something else, but he did as she asked and turned on the playback, returned a moment later, his eyes trained on her, as he wait for her next move.

As the opening strains of the piece began, she walked into his arms and kissed him with all the pent-up desire she'd held in check since their night in her bed.

Ned welcomed her lips with his own, echoed the gentle arpeggios of the music. As the volume increased, so did the ferocity of his kiss. His hands roamed over her body, took inventory of every inch.

Her passion unshackled, her insides tingling, Shae rubbed against him. She wanted to embed herself in his body and never leave. Locked together, they swayed, tottered as they struggled to get more of each other. Ned pressed her into the nearest wall, crushed the hard evidence of his arousal into her stomach. His hands grasped hers and pinned them above her head while he rocked against her, ravished her neck.

Shae's breath came in ragged spurts, but even if her heart stopped beating now from too much stimulation, this would be the way she wanted to go, pummeled by Ned's elevating need.

The melody grew more intense, the underlying accompaniment more elaborate. Ned broke away long enough to seek permission in her eyes. For what seemed like an eternity, they stared at each other, studied the other's intent. Then she nodded, pulled her blouse from her jeans. He quickly undid the front buttons and reached in to lift her bra over her breasts, didn't take time to unhook the garment. "Oh, babe," he moaned. He leaned down and laved his tongue across one exposed nipple, now firm with anticipation.

His mouth on her breast sent delicious waves of heat to her core. Did he have any idea how his touch sent her over the brink? Though she squirmed, anxious for him to move on, he held her to the wall with his body while he feasted on her breasts.

"Take me now, Ned. I'm about to explode."

With lightning speed, he unzipped her jeans, pulled them and her panties down to her knees. She shimmied enough to kick them off while he undid his own pants and slipped on protection.

He boosted her up, so her legs could go around his waist. She latched one ankle over the other behind him and nearly passed out as his hard-on met her exposed labia. She'd never experienced such exquisite torture.

"Oh, Ned. Oh, oh," she breathed. Other words eluded her.

"This feels so … right," he murmured as he penetrated her. In the background, deep, lingering chords replicated a no-nonsense storm while their joined bodies thrashed against the wall.

A frisson of worry cut into her reverie. "What about the housekeeper?"

"Day off. I lied."

"You're a bad boy, Ned," she whispered against his neck.

"You ain't seen nothin' yet, ma'am. I do bad very well."

"Show me."

He slid them both to the floor and rolled on top of her, ripped off her upper garments, his shirt. "I told myself this wouldn't happen again, but I can't seem to keep my hands off you."

"Same for me," she moaned. She arched her back as his hands and mouth claimed her.

His music had taken her to new sensations in sound. His ministrations now sent her to a different plane, one based on touch and taste and smell. The composer was now the conductor, who drew from her body notes it had never sung before.

Some sensual operating system deep inside her seized control from her brain. Her body reacted and initiated of its own accord. All her brain could do was sail along, surrender to the overpowering stimuli.

Though he'd begun gently, he quickly increased the pace. The tempo of the piece increased as well, as it built to a final throbbing, breathtaking finale as it matched Ned's thrusts. She opened her eyes to note he'd left her, gone to his own place of ecstasy. She'd done that to him. Other women in the past may have sent him the same direction, but for now, he was hers.

Spent, they fell back on the floor to catch their breath. Gradually, their surroundings came back into focus. She reclined in his arms, savored the moment and gave in to the utter comfort and security his embrace brought her. At least for this brief sliver of time. She felt so languorous, satiated. "Oh, Ned. That was—"

"Better than before? Yeah. For me, too." He leaned down to kiss the tip of her nose.

"We're fools."

"Because we couldn't resist each other?"

She breathed in deeply, closed her eyes before she gazed back at him. "This is such a wrong move while the project is underway. But it's, you're, all I can think of." *Dammit, Shae. Why did you have to go there?* She'd ruined it.

She steeled herself for his cool reaction. But he surprised her.

"Me, too." The words tumbled out before he thought them through, but once uttered, he knew he meant them. They weren't just something a guy said to a woman after sex. Stupid move, but hell, there it was. He wanted her more than any other woman he'd ever known.

"Don't worry. I know there's no commitment. But I enjoyed the moment immensely," she told him.

He placed a tender kiss on her cheek. "I can't see beyond right now, either. This is so good."

"Play your concerto one more time. I want to savor it here in your arms. Just like this."

"Babe, my body's not ready to go where the music goes yet. Give me a few minutes."

"No, play it again now. We got caught up in the drama of the piece, but there were slower, more tender parts as well."

Give the lady what she wanted. She'd certainly given him her all. He left her long enough to play back the piece and returned to embrace her, kissed her again, slower with feeling, as he now concentrated on the more *adagio* parts of the music.

The alluring, seductive tone of the melody swept over him. He'd been more focused on the optimistic carol of the land and hadn't paid much attention to this section. It had slipped into the music on its own. Had Shae been in his thoughts as this part came to him?

Whatever the motivation, the music and Shae did things to him now despite the need to let his guys rest. Condom removed and replaced, he nuzzled her neck, while his arm drew her closer. He laid her on the floor and rose over her. "Can't stop myself," he said as he entered her again.

Sometime later, Shae unwound from the protective cocoon of his arms and legs. "Italian opera has nothing on you, Jake Bonneville, aka Ned Collier. This is the new go-to piece for lovemaking. Or should I say, for sex?" she quickly added. "I know the difference. I'm fine with it."

He'd heard that chestnut before, once or a hundred times, and regretted every time he'd been unwise enough to believe it. Unlike those times, though, he hadn't experienced the strong emotional need for the woman, like he felt for Shae. Scared him more than her words. "You don't expect anything more than, uh, sex?"

She nodded, although her eyes didn't quite meet his.

He wasn't convinced. "Not even dating?"

"Definitely not that. I don't want my dad or any of the crew to know about us. It's, uh, well, unprofessional. I shouldn't have given in to it now, but—"

"I know. We can't keep our hands off each other."

"What do we do about it?"

Did she want him to commit anyhow, or did she just seek a way they could both live with this overwhelming urge to get it on with each other? "Unprofessional or not, we have to keep this as professional as possible."

"Agreed."

"So, the project site is off limits." Although he didn't write off Mike's RV.

"And since my dad has moved back home, his house will no longer work, either."

He raised a brow. "Where besides one of our vehicles? The gear shift in mine could be mighty dangerous." A joke, but other than one of their cars or a motel, their options were pretty limited.

"How about the rest of this mansion? There have to be a zillion more rooms."

"Good thought, but you said you could only spare an hour to hear my music. We've already *used* all of that and more."

She returned a coquettish smile. "Funny thing. My schedule just cleared up for another hour. Or two."

They threw on their clothes but didn't button or zip anything, as they went off to discover more venues.

Shae grabbed his arm. "Just so we're clear, this doesn't negate our clashes about expenses or what you can or cannot do as project manager."

Surely she didn't think he'd set this up to get past her? That was so behind them. Now was not the time to quibble. "Foiled. Saw through my ploy, huh?"

She tugged his arm harder, her demeanor had gone way more serious. "I mean it, Ned. I don't think you've told me everything about your finances yet. Just enough to keep me quiet. I'll respect your need for secrecy, unless you go overboard with something else."

A chill ran through him. *You don't want to know anything more, Shae. Give me a chance to make this right, and you'll never have to know.*

CHAPTER 23

Four days into framing, Irv Farley called in his favor. "A little birdie told me your first houses are going up."

"Uh, yeah. That's right."

"Then congratulations are in order for both of us, because I've just opened my own business in the area."

Ned swallowed as deeply as he could without irritating his throat. His stomach churned like a washing machine in high agitation cycle. How could he get out of this? Farley wanted his pound of flesh, and Ned's skin couldn't afford it. "No kidding? Thought you'd focused on Southern California."

"That, uh, *market* seems to be drying up. You called it right. Much more opportunity in the Midwest right now. I now own a heavy equipment company not too far from your site."

Heavy equipment, like in cranes? The spin cycle in his gut kicked up a notch. As soon as the walls were up, the roofs came next. Cranes were used to lift the trusses supporting the roofs. Surely Farley didn't expect him to cancel the sub they'd already scheduled? *Get real, man. Of course, he does.* "Good for you."

"Good for you as well, because I plan to make the best of my fleet available to you. Say day after tomorrow? I'll have a crane there just in time for roofing."

The guy must have spies planted in the crew. No surprise. That's how Farley worked.

He'd promised Shae no more surprises. If he explained how his *friend* wanted their business, would she go along with this last-minute change? As loyal as she was to their subs, she'd want to know who this friend was and why they had to alter their plans now, so late in the process. If he revealed anything about Farley, she'd question him repeatedly until she learned he was the backer. From there, she was bound to figure out this backer had something on him. It wouldn't take much imagination for her to realize his finances were in more trouble than he'd let on.

He'd already gone to great lengths to keep the media, his fans, Mike, and his mother from learning he was out of money. Shae had been affected by those extreme measures. She'd ranted at first, but once he let her in on some of his difficulties, she'd helped him keep the project afloat.

He'd come to respect and admire her. He really didn't want to break his promise. It wouldn't be fair to make her go against her better judgment. Truth be told, he didn't want her to know what poor decisions he'd made. But there didn't seem to be any other way to deflect Farley.

Still, he could try. "That's mighty neighborly of you, Irv. Thing is, we've already got that business lined up. Maybe we could—"

"Cancel it. I told you I'd be back with a *request*. This is it. For starters."

For starters? Surely the guy didn't think he could pull more of this crap? "Why don't we postpone the services of your company until the next phase?"

The other end of the line went silent for a bit, as if Farley wanted that absurdity to hang in the air, draw out the humiliation. "Time for bargaining is over, Bonneville. My folks'll be there bright and early two days from now."

"But Irv—"

"You've had some pretty tough knocks to contend with lately, pal. Some of your critics have even suggested your career is over. It would be a cryin' shame if word got around you were also a poor business-man. One who's not only out of money to fund his project but one who also goes back on his word."

What a shi …

Mike had warned him. He himself had known this deal was a risky proposition. But he'd been desperate. At least, that's what he'd told himself. Ned didn't like this one bit, but at the moment, he didn't appear to have any other recourse than to go along with the guy.

"Okay, Irv. I'll expect your crane on the site first thing Wednesday morning." He didn't wait for the creep to hang up.

He had to find a way to get Farley's crane on-site without anyone being the wiser to the substitution. Not an easy task, since something so critical to the project— and that large—couldn't be ignored. While the walls continued to go up, he returned to the mansion. He thought best as he composed.

After an hour or so at the keyboard, he had a plan. Of sorts. If Triggs could try to postpone things, the crane operator could just as easily attempt the same maneuver. With his help. That way his promise to Shae could be sidestepped. Deep down, he knew that wasn't good enough. He could rationalize his action every which way, but in the end, he'd be doing the one thing that had angered and disappointed her the most, left her out of the picture.

But it was the best he could do with so little time. It all depended on his ability to call in some of his own favors and time the execution of his plan perfectly. He placed a call to one of the local television stations. Time to schmooze. "Hello. Cora, isn't it? Jake Bonneville."

"Bonneville? As in *the* Jake Bonneville, the singer?" the woman's voice on the other end asked. "We've tried to interview you for weeks. Have you decided you're ready to go public about your voice?"

"My voice is recovering nicely. Have to put off concert appearances a little while longer, but I've kept busy in the meantime. In fact, that's why I called." He briefly described Sullivan's Creek and his grandfa-ther's dreams for it.

"Sounds interesting. We'd like to do a story about it when you're further along."

"Actually, Cora, I'd like to publicize the project now and play up some of the locals who are involved." He suggested she start with a certain crane operator. "I'd really appreciate it if you'd go out there day after tomorrow.

"Doable," she agreed.

"Here's a thought, why not stage some sort of competition for the crew? They'll probably have to call off other work for the day, but what a great opportunity to showcase their business."

"Great idea, Jake, although I'm not sure they'll be able to pull off something so ambitious in just two days."

"I'd, uh, consider it a favor to me if you can make it happen. Talk to your general manager. Get her to help. Might even be an exclusive with me if you can do it." He'd navigated the media waters for years and knew exactly what buttons to press to get her cooperation. He even got her to wait an hour to call the crane company owner, so he could get back to the site and station himself near Dave when the inevitable call came.

Before he left for the site, though, he placed one more call. To Jesse Swink, owner of the Swink Crane Company. "Seems we've double-booked, Jesse. We won't need you folks this week after all."

"Too bad, Bonneville. We'll be glad to take the day off, but we'll have to charge you folks, just the same."

"Well now, let's talk about that, Jesse. How 'bout instead of pay you, we send you more publicity than you've ever had? Publicity that not only advertises your business but also makes you and your crew look like good guys in the community. You can't pay for that kind of promotion."

Swink didn't reply at once, hopefully to consider the proposition. "What're you suggesting?"

Ned went through the same ideas he'd suggested to Cora at the TV station. "I can have them call within the hour, if you're interested."

"You guarantee this'll run on TV?"

"All I can guarantee is they'll show up. You and your crew have to give them something they can use. Something entertaining. C'mon, you don't want to deny your wife and family the chance to appear on TV, do you?"

That clinched the deal. He hung up and raced to Sullivan's Creek.

"What'd'ya mean you have to postpone?" Dave asked the party on the other end. "Yeah, I suppose we could hold off another day for the trusses, but this isn't like you. In the past, you've always given us at least three days' notice to find an alternate. This really puts us in a bind."

Dave listened to an apparent explanation on the other end of the line. "Yeah, well, gimme a while to find someone else. If I can't, I'll call you back."

He clicked off. "Damn!" Apparently his typical response to sub problems.

Ned made sure he was conveniently near. "What's up?"

Dave stared at him, apparently debated how much to say. "Just a delay. Only a day, but I know how much that irritates you. We'll try to find someone else to do the job."

"What job?" Ned asked. He kept his tone innocent.

Dave went over the highlights of his phone conversation, attempted to bring him up to speed.

Ned appeared to consider Dave's dilemma. "You've probably got a few other companies in mind that you use on occasion, but by pure coincidence, a friend of mine just started up his own small crane operation not too far from here. I'd, uh, appreciate it if you'd give him the business."

A long time ago, he learned when a hopeful smile accompanied a seemingly innocuous request, it achieved more mileage than a heavy demand. Dave seemed to need encouragement to do right by the client rather than trust his own instincts.

"Who do I call?" Dave asked after considerable deliberation.

～

THE DAY the crane was to appear, Ned beat everyone else to the site. So far, so good. Everything was on the up and up with Shae, because Dave made the call to Farley's people, not him. How could she fault him? Who was he kidding? He'd still maneuvered things to happen. He'd just have to live with what he'd done. If this substitution worked, the end would justify the means. Sure. His stomach hadn't settled since the guy's call two days earlier.

Dave arrived a few minutes later. As soon as he spotted Ned, he trudged over. "I don't see a crane yet. Should've been here by now."

"It's early. I'm sure it'll show up any minute." He almost hoped he was wrong. He'd rather wait a day for the other company. Then he could tell Farley his people hadn't shown up. Like Farley would allow such a thing to happen. Unfortunately, further speculation was unnecessary, because within minutes, the crane drove in and came to a stop in front of the site of what was to be his mother's house.

Dave went to talk to the driver, who seemed hesitant to discuss much of anything. When that proved futile, Dave left the guy and circled the rig. He scratched his chin every so often, then glanced toward the top of the boom.

Dave apparently sensed something wasn't right. Had the crane operator spilled the beans?

Ned drifted to them as nonchalantly as his leaden feet would allow. "What's up?"

"Not sure."

Shae joined them. "Not sure about what, Dave?"

"It's SOP for the crane operator to check out his equipment before it's brought in as well as once it arrives. This guy says he's done that. But something doesn't look right."

"Tell me what's got you bothered," she said.

Tiny hammers whacked away at Ned's brains. What had Farley done?

Dave pointed to the rigging near the top of the crane. "See that wire rope? That's all part of the sling that holds the trusses and hoists them to the roof so the crew can move them into place. My eyesight's not as good as it used to be, but things don't look right."

Shae shielded her eyes with her hand in the morning sun to see for herself what concerned Dave. "Nothing seems out of the ordinary from here. What doesn't look right?"

"Can't say for sure. Those wires just look funny."

Usually, Ned appreciated Dave's overly cautious nature, since it only served to improve the quality of the work. But he didn't need Dave's vigilance today. The sooner those trusses and the others slated for today were put in place, the sooner Farley's crew could be on their way. "Sure your eyes aren't playing tricks on you, Dave? I don't see anything that looks wonky."

"A year or so back, I took a course on counterfeit or faulty rigging. Wouldn't have paid much attention today, except I didn't recognize the operator, and he seemed real antsy when I questioned him."

The thought of being found out so soon paralyzed him. How could he stop this? Although if something really was wrong with the equipment, he didn't want to.

Shae shot around the crane to the spot where the company name appeared in small letters. "This a new outfit? I've never heard of them."

"Guy says they've been around a few years, but ownership just changed hands. New owner sent in some of his own equipment."

"Have him lower the boom," Shae said. "Let's check it out."

Once the boom was closer to eye level, Dave ran his work-gloved hands along the wire ropes at several junctures along the sling. Within minutes, he scratched his head, even more concerned than before. "Not good."

"What's wrong?" Shae asked.

"You know much about this equipment?"

"A little, but educate me."

"Wire rope slings like this one are made from a wire or synthetic core wrapped with several strands of wire rope. Over time, the strength of the rope diminishes due to continued metal fatigue and stress from bending."

"Okay. I get that. What's wrong here?" Shae returned.

"If not replaced periodically, the individual wire strands begin to break or develop kinks. That's what I'm seeing here. That, plus corrosion."

He motioned for the operator to join them. He checked the pocket tab on the operator's shirt. "Look, Joe, we got a problem with your crane. Appears the wire rope in the sling could give way and break. We can't let you proceed."

"In fact," Shae added, "we can't let you or the crane leave until someone from the state inspects it." *God, Farley, we are so screwed.*

"Looks okay to me," the operator nearly screamed, although the panic in his tone and eyes indicated otherwise. "I done this for years. Never had a bit of trouble."

"Been usin' the same crane all that time?" Dave wanted to know.

The operator glanced back at the rig, then down at his hands before he muttered, "Well, uh—"

"The new boss sent this in?" Shae guessed.

For the first time, the operator noticed Shae. "Look, lady, I got a good record. I can't afford for the State to cite me or the company."

Shae didn't appear to sympathize. "Then you should have caught these problems. They test you for that when you sit for your operator's license, don't they?"

The crane guy, Joe, took a step back; his eyes grew wide. His lips moved, but no words came out.

"Or maybe you never got your license?" she speculated. "Call your boss," she said when the operator still didn't answer. "Who is that, by the way?"

"I-I don't know." So far, Farley was safe.

"Okay, give me the office number." The operator did know that much. "Hello," Shae said when someone apparently picked up on the other end. "This is Shae Harriman, acting head of Two Rivers Construction. I want to speak to whoever's in charge there. Now."

"Aren't you getting a little carried away, Shae?" Ned asked, trying unsuccessfully to call back this runaway train. "Nothing looks amiss to me."

"You're now an expert on hoisting equipment?" she shot back.

She had him there.

She continued to wait, far too long for the person who answered to have located their supervisor. "I hear doors slamming in the background. Call the sheriff, Dave. Get someone over there before everyone disappears."

Within the hour, the state inspector arrived and verified the sling was indeed unsafe. "Good thing you called, Ms. Harriman. These ropes could have broken, which might have caused no small amount of damage. Possibly injury."

"Or … worse?" she guessed.

He nodded. "I've already got the basic details, and my associate will photograph evidence. But it will take us several more hours at a minimum to close out our report. You'll need to shut down this site, at least for the rest of the day, maybe longer."

Shae blinked, like the thought hadn't occurred to her yet, but her voice remained calm and in control. "Yes, of course. Are you going to cite us?"

The inspector considered. "They're on your site. You hired them, supposedly after you did your due diligence. But you also caught it in time and reported it to us immediately."

The sheriff arrived in the middle of this discussion. "Your quick thinking helped us gather as much of the company's evidence as they didn't carry off. We'll track them down, but we don't have much to go on from the neighboring businesses. Though the company has been around for years, ownership changed recently," he said.

ALL THESE LAW enforcement agencies involved? Ned's insides ripped apart. Farley was such a criminal. And he'd been the guy's accomplice. This nightmare just got worse.

"Who'd you talk to over there?" the sheriff asked Dave.

"Ned said the owner was a friend of his. That's why I called them, even though we've never worked with these guys before."

"Ned? Who's that?" the sheriff asked.

Aw, Dave, do you have to be such a stickler for the truth? The guy didn't tattle or even try to cover his own behind. He was just a straight shooter who wanted all the facts to come out. Ned didn't have much choice but to step up. "I'm Ned. Ned Collier. I'm the developer. The guy you want is Irvin Farley. He lives in Malibu, California."

Everyone's eyes shifted to him.

He gulped air, which was ironic, since he was about to cut his almost fully recovered throat. "I set up the job with Farley."

"What?" Shae's voice rose.

Time to face the music. Music? Another irony. His poor judgment had laid the groundwork for this near disaster. "Farley is a business associate. He wanted in on our project, so when the other outfit had to postpone, I told Dave about my friend."

Shae quirked a brow. "The other group postponed?" She looked at Dave.

Dave swiped a hand across his jaw. "Strangest thing. It was late in the day Monday. I got a call from Jesse Swink, the owner of the crane company we'd scheduled. Said something had come up and none of his people could be here today. Tomorrow, yes, but not today." Dave continued. "Ned had just come into the office and asked what the problem was. When I explained, he suggested this guy. I told him we have a couple alternates we could try, but he kinda, uh, *strongly suggested* for us to use this outfit."

"Strongly suggested?" Shae repeated as she turned to Ned, a brow raised.

"Why shouldn't I?" Ned attempted to defend his actions.

"Interesting," she commented. "Excuse us a minute, Ned. Dave, follow me." The two of them headed off until they were several feet away, at which point they stopped and conferred.

Geez, was she going to ream Dave for this? Hadn't meant to get the guy in trouble.

From where he stood, he could see Shae make another call on her cell. At one point, she nodded, then glanced over at him, then quickly away. When she got off the phone, she and Dave returned to him.

"It seems our friends at Swink Crane Service are to be interviewed by the local news today as one of the groups involved in this very project. Came up rather suddenly, they said. Monday afternoon. Apparently it had to be today, and everyone was needed there for the story. Strange coincidence, wouldn't you say, Ned? You showed up in our office just when Swink called to postpone?"

She didn't say anything more, she simply glared at him and clenched her fists. The space between them seemed to glow with the tension.

Apparently Swink hadn't ratted on him. Only that link remained, where the reporter got the idea for the story, and then all the dots in the trail that led back to him would be connected. If Shae could call the crane people, she could just as easily contact the reporter. Might as well save her the trouble. "I owed the guy a favor. Okay? I told you I wouldn't go behind your back with any more changes, so I had to find another way to make this happen. I suggested the story to the TV station in return for an exclusive with me."

Shae's eyes narrowed to mere slits and her breathing became labored. She was about to erupt. Before she burst, though, the sheriff approached. "Guess we got enough to go on. For now." He said his good-byes and left.

Shae turned to the inspector, who'd also come up to them. "I need a few more minutes with my people," she told him.

The state guy nodded and drew his assistant aside.

Shae addressed the crew, who'd remained nearby, although they kept their distance from Shae, Dave and Ned. "Though this incident is an embarrassment for the company, I don't hold any of you accountable. Dave and I will work with the state people and get this cleared up as fast as we can, so we can all get back to work. Dave will let you know when to return."

The group started to disperse. "Wait. You were all here when this happened, you're entitled to witness the next part." She turned to Ned. "This is the last straw, Ned," she said in a deliberate, even tone. "Technically, you may have kept your promise not to make any more changes without our knowledge, but to manufacture this incredible scam to pay off your friend is even worse. You not only destroyed your own credibility and the good name of Two Rivers, you endangered everyone here today."

"Let me explain."

She held up a hand. "No. The time for explanations is over. We are all committed to your project, Mr. Collier. We want it to be the best of its kind. But with you as the developer, not the project manager. Consider yourself fired." Point made, she pivoted and walked off toward the mobile office, leaving a stunned crew in her wake.

The most surprised of all was Ned. He knew she'd be angry. He didn't blame her. But to fire him? He was the client, for God's sake!

SHAE BOUNDED BACK to the trailer, all the while biting back tears. She went five feet past the entrance before she realized what she'd done and retraced her steps. That delay was all the time Ned needed to catch up.

"You can't fire me."

"I just did." She kept her voice flat, dispassionate. As she started up the steps, he placed a hand on her arm.

"At least hear me out. I didn't have a choice. I owed Farley a favor, and when he called it in—"

She ripped her arm away. "Favor? For what?" Before he could answer, the name clicked in her mind. "Wait. Farley. He's the backer Mike took issue with and left town because he couldn't stand the man. You said you lost your voice at this guy's charity benefit, because he had you sing out on the beach."

"Let's discuss this inside."

"Inside, where you can put the moves on me, take my mind off this with your body?" a new thought occurred. She froze, her heart turning to stone. "That's been your plan all along, hasn't it? Romance me, keep me off-balance enough to dismiss all the problems you've caused."

"No, of course not. What I feel for you is … never mind. You've confused the issue. This isn't about you and me. It's about why I didn't have a choice on this."

Her throat constricted. He'd dismissed their affair like it didn't count. Truth was, it didn't. It had only been sex. She'd known all along, but she'd still allowed feelings for him to develop. She'd been such a fool.

"I can't keep you away from the site when you come to check on progress. But please have the decency to keep your distance until this dies down. For all I know, you may have cost my father his company."

"I never intended—"

"Of course, not! You haven't thought about anything or anyone else except your project. Go, Ned. Don't waste my time any longer. Here or in your bed." She ran up the steps and entered the trailer and pulled the door tight.

CHAPTER 24

ired! She couldn't do that.

But she had. All the ammunition Ned needed to pull the plug on the contract. Get himself a new contractor who'd listen to him. Understand his money woes. Right. Like he'd now find someone dumb enough to work for a near-broke developer. The only reason Shae had put up with him this long was her need to show her father she could handle the job.

She wouldn't give him a chance to explain. Fine. He didn't want to remain here longer anyhow. He avoided the rest of the crew and thundered off to his car to make a speedy getaway.

He no sooner got on the road when his cell rang. "Thanks for ratting me out, Bonneville."

Like he planned it? "You sent inferior equipment, Irv. Someone could've gotten hurt or even killed."

"Don't be so dramatic. I may have acquired older equipment on the cheap, but it remains to be proved that it was unsafe. I expected you to clam up and play dumb about who owned the company."

"They would've known your identity within an hour anyhow. What's the big deal?"

"The sheriff impounded all my equipment and files. They've

already checked into my other holdings, so I'm unable to go home. In time, my attorneys should be able to overturn the mess you've made, but in the meantime, you've inconvenienced me considerably. I don't like to be inconvenienced. Consider our deal off. I'm withdrawing my funding immediately."

"What? You can't do that. The bank already has the money."

"Read our agreement, buddy. I can demand payment on my loan anytime I want, bank or no bank."

"But if you do, the bank will call in the rest of my loan. I'll be ruined."

"Shoulda thought of that when you dropped my name." He clicked off.

No more Farley money. No more bank support. He was a dead man.

His hands shook so much, the car swerved several times before he got it under control. He pulled to the side of the road, turned off the engine and slumped over the steering wheel. As a young teen, he'd ridden his first and last rollercoaster. He was barely off the machinery before he regurgitated his last three meals. He felt worse now. In fact ...

He sprang from the car, fell to his knees at the ditch that bordered the road and heaved. He remained in that position even after he'd emptied his stomach, until the onset of nausea threatened to topple him. To straighten, Ned grabbed for the car and leaned against it to steady himself. As the countryside stopped spinning, he stumbled back inside, though he didn't turn over the ignition.

Damn Farley! And his throat. Damn his life in general. This project had been well within his grasp and then everything conspired against him. He would lose it all. His reputation, his money, his mother's respect and Shae. No, he'd already lost her.

He caught a glimpse of himself in the mirror. God, he looked terrible. Pale, eyes watery, hair disheveled. How had his life sunk so low?

Who was he kidding? He was the source of his problems. He had only himself to blame. He leaned back in the seat, rubbed his neck. His attention went to a nearby billboard that extolled a diet product.

"Stop kidding yourself," it read. "It's time to get real and lose that weight."

He didn't need to shed any pounds, but the rest of the message resonated.

"Stop kidding yourself."

"It's time to get real."

Okay. He'd finally stopped kidding himself about his finances. Get real? He'd just acknowledged he'd reached the end of the road that led to Sullivan's Creek.

What would he do? His life wasn't worth the crap he'd just upchucked in the ditch. His gut ached like someone had ripped away part of it.

To climb under the covers and stay there for the next month sounded pretty appealing about now. But before that, he needed to make one stop.

~

I WILL NOT CRY. *I will not cry.* Shae repeated the mantra all the way to her father's house as she swiped at her eyes. She'd done what she had to, fired Ned and broken things off with him. But that was just half of it. They faced possible charges and fines from the State, and now that she'd let Ned go, they could also lose his contract.

Sullivan's Creek could have been the company's financial salvation and their showcase for years to come. It could have been her chance to show her father she could run the company. At the moment, it appeared to be their downfall. She'd let her father down as well as herself. Moreover, the results of her poor judgment might be more stress than her father could handle, despite the apparent strides he'd made in his recovery.

Try as she might to put him out of her mind, her disobedient brain, or was it her heart, continued to think about Ned. How could he disappoint her so much and at the same time make her almost cry from his misguided intentions? Because she cared for him, dammit! Cared way too much for her own good.

She'd remained at the site only as long as it took to send the crew home and turn things over to the state people. She raced for home now, because she wanted to be the one to tell her dad about the crane incident. Dave assured her he wouldn't call, but she couldn't be sure about the crew.

Fortunately, no one had gotten in touch with her dad. The briefing about today's incident was all hers. She hit the high points for him. "No one was hurt?" He asked when she'd finished. His voice was unusually low.

"It never got that far, thanks to Dave's keen eyesight and odd feelings about the operator. The rig made it on-site but no farther."

"Why'd you decide to go with that outfit? Never heard of 'em."

"Nor I. The Swink people cancelled two days ago. Dave called this group on Ned's recommendation."

"Ned? How the hell did he know about 'em?"

"The new owner of the crane company was a friend." She didn't want to tell him the rest, but he deserved to know. She stuck with the headlines.

"Collier's money problems are worse than you led me to believe?"

"I just found out myself. Had this incident not happened, we still wouldn't know."

His telltale intake of breath, then several snorts sent a shiver of ice up her spine. Warning signs of a pending outburst she hadn't heard since his hospitalization. No! This couldn't be happening again.

A wave of pink crept up his neck, suffused his face in an even deeper shade.

She had to stop this before they were back to Square One. Or worse, he suffered a heart attack.

Before she could do anything, though, he burst from his chair and began to pace back and forth in front of the sofa, bumping into the coffee table a couple times, knocking magazines to the floor. "Where's Collier now? Gotta give him a piece of my mind."

She rushed to his side as she tried to recall the calming techniques his doctors had taught her. "Calm down, Dad. I already took care of that. I didn't want to tell you any of this, but as owner, you had to be told. But now that you know, let me handle the rest. You can't stress over this."

"Fool … jeopardized … company. Criminal."

"True, he acted without our knowledge. Well, without mine. He got Dave to act for him. But Ned had no idea his friend's company was using defective equipment."

Her dad pulled up. "You defending him?"

"No." She wasn't, was she? "Technically, he got around his promise not to act on his own. But using Dave as his pawn was even worse. If Ned hadn't been so desperate to get this guy off his back, he would have seen that himself."

"Someone coulda been killed."

She hung her head. "I know, Dad." She took his hand and faced him. "Go ahead. Blame me for trusting him. Fire me, if you must. But don't let this undo all the progress you've made regaining your health."

He shook his head repeatedly, as if trying to grasp the totality of this disaster. Then, abruptly, he backed up a step, released her hand. Straightening his shoulders, he inhaled deeply and let out his breath slowly, repeated the process several more times. "Right. Can't go down that road any more. Therapist showed me how to relax."

"Go for it. Do you need me to help, get you anything?"

He held up a hand. "Give me … few minutes."

She tried to do just that, as her own heart pumped faster than usual at the prospect of losing him.

After a minute or so, the color of his complexion returned to normal. He offered a lopsided smile. "Damn therapist was right. Made me practice the technique over and over. Until now, never saw much good in it."

"I'm so glad you paid attention. You're doing much better, Dad."

"Doesn't mean I'm happy about any of this."

"It was a mistake to let Ned serve as project manager. But I knew how important it was to you to keep the Sullivan's Creek project. You never would have allowed me to step in for you if you hadn't thought a Harriman at the helm was the only way to reassure Ned."

He settled onto the sofa and indicated for her to join him. "Thought it could work with Dave there to watch over you."

"Don't blame Dave for any of this. He took his cues from me. He's seen me accommodate and accede to Ned's demands often enough to think that's what I expected of him, too."

"Sounds like the two of you got a little too close to Collier for your own good."

If he only knew how close she'd gotten to their client. On second thought, bad idea. "I fired Ned as project manager, a long overdue decision, but something that may also cost us the contract." She paused to catch her breath. Her father opened his mouth to reply, but she continued. "It was my decision to call the State. I didn't want to take any chances with either the safety of the crew or the company's reputation.

"All these years since Sean, uh, left us, I thought it was your unreasonable fear of industrial accidents that kept me off the worksite. I learned today how wrong I'd been. In our business, accidents are just one poor decision away."

She paused. "That it? You got anything more to tell me?" he asked.

"As a matter of fact, yes. I gave up a new job and a new start to run the company in your absence. I want to stay in charge, until you're ready to come back, and you're not quite there yet. After that, I want to stay on as your partner—assistant, at the very least. Yes, I made a mistake trusting Ned. But when corrective action was called for, I took it. I've kept this project on schedule, and the crew has come to respect me." She felt her jaw snap as she finished. She'd forced the question, but her gut told her it was time.

Her father studied her. "Done? Finally?"

She nodded.

"If the guy's got money problems like you described, maybe we want out anyway."

His response surprised her. "Are you suggesting we terminate the contract ourselves?"

"That what you think we should do?"

He wanted her opinion. *Okay. Go for it.* "Not yet. We need this project to get our books in the black, but we can't afford to give him more than a week to get his own finances in order. Now that we know how broke he is, he has to accept that fact and do something about it or give it up. He either gets his act together—"

"Or what?"

"We drop him."

"Does his mother know about his money problems?"

Why had he asked about Janice? "Maybe by now, if he's smart. But I got the impression this whole charade about his finances was to keep her from worrying."

"Damn fool," he muttered once again. "Check in with the state people and find out how soon we can get back on the site," he said, as if he'd turned the page on the matter. "Tell them to expect a call from me. I've got a few contacts at that office. Time to work them. Soon as you know when we can go back, call the Swink people and see how soon they can get there."

Her heart nearly stopped. "Does that mean you'll keep me on? Let me remain in charge?"

"As much trouble as Collier has brought upon us, the real blame rests with me. If I'd stopped dwelling on your brother's death and paid more attention to the warning signs about my heart, I might've avoided being sidelined the last several weeks."

Her dad was full of surprises. Though she never would have wished for him to experience his recent health scare, his time in rehab seemed to have prompted some positive self-reflection. The old Tim Harriman wouldn't have taken responsibility for this mess. "You wouldn't have allowed Ned to be his own project manager."

"Probably not. But I shouldn't have allowed you to run the company with no experience. Or I should've listened to your pleas for more responsibility the last few years so you would've been prepared to step in for me.

She never thought he'd admit as much. "All I wanted was to take Sean's place. Not in your heart, of course, but to help you run the company."

"You've gone through a real baptism of fire. I probably would've canned him long before you, but at least you finally came around. As for your call to the State, you did good, kid. That's what I would've done, although it wouldn't've occurred to me to get the sheriff involved. Smart move."

"Th-thanks." A compliment?

"I still plan to take back the reins."

And there it was. Stuck in like the swift jab of a dagger. "But not yet. Doc won't let me."

She let out the breath she'd held. "Oh."

"Accidents happen. Our trip to the place where Sean skidded off the road brought that home to me. He was a good cyclist. Great, if he competed in as many races as I've learned about since his death. He lost control because he was worried that if he returned late"—he choked here but quickly regained his composure—"I'd find out he was more interested in motocross than working for me."

Where was he going with this?

"You're right. After his death, I worried I'd lose you, too. Not necessarily an accident, but that you'd let something cloud your judgment as well."

Like letting Ned serve as project manager?

"You proved me wrong today," he added before she could ask. "You handled that near disaster better than I could've ever imagined."

Something "pinged" in the region near her heart.

"You need a new project manager. Any ideas?"

She'd considered the possibilities on the drive home, as she figured out how to tell her dad about their near catastrophe. "What if we made Dave project manager and moved Pete Martin into Dave's position? We need someone who's already familiar with the project and who knows construction. That's Dave. Pete's a natural leader, despite his early clashes with me. I think he's ready to step up."

"You know your people, kiddo. That's crucial for the person in charge."

~

Ned hesitated before the door to his mother's gallery, gathered his courage. He had to do this, as much as he hated to let her down and look like a schmuck. He pulled the handle and shoved in.

He found her in her office huddled over paperwork.

"Ned! What a pleasant surprise."

"Got a few minutes?"

She cocked her head to study him, like she stared into his mind.

"We need to talk."

She lifted a speculative brow. "Okay. Will I need headache tablets? Or tissues?"

"Not sure." He stayed near the door. *Just spit it out. Get it over with.* "Sullivan's Creek is in danger. I've spent beyond my means."

He waited for a reaction, but her expression didn't change. Her eyes didn't even flicker. He revealed the whole sordid story, ended with the day's near disaster. While he spoke, he drifted from one spot in the room to another, unable to sit.

"You've had quite a day," she said at length.

"There's more. I'm no longer project manager. Shae fired me."

Now she did blink. "Really? Why?"

"I changed things to cut costs and didn't tell her. Today was the last straw. I knew this guy was bad news, yet I agreed to his terms. God, Mom, if Dave Hale hadn't caught that faulty rigging, we could've had a serious accident."

"Why didn't you tell me you couldn't pay for it?"

"You're the last person I wanted to know I was a failure. I've let you down too many times already."

Her brows furrowed. "How on earth do you think you've done that? I couldn't be prouder of you and your success."

He slammed a fist into his palm. "Success? Look at what I've done to my life. And yours."

"You've made a respected name for yourself in the music world while you've remained a decent human being. You were even at a charity event when you lost your voice."

He shook his head. "I only agreed to sing because I wanted to get in

Irv Farley's good graces. Poetic justice, huh? Not only did I lose my voice that night, when I turned to Farley for money, I lost everything."

She flew to his side. "Don't say that, Ned. Your money may be gone, but it's not the end of the road. You have so much more."

"Like what?"

"You're a great composer and musician."

"Haven't sold anything lately. Once Farley spreads his tale, no one will to want to be associated with me."

"Even if that horrible man does attempt to darken your name, think how many other entertainers have revived their careers after setbacks."

"Those folks spent big bucks, which I no longer have, to pay PR people to clean up their images."

"I suppose you'll say the same about your singing career."

"That's still months off. The doc doesn't want me to rush it."

"What about Mike? Not only would he come to your rescue, but his friendship is worth even more. All you'd have to do is ask, and he'd be back here immediately."

Mike. May have hit rock bottom, but Ned still couldn't bring himself to go to his friend for help. "Haven't forgotten Mike."

"How about me?" It came out so quietly, he wasn't sure she'd actually spoken.

"You, Mom?" He put his arms around her and pulled her close. He stepped away. "Why do you think I'm here? Even though I let you down, I need to know I haven't lost you."

"You have to ask? You are my everything. I never wanted the new house. I agreed to move there because it seemed to please you so much to give it to me. I can do quite well with what I have."

"That's the point. I remember a day more than two years ago when I made a surprise visit to town. I dropped in at the gallery and found you so involved talking to customers, chatting on the phone, giving orders to your assistant, you didn't notice me for several minutes. You were in your element."

She cocked a brow. "Isn't that what I just said?"

"I should've been relieved. Instead, I was crushed. All the guilt I'd carried because of my absence during Dad's last days morphed into something else. You'd moved on. You didn't need me. That bothered me more than the guilt."

He hadn't thought much about that day since, not consciously anyhow. Funny, how he'd repressed that yearning for his mom to need him again. Instead, he'd used the break-in several months later to rationalize her move.

"I wanted you to rely on me again. Hence, the new house." Not for all the reasons he'd cited to her and everyone else. God, the second part of that billboard had been right. He had been kidding himself. How had he gotten to this sad state of affairs?

"Let me get this straight. My house, this whole project, is because I didn't need you enough?"

"It sounds so much worse, so egotistical and childish, when you say it."

She shook her head, backed away, and returned to her desk. She remained silent a bit, apparently to absorb what he'd told her. "You disappoint me, Ned."

"I know. I screwed up royally."

"I don't mean your housing development. Your dad and I raised you to stand on your own two feet. Our lifestyle was so different from yours, we knew you had to be strong to follow your own path. I guess we expected the same respect from you in return. You needed me to need you?"

He flopped into the rocker, ran a hand through his hair. "I don't know, Mom. I guess I got to a point in my career where I wondered if it was all worth it. I was on the road so much of the time, had to starve myself so I could stay in shape for my fans, had to schmooze jokers like Farley to get an album produced, land a performance contract. I began to question why I drove myself so."

"Sullivan's Creek justified it all?"

He wrung his hands. Thought through her question. "Yeah. Stupid, huh?"

"Well, yes. But most of us at some time or another wonder about our existence. Your path was simply more ambitious."

"Will you ever be able to forgive me?"

Her eyes softened. "There's nothing for me to forgive, though perhaps you have to forgive yourself."

Was she right?

"You're trying on my words for size. Good. But don't be surprised if it takes more than a few minutes to make sense of your actions. In the meantime, what do you plan to do about the project?"

Trust his mother to consider the immediate problem. "Either I find more money right away to satisfy the bank or I sell. Or"—here, he had to swallow just so he could form the words—"declare bankruptcy."

"Offer the bank this gallery for collateral. It won't cover it all, but it will show good faith."

A lump that had nothing to do with the nodules on his vocal cords formed in his throat. He bit his lips, hoped she wouldn't see the tears that had come unbidden to his eyes. "No, Mom. Thanks, but I can't do that to you."

"Maybe I want you to need me for once. Let me do this."

He shot from the chair and pulled her into his arms again. "I don't deserve you."

"Love is not about deserving, Ned. It's about accepting what's offered free of any strings."

The embrace lingered, his mother's strength seeped into him. "I love you, Mom. But I've gotta to take care of this on my own. Don't do anything with the bank until you hear from me. Okay?"

"Where are you going?"

"Gotta talk to Gramps."

He returned to the site, stayed clear of the state investigators, and instead headed toward the fields he'd worked so many years ago with his grandfather. Though he stumbled at times, he dragged himself forward for several minutes before he stopped at the top of one of the rolling hills. Before him lay untrammeled ground that reminded him of the rich legacy he'd inherited.

When he turned around, he could barely discern any signs of construction. Here alone, planted in knee-high field grass that rippled from the wind's breath, he closed his eyes—not quite sure what picture his brain was trying to form—and inhaled the fresh prairie air. Even the smells were different here—fresh, verdant, redolent. He could almost feel Grandpa Jake alongside him, ready to lend his wisdom.

"My life is falling apart, Gramps. I don't know what to do. I tried to follow through on your wishes. But that was just a front to grab Mom's attention. Now, I've bankrupted myself in the process."

It helped to confess. "I also jeopardized my friendship with Mike. All he ever wanted to do was help, and my pride and ego refused him. Instead, I took money from Farley and left myself open to his demands. God, I might have caused a bad accident today. If Dave hadn't been concerned about that rig …"

Then there was Shae. "I went behind her back to cut corners and foisted myself on her as project manager when, with her lack of experience, she really needed someone who knew his stuff. As I attempted to make things right with my mother, I probably made things even worse between her and her dad."

More than any of his other failings, the fact he'd disappointed Shae cut the most. When his throat had gone bad and his money started to dry up, she'd been a means to an end. She said he'd played up to her, had sex with her to get his way with the project, and she was right. Not that making love to her was a chore. She'd even agreed to no commitments. But …"

Therein lay the rub. Ned had grown to care for her much more than he ever intended. He, the guy who could have his pick of almost any Hollywood honey, had fallen for a real woman from his hometown. But that hadn't stopped him from taking advantage of her when it came to the project.

All these issues swirled around him like a swarm of bees. He could bat his defenseless mitts at the pests all he wanted, but they wouldn't disperse until he figured out where the course ahead lay.

His breathing seemed to even out, as if the weight of his current problems might have lifted. That had to be Gramps.

"What do I do now, Gramps? It's one thing to realize what a fool I've been, but how do I fix this? I can't let Mom sacrifice her gallery. She lives for it."

What did he live for? His music? To a point. But while he'd been laid up, unable to sing, it hadn't been his music that got him through. His mother and the refuge of her home had been there when he needed to escape the press. Besides financial assistance, Mike had offered his advice and his home. Until today, Shae had believed in him and his dream.

He'd begun to make things right with his mother. Until he cleaned up this mess, he couldn't face Shae. That left Mike.

He'd told both his mother and Mike it would jeopardize Mike's rebuilt relationship with his family if he loaned Ned money again. But if he was honest with himself, that wasn't the real reason he'd refused Mike's help. His pride had prevented him from letting his friend come to his aid. He been unable to accept being the one who needed help yet again. Pride, geez. Such a debilitating emotion. Thanks to his pride, he'd paid a terrible price. He could no longer afford it.

Only one thing left to do. He pulled out his cell and hit a button. "Hi, pal. How's it going?"

CHAPTER 25

Mike returned to Des Moines around nine that evening. As he and Ned sat around the kitchen island, Mike with a late snack and Ned with water, Ned filled his friend in on all the distasteful details about his collapsed world, which he'd skirted over the phone.

"Bottom line—I've been a jerk."

"Naïve fool's more like it."

Ned wanted to object but held his tongue. "Yeah, you're right."

An amused expression curved a corner of Mike's mouth. He set down his sandwich, turned to his beer. Ned waited for the lecture Mike had every right to deliver. "She really fired you?" he asked.

"Humiliating, huh? Fired from my own project."

"For the shit you've pulled, she should've done it weeks ago."

"But in front of her crew?"

"Probably to show them she was still in charge."

"Thought you didn't like her."

Mike went back to his sandwich. "Never said that. Didn't like that you'd entrusted a multi-million-dollar project to someone with no experience. From what you've told me about the project, seems to have been the one thing you did right."

Ned recalled Shae's first meeting with the crew. Disastrous. She hadn't wanted to admit she'd invited the crew's heckling. But she hadn't given up. Had even gone along with his idea to treat them to lunch as her way to apologize. She'd come a long way since then.

Mike broke into his thoughts. "So? Where do things stand between the two of you?"

"Just told you."

"Not the firing part. The personal part. Understand in my absence she's been a guest here several times. Even a few nights."

"You know?" Damn! They'd been so careful to keep things on the down-low. Now he'd have to suffer through Mike's warnings not to get involved again.

"Housekeepers do more than dust, buddy. Mine wanted to make sure it was okay. So?'

"It was a convenient arrangement while it lasted. Now, obviously, it's over."

Mike cocked his head, studied him. "That for my benefit or yours?"

Ned started to refute Mike's supposition but heaved a huge sigh instead. "Mine. That was a load of crap. Shae's no one-night stand or hometown hottie. She's real. She didn't deserve the way I treated her."

"What you gonna do about it?"

Ned shrugged. "She no longer wants a thing to do with me on a personal basis."

"Gonna let that stop you?"

"Gotta make things right with my business affairs first."

Mike scrubbed a hand across his face. "Okay, I can buy that. But she's no Gillian or Julie. That crane fiasco may have pissed her off enough to fire you, but I suspect she did it for you, too, since you weren't smart enough to see your life crumbling around you. If I had someone care enough about me to risk her father's company by firing me, even I might consider a more serious relationship with the woman."

Some admission. "You mean that?"

Mike considered. "Not gonna happen with my crazy lifestyle, but sure." Then, as if he'd said too much, he changed the subject. "So? What're we gonna do to get you back on your feet?"

"First, deal with Farley. If you're still willing to pay him off, like you offered."

"That's why I'm here, pal."

His shoulder muscles relaxed. Until Mike actually confirmed his support, there'd still been a niggling doubt in Ned's mind. "Thanks. That SOB Farley is history with me."

"From what you told me about the State's investigation, may be a moot point, if they bring charges of negligence against him."

"Won't break my heart."

"What else?"

Ned took a long, deliberate breath. He was pretty sure Mike would agree to this next point, but what if he didn't? Mike was his last option. "What say we team up on this project? I contribute the property and you the money. At least the bulk of it for now. I'm not completely broke, just don't have enough to continue this project as I'd anticipated. Once my throat recovers and I make personal appearances again, I'll throw in what I make from that as well."

Mike started to speak, but Ned stopped him. "Before you say or agree to anything, we'll do an audit, so you can see the full financial picture."

"That mean a formal partnership?"

The guy was going to make him say it. "Uh, yeah."

"Woodley and Collier. I like the sound of it."

"Collier comes first alphabetically," Ned said, knowing full well that wouldn't happen.

"Woodley has the bucks."

"Woodley and Collier it is."

They toasted, water bottle to beer bottle, and the deal was done.

Ned marveled at how easy it had gone down, once he'd gotten past his ego and admitted his mistakes to Mike. There'd be times ahead when Mike would remind him of the mistakes he'd made, but Mike would never remind him that he'd come to his rescue. Not his style.

Mike went to bed once the initial plan for their new partnership had been discussed, despite still being on Pacific Time. However, even with his money problems behind him, restlessness plagued Ned. Something was still off. He felt unsettled.

When sleep wouldn't come, he found himself once again at his keyboard in the music room. His mind wandered back to the first time he brought Shae to hear his composition. The two of them had thrown caution to the wind that day, as they had ever since, enjoyed each other's bodies and collapse in fatigue afterwards, though they'd kept their relationship a secret from everyone else except apparently the Woodley housekeeper, who'd informed Mike.

Even though both his mother and Mike asked about Shae, they'd mercifully let the subject drop when he skated past anything that resembled a straight answer. Nor did either mention the L word. He'd been burned not once but twice by what he thought was love. He no longer believed in commitments, and Shae agreed. After today, she was probably more than happy she had.

Although he and Shae had been lovers, what they shared wasn't love. Was it? Love was the kind of thing his parents had. Belief in the other person, like when they started the art gallery together. Willing-ness to see things through together, even when times were bad, like his dad's illness. Inability to hold back a smile whenever the other person came into the room. He'd witnessed those private looks between his parents many times. Hadn't really understood them until he was a teen.

He hardly knew Shae. They hadn't even been on a date. Wouldn't happen now.

His stomach clenched. Maybe he should've had a sandwich with Mike. Nah, this ache wasn't from hunger. Nor was it the queasy sick feeling that had sent him to the side of the road to barf earlier in the day, after Farley pulled the plug. He just felt empty.

He played the piece he'd shared that day for Shae. Though his mind traveled elsewhere, his recorder continued to run. When he emerged from his woolgathering and listened to what he'd done, the playback shocked him. The same melody was there, but somehow, in his reverie he'd changed the key and the beat. He repeated the play-back and afterwards simply sat there, surprised.

Ned had been more than pleased with his progress on the piece when he'd first played it for Shae. But this? This version blew the other out of the water. Had relief about his money problems seeped into his subconscious and freed up his creativity? No, as his hands stroked the keys, he hadn't thought about the project. His mind had been on Shae.

How about that? His fingers knew better than his brain. He and Shae weren't over.

THE FOLLOWING MORNING, Ned drove Mike to the site to pick up the RV.

"You don't have to do this," Mike told him before they started. "I can arrange for someone to return it. Or it can stay for the duration of the project. I don't need it, and I doubt my parents will be back in town any time soon."

"Thanks, but I think Shae will rest easier once this reminder of me is off the premises."

Mike shrugged. "Okay, your call."

The plan was for Mike to drive the RV back to town with Ned to follow in his own car. Keep it short and sweet and get the hell out of there. Though Ned now knew what he had to do, he wasn't sure how to get there. Like he did so often in his music, he counted on inspiration to strike when he most needed it.

Upon his arrival, he spotted Shae near the site of his mother's house. She stared up at the suspect crane. Her father, Dave and Pete Martin flanked her.

He started their direction, but Mike caught his arm. "You go over there, you'd better be prepared to face the consequences."

"I just wanted to tell her …" What? That he was sorry? That he didn't want to lose her? "Meet you back in town."

"I know it's too soon to make amends with her, but a guy's gotta try."

Mike didn't stop him.

He caught up with the group before his brain figured out what words to supply his mouth. "Mornin', folks."

The three men nodded.

"I, uh, left some notes back in the office," Shae stammered before he could speak to her.

His spirits sank. The knot that had formed in his gut tightened. She definitely hadn't changed her mind about him. Until then, he hadn't realized how much he'd hoped she had.

The others didn't say anything or try to stop her. Her father didn't even glance in his direction.

"My friend and I are here to pick up his RV. Just wanted you to know I don't plan to switch to another contractor."

Shae's father replied. "Thanks."

Terse, Well, what did he expect. He'd compromised the integrity of the guy's company. "Should you be fined by the State, I plan to reimburse you," he felt compelled to add. "Once my friend Mike over there gets the RV back to town, he'll contact the State to see what we can do to mitigate the charges."

"Not necessary. I've already been in touch with the state people," Tim Harriman said as if to dismiss him.

So much for his chance to redeem himself in Shae's eyes. But he had to try. "Don't blame your daughter for any of this, Tim. She's done a great job on my project."

"Yes, she has," her father said.

Could he sound more awkward and guilty? "Uh, well. Just wanted to let you know." He pivoted and slinked toward his car. Then it hit him. If they really were over, Shae would've stuck around and ignored him. Instead, she'd run off. Not given him a chance to talk to her.

She still cared.

Now or never. This was his best chance to make things right.

～

SHAE STOOD AWAY from the trailer window and observed the Ned Collier show outside. Or should she call it *The Jake Bonneville Show*, since he'd clearly assumed his entertainer persona to worm his way back into her father's good graces. Her chest felt like someone had spilled liquid fire inside. She couldn't catch her breath. How dare Ned return to the site barely twenty-four hours after he'd subjected them all to professional humiliation and possible charges from the State?

At least her dad and the guys didn't appear to welcome him. He was the one who talked most, and at times, none of them spoke. What did he expect?

How could she have trusted him? And … and what? Cared for him? Surely her feelings hadn't evolved beyond that? For Pete's sake, of course she had feelings for him. Ever since the first time they made love. She'd been so anxious to get him into her bed, she made herself vulnerable to whatever came afterward.

There'd been times, especially when he coached her on how to be a boss, or when he'd listened to her go on about her dad's lack of support, he'd been so human and understanding. At those times, she'd almost let herself believe more was possible. But the minute he realized he was in over his head monetarily, he'd turned manipulative.

He started to leave. Good. Good riddance.

No, wait. He stopped. Now he was … oh, God, he was headed in her direction!

He planned to force the issue. Not if she could help it. All she had to do was flip the lock on the door. Surely he wouldn't make an ass of himself and stand outside and beg to come in?

But she didn't. And he didn't. Instead, he simply turned the knob and let himself in.

"I thought I made it clear yesterday your presence on the site would not be appreciated for some time. You adhered to that statement as well as you listened to everything else I've told you."

He pointed his index finger like a gun and shot. "Bingo. That's been our problem in a nutshell."

His reaction caught her off guard. What was he up to? "Why are you here, Ned?"

"If you'd remained with your dad and the others, you'd know I drove Mike out to pick up the RV. You don't want me here, so I've come to remove the last vestige of my presence."

Sounded unexpectedly reasonable. "Oh." *Okay, you've said your piece. Now go.*

But he didn't. He edged his way farther into the trailer. She backed up. "Before I go, there are a few things you should know."

Don't give an inch. Make him leave now. "And those would be?"

He ticked them off on his fingers, reminiscent of the night she'd pointed out his flaws when they'd shared fast food in her dad's kitchen. "First, thanks for firing me. You knew before I did that serving as my own project manager was a bad idea."

"From the first time you mentioned it. Too bad I didn't stick to my guns."

"Second, you forced me to face my problems and not attempt to cover them up with bizarre cost-cutting measures. I've now told both my mom and Mike about the sorry state of my finances. Should have trusted them with that knowledge ages ago."

Progress, although overdue. "Glad to hear it."

"Next, I got rid of Farley. Mike's my new partner."

Probably the smartest move he'd made yet. *Watch out, Mike, if you have any intention to be part of the decisionmaking.* "He will provide the financing?"

"Yep. So the project's back on. With Two Rivers Construction as my general contractor. I told your dad as much."

That was a relief. She'd called it correctly when she recommended they give him a few days to find more backers. Her dad should be thrilled.

"And I love you."

Her heart bounced. She gulped. "What?"

"Would've told you sooner, but I just figured it out myself. How 'bout you?"

"Huh?"

"Have you figured out you love me yet?"

She backed up farther and fell into her seat. How was she supposed to answer?

Ned moved around to the visitor chair. He leaned into the desk and watched her intently.

"We hardly know each other," she said.

"I know about that small tat on your back shoulder. Pretty intimate in my book."

"Okay. Sure. We've had sex. Lots. But I thought we agreed on no commitments."

"Yeah, well, two failed engagements made me commitment-shy. I didn't think I'd ever find someone I could trust again. What I failed to take into account is neither of those two relationships was real." He came around the desk and drew her into his arms. "You and I have something far different. Something that's strong enough to give me the audacity to return to the scene of my incredible folly just to tell you how special you are to me. I don't want to lose you."

He loved her? He said something about commitment? She'd barely heard the rest of his words once he said, "I love you."

Her mind snapped back to the present. "I want to relocate to Iowa. I have my own lot out here. Did that mainly for my mom. Can't wait to see it finished and move in."

"What are you saying, Ned?"

He stared into her eyes. "I've said I love you a couple times. I've also said our relationship is real. Beyond is up to you."

"Yes."

"Yes, what?"

"Yes, I love you, too. I realized it a long time ago, but I thought it would never be reciprocated."

"Came as a whopping surprise to me. Then I realized it had been in development all along. We just nurtured it the wrong way, limited ourselves just to sex. Not that I minded that part, but like you said, we hardly know each other. We should remedy that."

The blood pounded in her ears so frantically, she could hardly hear him. "You mean, socially?"

"Yeah. Date. Go to movies, out to dinner, things like that."

She winced. "As I recall, I didn't do so well the last time we dined out. I got a bit tipsy, even spilled wine on you."

"That night I got a glimpse of a woman who was so determined to succeed at her job she'd venture way out of her comfort zone to snag her client. At a time when I questioned my ability to get through my own problems, you were the role model I didn't expect."

Her? Role model? It wasn't so long ago she'd compared herself to the Hollywood glamour girls she thought he spent his time with and saw herself come up short. That made her remember something. "What happens when your throat recovers?"

"I plan to go back to my concerts and recordings. You can come with me if you want. As your job permits. I'll try to make my road trips shorter. But my heart's in Iowa. Wherever I go, I'll always come back here. To you."

Had she heard him correctly? Ned Collier, aka Jake Bonneville, the megastar, would be willing to trade Hollywood for a Harriman? Before she could clarify, his lips sought hers with a new urgency. His tongue began the now-familiar foreplay.

She remembered the night at her father's when she'd told him she was up to tango-ing with him. They may not be on a dance floor at the moment, but the mating of their tongues assured her the dare had taken. He loved her! Despite her sexual naïveté and their continual run-ins.

"By the time my house is ready, I hope we'll know each other well enough to take the next step," he said when he came up for air. "If I have my way, you'll consider co-ownership, as my wife. It only took three tries, but this time I know I've got it right."

EPILOGUE

Thanks to the infusion of Woodley money into the project, they were back at work on Sullivan's Creek in a few days. Ned kept his promise and stayed away, although at night, Shae saw him more than ever.

A few weeks later, she was at work on the revised work schedule in her office in town when Pete Martin stuck his head in her door. "Got a minute?"

"Sure. Come in." She gestured toward one of the two guest chairs. "What's up?"

The large man ambled over to the chair and, once seated, ran his hands down his jeans, as if to brush off stray debris. "Came in to pick up supplies for the mobile office. Thought I'd stop by and thank you again for naming me Dave's replacement when you appointed him project manager. I never would've thought you could look past some of the things I said to you when you first took over."

"At the time, I probably wouldn't have imagined you in your new position either. But I'm glad we got past those days. You're more than a good worker, Pete. You're a good leader."

"Thanks. You're not your dad, but you've done a pretty good job as his stand-in." He gazed down at his hands, then up again. "I would've said that even without the promotion."

She couldn't help smile. Quite a turn of events.

"You chose a great project manager in Dave Hale. He knows the business and this project better than anyone, even you." He rose and held out his hand. She grasped it and shook enthusiastically.

Too bad her dad hadn't been here to hear Pete's words, although that was no longer as important. Her dad already acknowledged his satisfaction with her work.

Ironically, shortly after Pete left, her dad appeared at the door. "Brought you a visitor."

He stepped back and Janice Collier entered the room. "Hi, Shae. Hope we're not disturbing you. Your dad and I stopped by to tell you we're off on a day trip." She glanced over her shoulder at Tim Harriman.

Shae and Ned told their parents about their relationship the day after they'd reconciled. Janice had not seemed particularly surprised or disappointed to hear the news. She was fast convincing Shae's dad to get past Ned's blunders, especially since Shae had. "You aren't concerned about my personal involvement with the client?" she'd asked her dad.

"I'd say the time to ask that question has long passed. Water under the bridge now. Besides, Ned's no longer project manager, and that pal of his, Woodley, will be the one hanging around the site now."

She'd hugged her dad profusely, which embarrassed them both, although neither moved away from the other all that fast. "I'd never do anything to embarrass you."

"Well, damn! Then you're not having enough fun." Fun. Imagine. That word emerged from her dad. On the other hand, *fun* seemed to be on his mind a lot these days. She turned to him now, an eyebrow raised. "Day trip?"

Her dad fidgeted in his seat, adjusted his casual slacks. No jeans or work pants? Or even the sweats he'd worn at Blackhawk Hills? "Ever since I deigned to help her out with her still life class, Janice has gotten the notion I should be exposed to other kinds of art. Today, she wants me to *experience* an art fair in Iowa City." Though his tone was typically churlish, it also carried a note of excitement.

Janice appeared to have taken seriously her task to interest Tim Harriman in something else other than sitting around during his rehabilitation and complaining. Though from the way the two exchanged private looks, Shae wondered if art had anything to do with the time they spent together.

Her dad surveyed his former office. "Place looks pretty much the same."

"I haven't done anything to it, other than clear all the clutter off the desk. Our organizational methods differ somewhat." She chuckled.

"Is this the first time you've been back here, Tim?" Janice asked.

He nodded. "I was more or less prisoner in that rehab joint. I promised Shae and my doc I'd be a good boy in order to go home. It's only been since"—he had the grace to look away from Janice briefly—"uh, you know, that I've been out at all."

"Well, I'm glad what happened at my house site was good for something," Janice said. "Although I guess I can't refer to the house as mine much longer."

"I heard Mike Woodley has offered to buy it," Shae said.

"Before I've even taken occupancy," Janice beamed. "Ned and I had a long talk after the incident. We both realized the house was his dream for me, not mine. Not that I wouldn't want to live out there. I grew up on that farm, as you know. Pretty strange turn of events since my house seems to be the impetus for this entire project." She gave Tim a quick, shy glance. "Maybe someday I'll move there. But for now, I'm happy where I am with the life I've carved out for myself."

"I was surprised Mike wanted to move out of that incredible mansion," Shae replied. "Apparently his parents may come back to town and he wants to give them their space." Translation provided by Ned: Mike wanted to get as far away from them as he could without totally leaving the area.

"Give them their space, my eye," her father said. "You kids pussy-foot around language more than us oldtimers. That young millionaire wants to sow his oats in his own pasture without his folks around.

Mark my words, Janice's place is going to turn into a rural bachelor pad."

"Good thing my son seems to be past that phase," Janice observed, her eyes twinkling.

Shae returned the exchange. "He certainly is, although that's hasn't prevented him from wanting to make his own new home the showplace of Sullivan's Creek."

"I, for one, couldn't be happier that Janice has decided to stay in town. If I'm gonna chauffeur her to all these art things, I won't have to drive out to the country to pick her up."

So, their relationship was going to continue. Who would have thought? But what better companion for her dad than this lovely woman who'd befriended her? Only then did she notice Janice wore white crop pants and a navy and white striped knit top, all very form-fitting. Gone were the gaudy long skirt and the loose overblouse. "What happened to the faux hippie look?"

Janice spread her hands in front of her. "Your dad convinced me we'd both lived through the seventies during the seventies. My gallery's reputation can succeed on its own without all the costumes."

Wow. When had all this happened? Shae still stayed at her dad's, although she planned to move to her own place once he came back to work in a few weeks. She would stay on as her dad's assistant— partner, really—but there was no need to debate titles. Yet.

The couple rose, almost in unison, like each anticipated the other's moves. "Better hit the road," her dad said. "By the way, I heard from our attorney before I left home. No citation from the State. In fact, there's a letter of commendation on its way to you, Shae, and to Dave, to thank you for your safety consciousness and quick thinking."

A wave of relief swept through her, caused her to fall back in her seat. Until she'd actually heard this decision, she hadn't realized how much she'd dreaded a citation.

As her dad reached the door, he hung back. "I'm off to the art world. Figure more of these day trips are in my future. Especially since Two Rivers Construction is in very good hands. Bye, Sweetheart."

Good thing he didn't see the tears his remark had generated. *Sweetheart? Thank you, Janice.*

Time to get back to work. Her visitors had cut into her day.

Not to be. Her phone rang. "Hi, babe. Got a question for you. I'm about to meet with Lacey and Scott to go over the floor plans for our place."

No. Not this again. He'd had those plans out every day since they'd decided to *date*. Every new idea, he asked her opinion. "Don't want to leave you out of any of these decisions."

A huge concession. She appreciated his consideration. Even though neither of them had yet to commit to anything permanent, that was pretty much a foregone conclusion. But she didn't need to be consulted about the height of the dining room windows or dimensions of the master bath linen closet. Nonetheless, she played along. "What question?'

"I ran into this guy at my doctor's office. He owns a small tile business in Ottumwa. We talked about our new place, and the upshot is, I can get quite a deal if we go through him rather than your regular subs."

Shae rolled her eyes. Some things never changed.

AFTERWORD

Dear Reader,

Thank you for reading this book. If you liked it, won't you please take a minute to leave a review?

To learn more about the eleven contemporary romances and two novellas I've written, sign up for my newsletter at https://www.subscribepage.com/BBContempRom

I've also written two cozy mystery series, the Mah Jongg Mysteries and Nailed It Home Reno Mysteries. You can learn more about them on my website, www.barbarabarrettbooks.com.

Follow me on Facebook: https://bit.ly/2aXZvG9
Follow me on Twitter: https://twitter.com/bbarrettbooks

SNEAK PEEK

NOT YOUR MAMA'S MAMBO

Read an excerpt from the next book
in the Sullivan's Creek series, *Not Your Mama's Mambo.*

"Am I interrupting?" an unfamiliar but surprisingly seductive female voice asked. "The woman who answered the door said to come right in."

Ned recognized her first, though Mike was just a split second behind. "Darren? You're Darren Williams, the artist, right?"

She turned toward Ned, offered a killer smile. "That's me. I'm surprised you recognized me, Mr. Bonneville. It's been a few months since my showing at your mother's gallery."

Mike took in their visitor while Ned made chit-chat. A tad below shoulder length, her black hair was slightly longer than the last time he'd seen her, but she still looked damned good, especially in her white leather jacket and tight navy jeans, which revealed a slim but curvy figure. Something about her had registered that night at the showing, enough for him to hassle her to gain her attention, but business and later his partnership with Ned had prevented him from following up. "Come in, Ms. Williams. Ned and I were just finishing our discussion."

She made her way into the room. Only then did he notice she was carrying a package, which she rested against the side of the empty den chair. She removed red knit gloves and then undid the red plaid scarf protecting her neck from the day's chill. "I've finished the seascape you commissioned last summer."

Right. He vaguely remembered calling her afterward and placing the order. God, had this project taken over his brain so much he'd forgotten about a looker like her?

Ned's phone pinged. He shot it a brief glance. "Gotta go. Wish I could stay for the reveal, but Shae—Shae Harriman, our general contractor and my lady, who you met that night, too—needs me back at my house. The special synthesizer I ordered for my music room just arrived, and I have to approve it before it's installed. Nice to see you again, Ms. Williams."

She nodded. Unlike most people who met Ned, she didn't appear intimidated by the superstar. "Please call me Darren. Both of you."

"Then I'm Ned, not my alter ego, Jake Bonneville, and he's Mike," Ned called as he grabbed his jacket and slipped from the room. "Catch you later, man."

"You arrived just in time," Mike told her. "My bud there wanted to discuss a subject I'd rather put off."

She lifted a brow. "Oh? What would that be?"

"How to promote our housing development so we can sell the remaining lots. He wants to do a concert to raise interest."

"There's no denying his name could be a draw. It certainly helped at his mother's showing."

"True. But we want to attract bona fide buyers, not just his fans. I was trying to figure out a diplomatic way to tell him when you appeared."

"Maybe his mother could share with you how she was able to draw actual patrons to her showing rather than just those who wanted to meet her son."

He studied her with new appreciation. Gorgeous, talented *and* smart. "Good idea. Thanks."

"Glad to help." She hefted the package and held it toward him. "Would you like to do the honors?"

His parents and the rest of his siblings lived in various parts of the country, so he had the old homestead, one of the town's major mansions south of Grand Avenue, to himself. Except for Ned. At his invitation, Ned was staying with him while his new home in Sullivan's Creek was going up. It was almost finished.

Mike also had a place under construction in Sullivan's Creek, but he was less anxious to move in than his pal. He'd purchased the home Ned had been building for his mother, Janice, when she decided to remain in town. Mike had purchased it more as a favor than as an intent to settle in the country. The shell was done, but he never seemed to have time to deal with the interior. He'd get to it. Sometime. Right now, his focus was on selling more lots.

He came out of his reverie to find Darren staring at him, still holding the package. "Don't you want to unwrap it?" A tinge of hurt underlay her tone.

"Uh, sure. Sorry. My head's still back in my meeting with Ned." He made a big deal of taking the parcel from her and ripping off the brown paper. He propped it against the end table and stepped back to examine it. Something didn't equate. This was supposed to be a picture of the Pacific Ocean as seen from his beach house in Malibu. He'd emailed her several shots he'd taken at sunrise. He'd expected shades of gray, blue, mauve. Maybe even some morning mist. Instead, reds and yellows dominated this seascape.

"You did receive the photos I sent you, didn't you?" he asked.

Her eyes narrowed. Apparently she hadn't expected his question. "Uh, yes. They helped me get a feel for what you see daily when you're there."

"A feel?" His voice rose. "I intended to see one of these scenes replicated in your work. Not this, what should I call it, *impression* of my view."

"I, uh, I'm an artist, Mike. I interpret what I see. I don't *replicate* views." She bit out the last sentence.

Neither spoke for a few seconds. Was nothing going his way today?

As pleasing as she was on the eyes, he couldn't deal with her artist's temperament at the moment. "Look, uh, no offense. You're a good artist. This picture just isn't what I anticipated." Hell, five minutes ago, he hadn't even remembered the painting, but now that it was here, it wasn't what he wanted. Go figure.

Her chin jutted out, and she seemed to grow two inches taller. "But I spent considerable time on this, even though I wasn't able to get started on it right away. Perhaps I could make a few alterations that would be more to your liking?"

"Yeah. Do that." What was with him? Why was he sending this beautiful woman away, her tail feathers in a bunch? Because he was that discouraged. Not with her. But with the latest loss of a sale. He needed to strike out at something. She was closest to his force field.

"I don't want a storm at sea. I want something peaceful, calm, tranquil," he said, attempting to soften the blow. "Come back when you can make it look like that."

Coffee-brown eyes now wide, Darren grabbed the painting, her gloves and neck scarf and headed out, leaving the paper behind. Within seconds, the front door slammed.

Learn more at BarbaraBarrettBooks.com

ACKNOWLEDGMENTS

Thank you to The Wild Rose Press, who initially published this book in 2014.

In order for this book to take on new life now that I'm publishing it myself, it needed a brand-new, intriguing cover. My grateful thanks to my cover artist, Chris Kridler of Sky Diary Productions, for taking the few snippets of ideas I fed her about this story and bringing this catchy cover to life. I also have her to thank for the formatting.

Thank you, Judie Stark, for proofing the re-edited version of this manuscript. Although many pairs of eyes have reviewed the book over its lifetime, the updates required one more look.

Thanks always to my husband, Veryl, for his continuing support of my writing career. He has seen me through more typewriters, tabletop computers and laptops than I can recall.

BOOKS BY BARBARA BARRETT

Cozy Mysteries

The Mah Jongg Mystery Series

Craks in a Marriage

Bamboozled

Connect the Dots

Beware the East Wind

Flower Power

Jokers Wild

The Charleston Challenge

The Dragon Lady Gets Her Due

Courtesy Call

also available in paperback

Nailed It Home Reno Mysteries

Measure Twice, Murder Once

Loose Screw

Death by Drywall

Homicide by Hammer

Nuts and Bolts

Snared by the Snake

Wrenched at the Reindeer Run

A LITTLE ABOUT
BARBARA BARRETT

Barbara Barrett skipped a midlife crisis by writing romance novels at night when she wasn't at her day job as human resources analyst for Iowa State Government. Her first book was published in 2012. She has now published eleven full-length contemporary romance novels and two novellas. More recently, she has published nine cozy mysteries in her Mah Jongg Mystery series and seven in her Nailed It Home Reno Mysteries series. This book is the second in the Sullivan's Creek series.

Barbara is married to the man she met her senior year at college. They have two grown children, eight grandchildren and two great grandchildren.

Now retired, she spends her time in Florida, Iowa and Minnesota. She earned her B.A. degree in History from the University of Iowa and her Master's Degree in History from Drake University.

When not in front of her laptop creating her next story, she plays Mah Jongg, is learning to paint with acrylics and enjoys lunches with friends.

www.ingramcontent.com/pod-product-compliance
Lightning Source LLC
Chambersburg PA
CBHW071219210726
48293CB00002B/498